FATALE

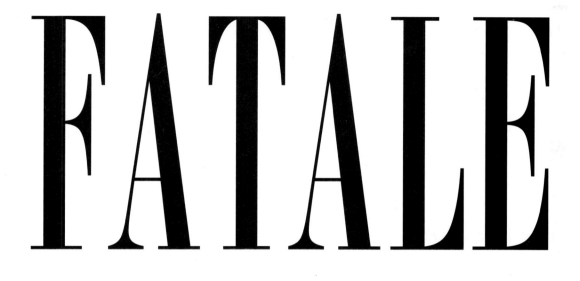

ED BRUBAKER SEAN PHILLIPS

FATALE

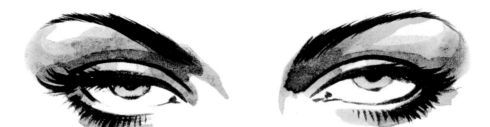

BOOK THREE
WEST OF HELL

By ED BRUBAKER and SEAN PHILLIPS

Colors by Elizabeth Breitweiser and Dave Stewart

MEDIA INQUIRIES SHOULD BE DIRECTED TO UTA - Agents Julien Thuan and Geoff Morley

IMAGE COMICS, INC.
Robert Kirkman - chief operating officer
Erik Larsen - chief financial officer
Todd McFarlane - president
Marc Silvestri - chief executive officer
Jim Valentino - vice-president

Eric Stephenson - publisher
Ron Richards - director of business development
Jennifer de Guzman - pr & marketing director
Branwyn Bigglestone - accounts manager
Emily Miller - administrative assistant
Jamie Parreno - marketing assistant
Jenna Savage - administrative assistant
Kevin Yuen - digital rights coordinator
Jonathan Chan - production manager
Drew Gill - art director
Tyler Shainline - print manager
Monica Garcia - production artist
Vincent Kukua - production artist
Jana Cook - production artist

www.imagecomics.com

FATALE, BOOK THREE: WEST OF HELL. First printing. June 2013. ISBN: 978-1-60706-743-6 Published by Image Comics, Inc. Office of publication: 2001 Center Street, 6th Floor, Berkeley, CA 94704.

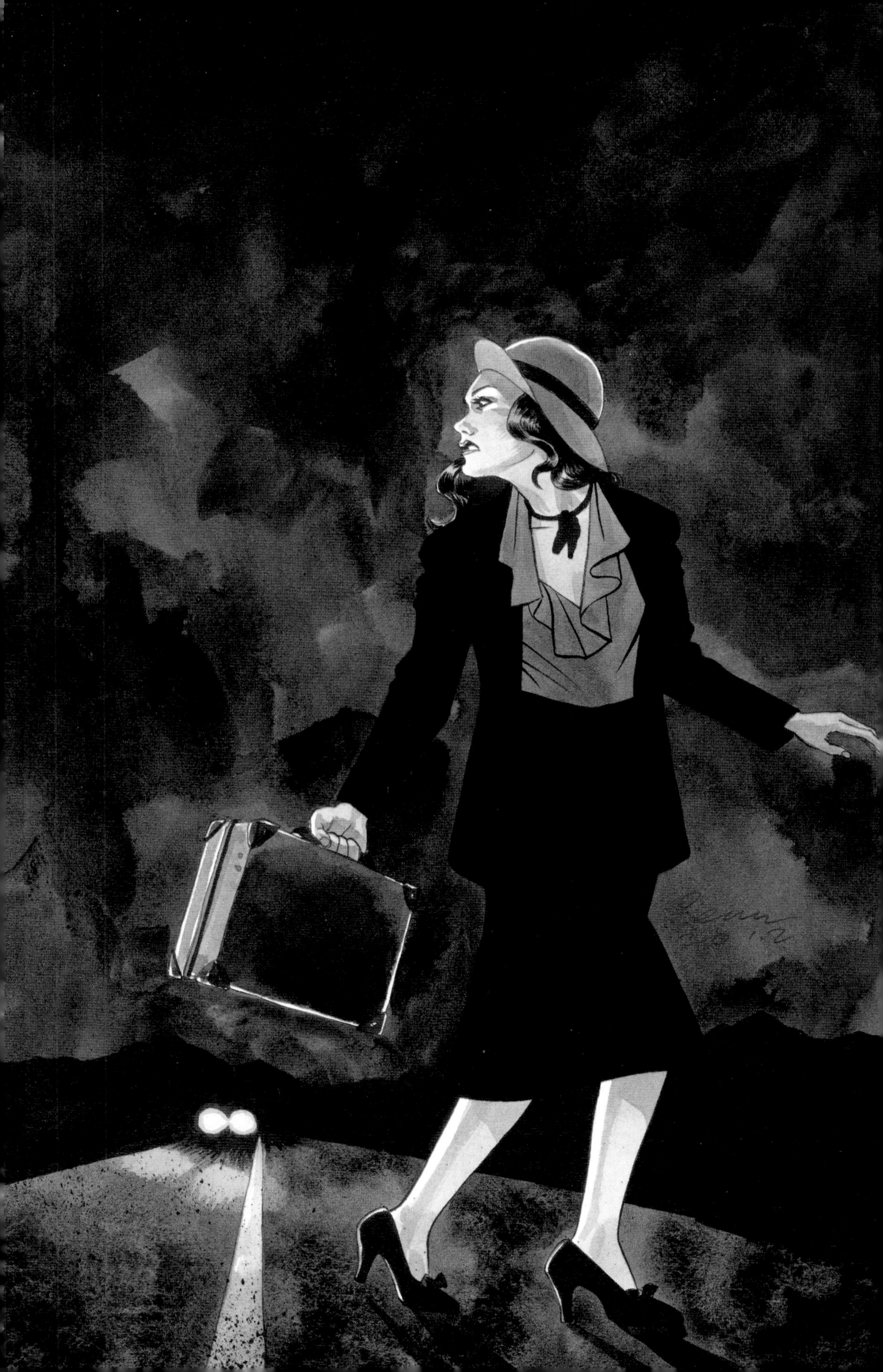

The Case Of Alfred Ravenscroft

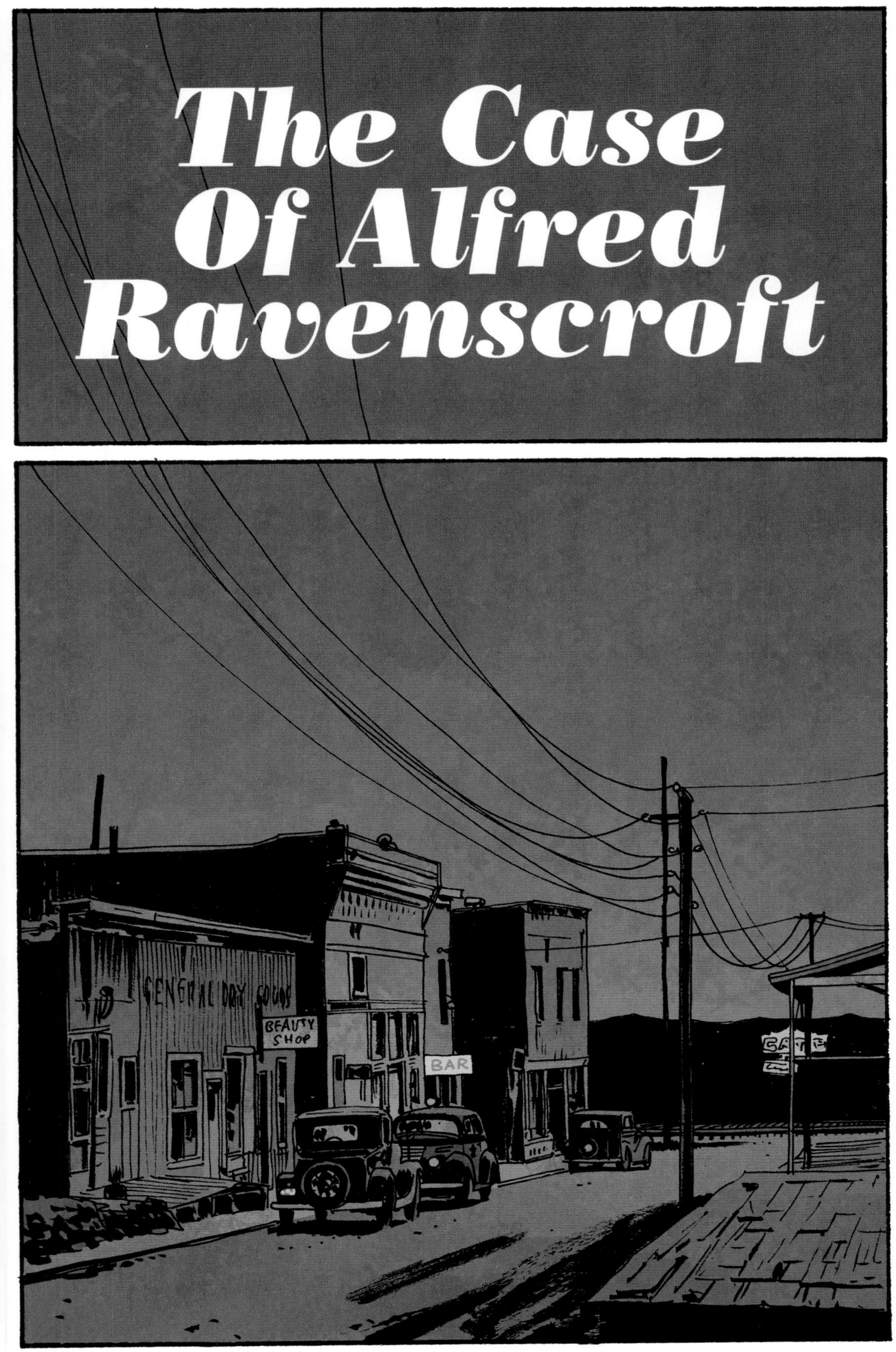
GENERAL DRY GOODS
BEAUTY SHOP
BAR

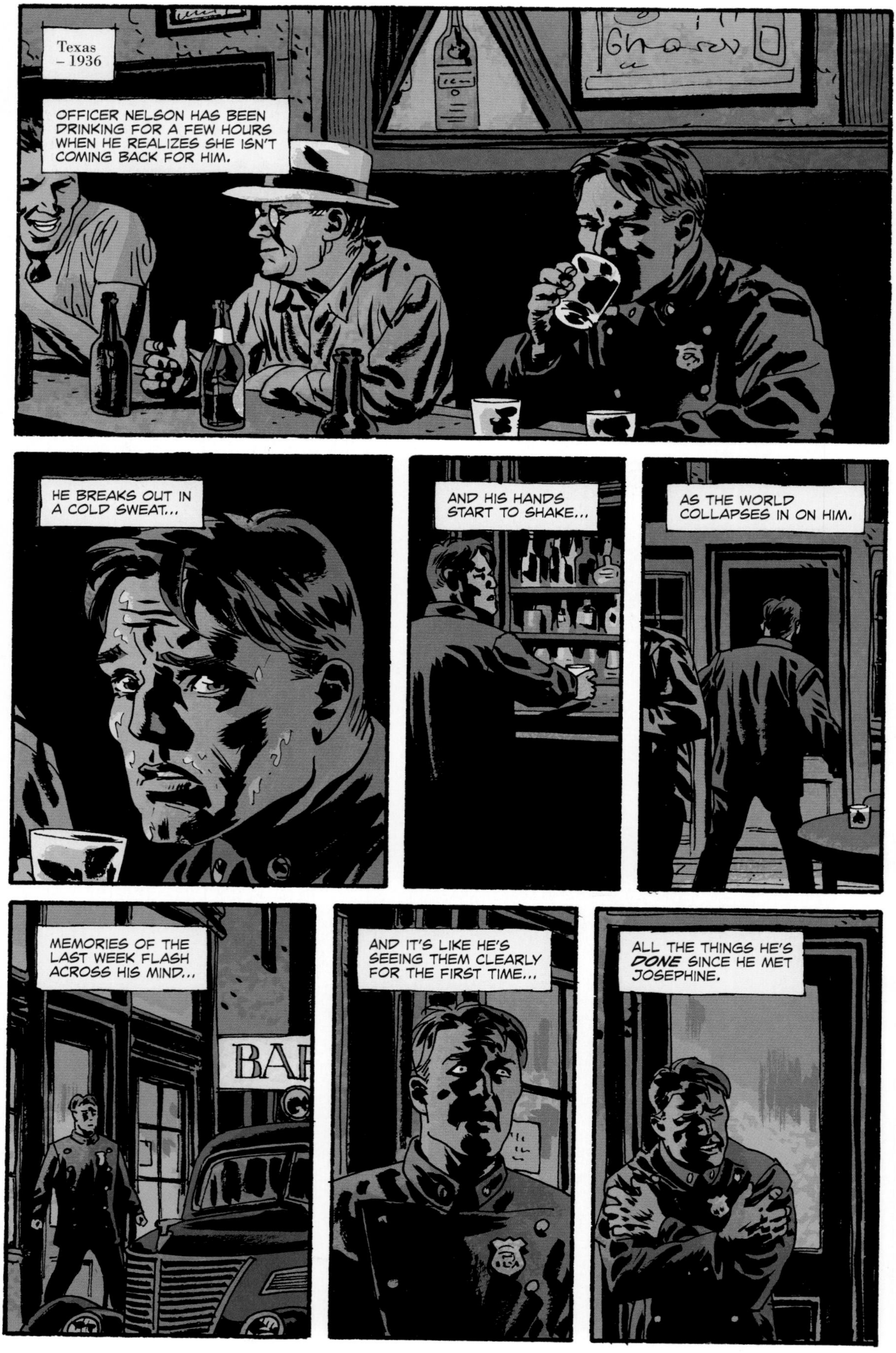
Texas – 1936
OFFICER NELSON HAS BEEN DRINKING FOR A FEW HOURS WHEN HE REALIZES SHE ISN'T COMING BACK FOR HIM.
HE BREAKS OUT IN A COLD SWEAT...
AND HIS HANDS START TO SHAKE...
AS THE WORLD COLLAPSES IN ON HIM.
MEMORIES OF THE LAST WEEK FLASH ACROSS HIS MIND...
BAR
AND IT'S LIKE HE'S SEEING THEM CLEARLY FOR THE FIRST TIME...
ALL THE THINGS HE'S DONE SINCE HE MET JOSEPHINE.

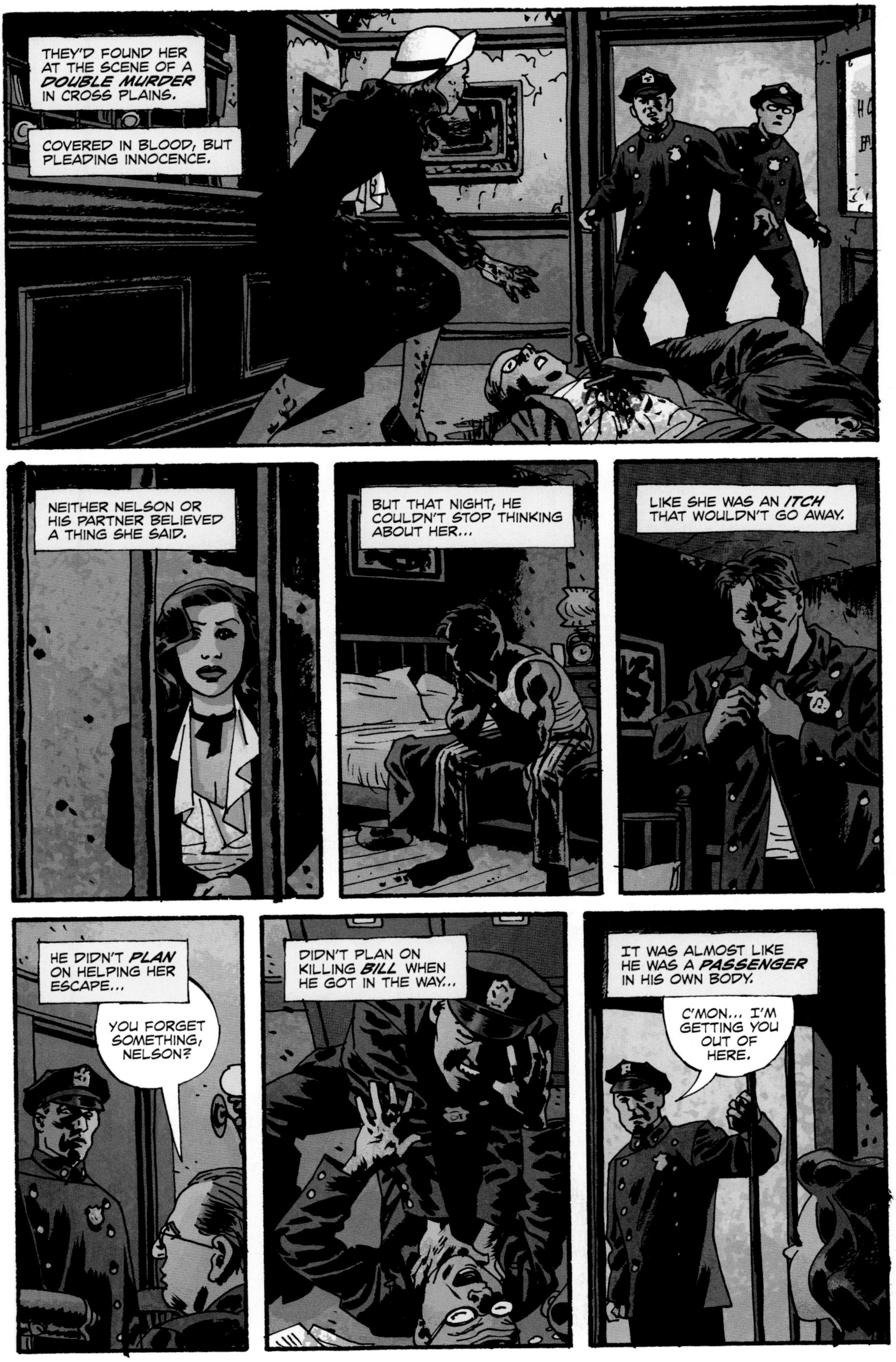

THEY'D FOUND HER AT THE SCENE OF A DOUBLE MURDER IN CROSS PLAINS.
COVERED IN BLOOD, BUT PLEADING INNOCENCE.
NEITHER NELSON OR HIS PARTNER BELIEVED A THING SHE SAID.
BUT THAT NIGHT, HE COULDN'T STOP THINKING ABOUT HER...
LIKE SHE WAS AN ITCH THAT WOULDN'T GO AWAY.
HE DIDN'T PLAN ON HELPING HER ESCAPE...
YOU FORGET SOMETHING, NELSON?
DIDN'T PLAN ON KILLING BILL WHEN HE GOT IN THE WAY...
IT WAS ALMOST LIKE HE WAS A PASSENGER IN HIS OWN BODY.
C'MON... I'M GETTING YOU OUT OF HERE.

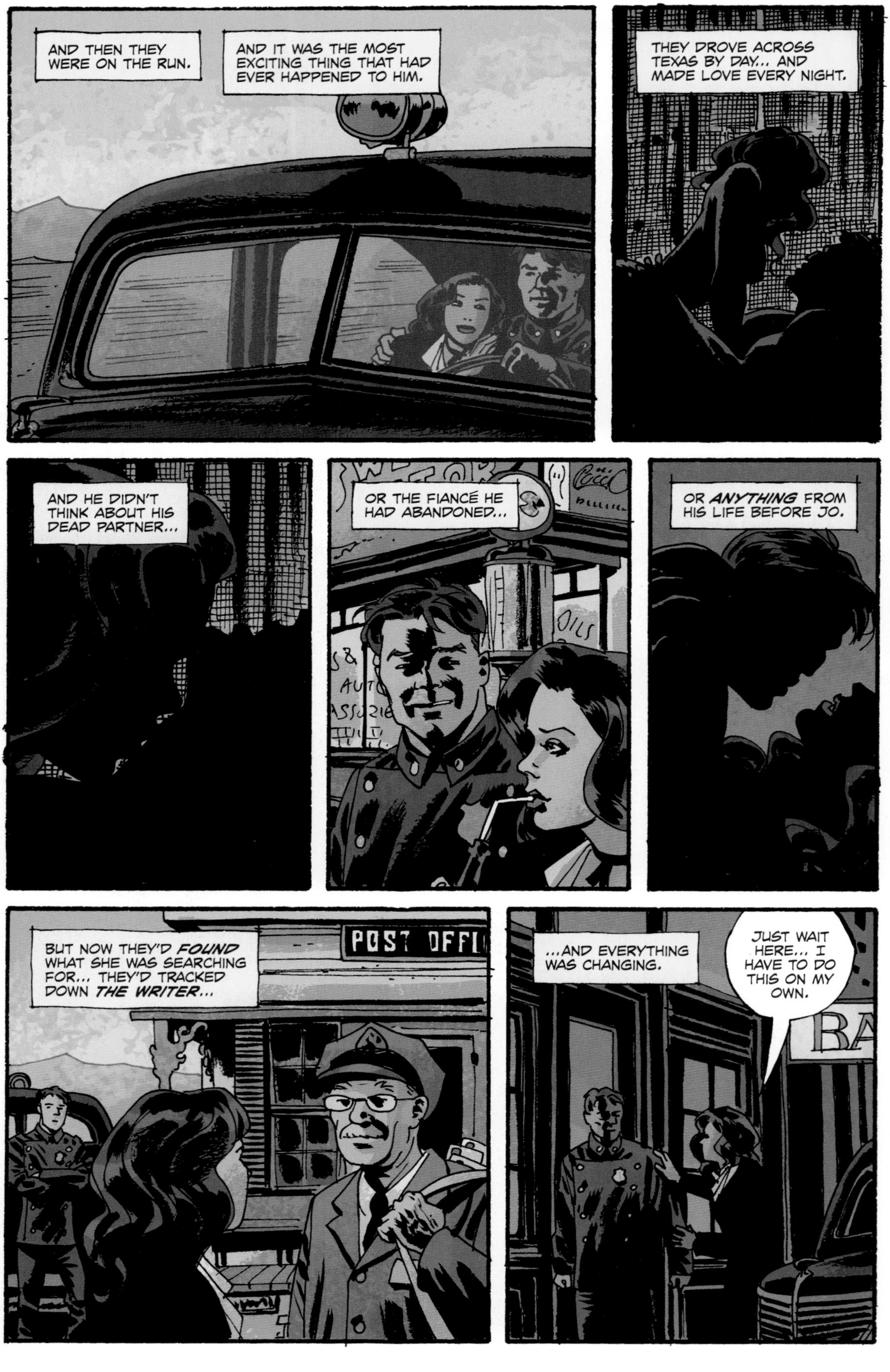
AND THEN THEY WERE ON THE RUN.
AND IT WAS THE MOST EXCITING THING THAT HAD EVER HAPPENED TO HIM.
THEY DROVE ACROSS TEXAS BY DAY... AND MADE LOVE EVERY NIGHT.
AND HE DIDN'T THINK ABOUT HIS DEAD PARTNER...
OR THE FIANCÉ HE HAD ABANDONED...
OR *ANYTHING* FROM HIS LIFE BEFORE JO.
BUT NOW THEY'D *FOUND* WHAT SHE WAS SEARCHING FOR... THEY'D TRACKED DOWN *THE WRITER*...
POST OFFI
...AND EVERYTHING WAS CHANGING.
JUST WAIT HERE... I HAVE TO DO THIS ON MY OWN.

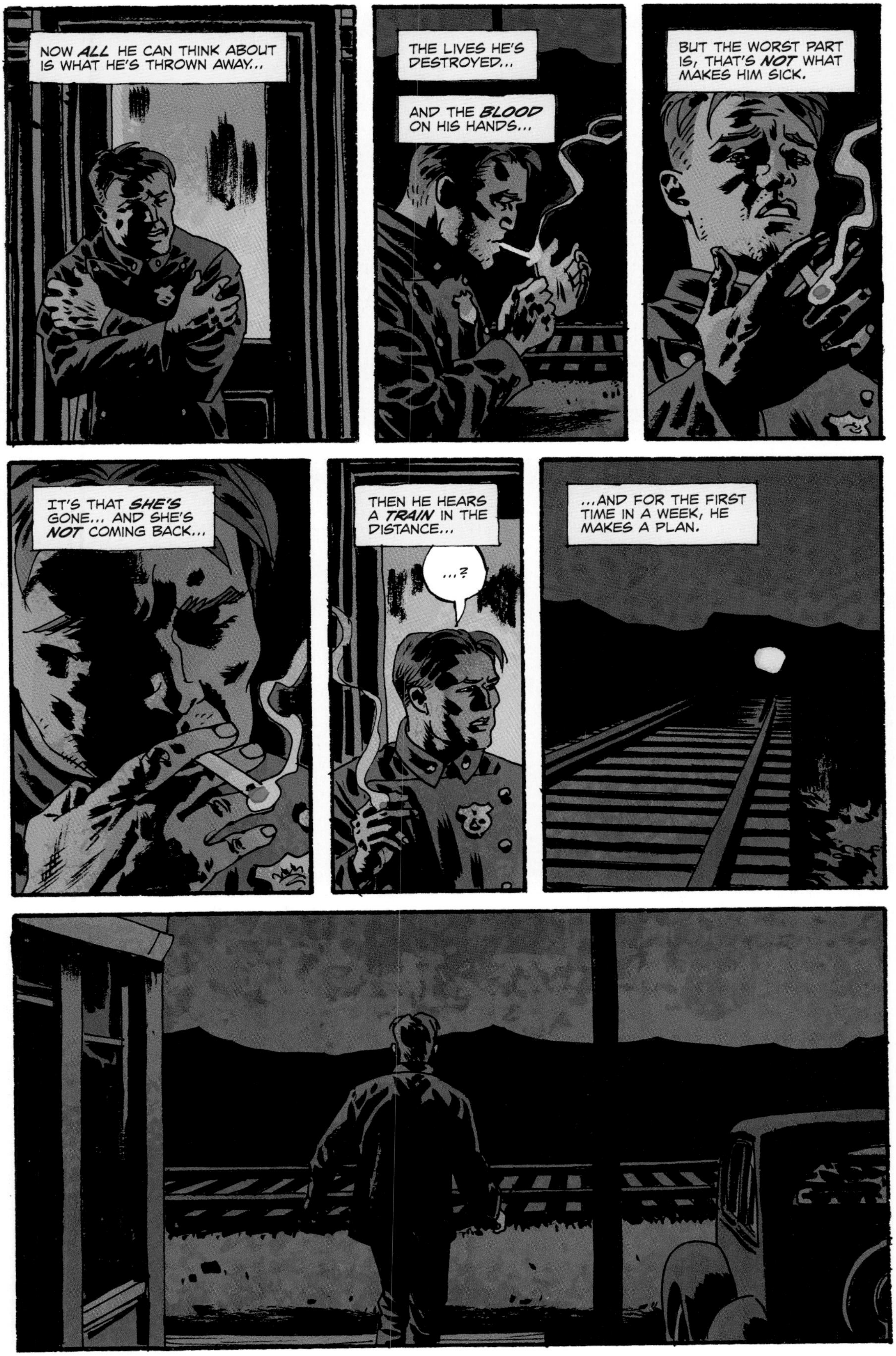
NOW ALL HE CAN THINK ABOUT IS WHAT HE'S THROWN AWAY...
THE LIVES HE'S DESTROYED...
AND THE BLOOD ON HIS HANDS...
BUT THE WORST PART IS, THAT'S NOT WHAT MAKES HIM SICK.
IT'S THAT SHE'S GONE... AND SHE'S NOT COMING BACK...
THEN HE HEARS A TRAIN IN THE DISTANCE...
...?
...AND FOR THE FIRST TIME IN A WEEK, HE MAKES A PLAN.

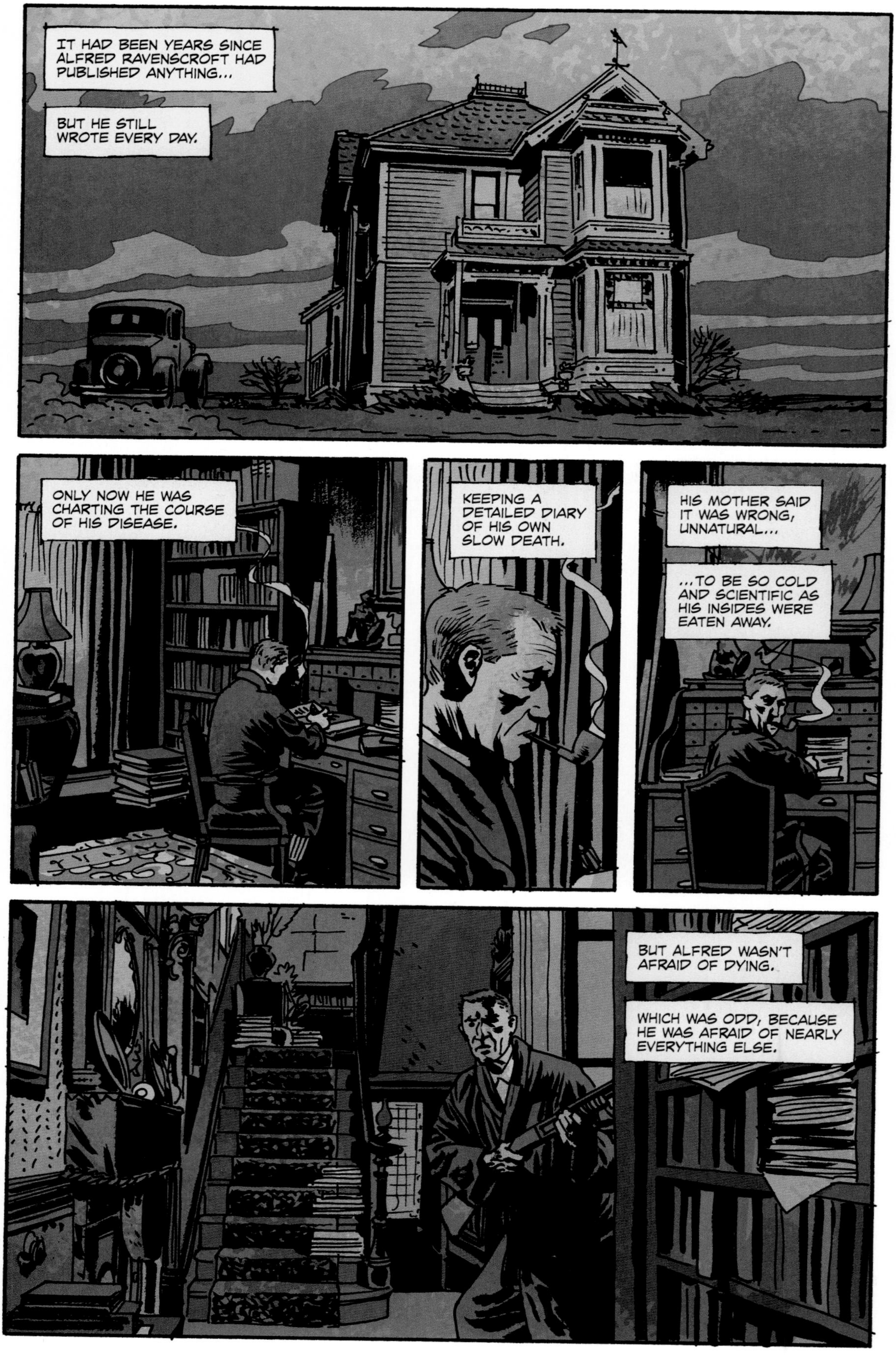
IT HAD BEEN YEARS SINCE ALFRED RAVENSCROFT HAD PUBLISHED ANYTHING...
BUT HE STILL WROTE EVERY DAY.
ONLY NOW HE WAS CHARTING THE COURSE OF HIS DISEASE.
KEEPING A DETAILED DIARY OF HIS OWN SLOW DEATH.
HIS MOTHER SAID IT WAS WRONG, UNNATURAL...
...TO BE SO COLD AND SCIENTIFIC AS HIS INSIDES WERE EATEN AWAY.
BUT ALFRED WASN'T AFRAID OF DYING.
WHICH WAS ODD, BECAUSE HE WAS AFRAID OF NEARLY EVERYTHING ELSE.

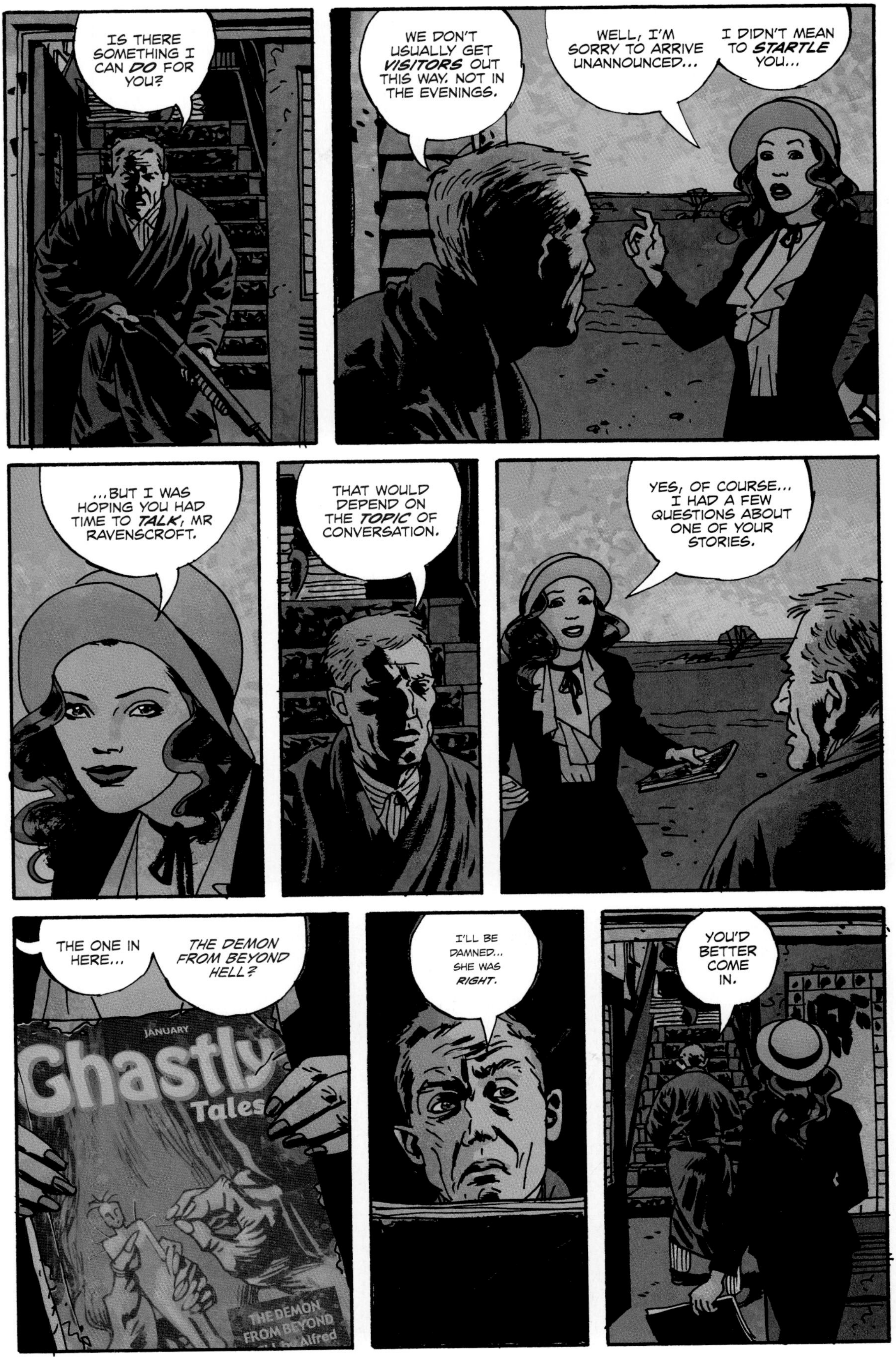
IS THERE SOMETHING I CAN *DO* FOR YOU?
WE DON'T USUALLY GET *VISITORS* OUT THIS WAY. NOT IN THE EVENINGS.
WELL, I'M SORRY TO ARRIVE UNANNOUNCED...
I DIDN'T MEAN TO *STARTLE* YOU...
...BUT I WAS HOPING YOU HAD TIME TO *TALK*, MR RAVENSCROFT.
THAT WOULD DEPEND ON THE *TOPIC* OF CONVERSATION.
YES, OF COURSE... I HAD A FEW QUESTIONS ABOUT ONE OF YOUR STORIES.
THE ONE IN HERE...
THE DEMON FROM BEYOND HELL?
JANUARY
Ghastly
Tales
THE DEMON FROM BEYOND
I'LL BE DAMNED... SHE WAS *RIGHT*.
YOU'D BETTER COME IN.

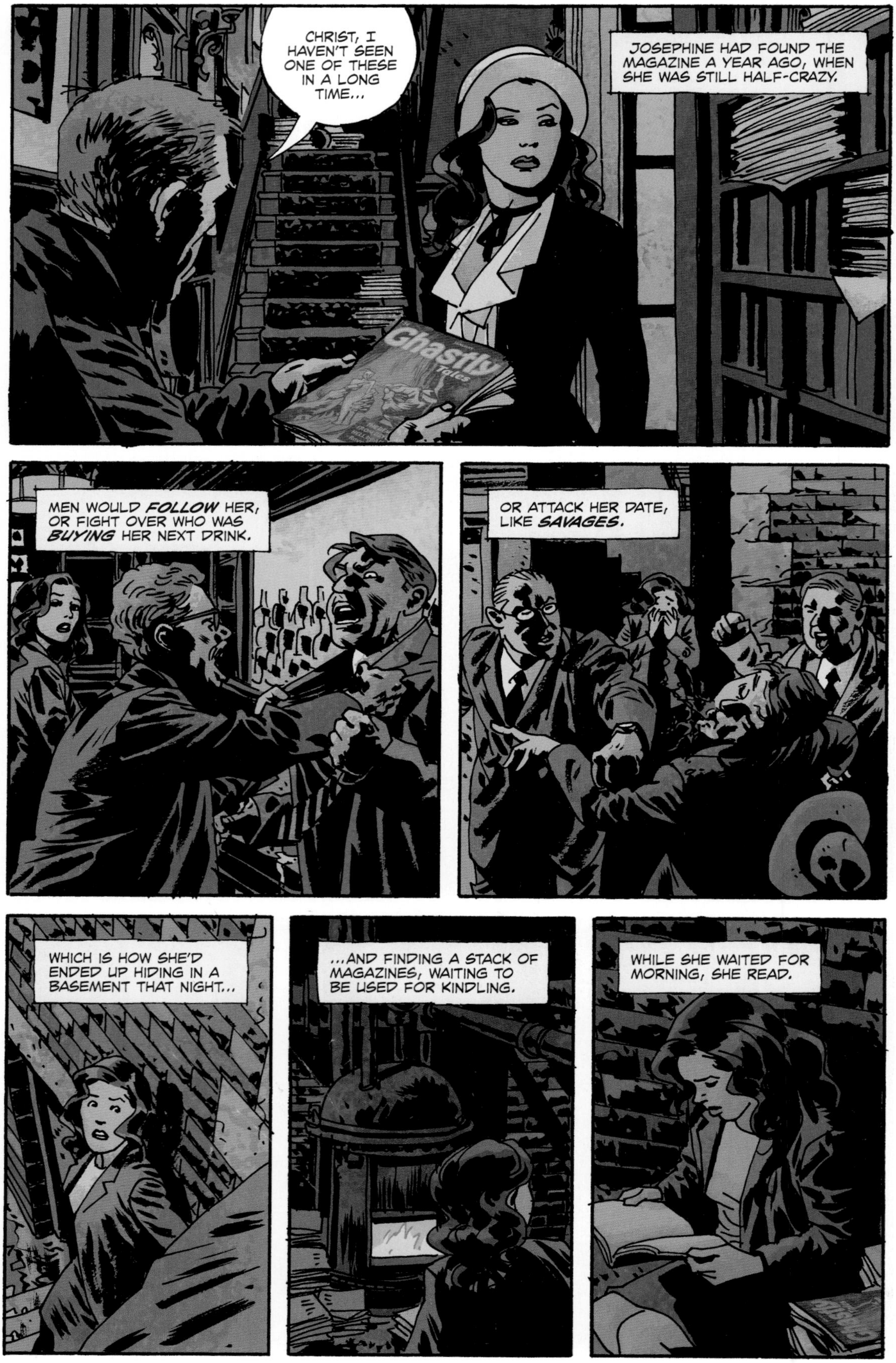

CHRIST, I HAVEN'T SEEN ONE OF THESE IN A LONG TIME...
JOSEPHINE HAD FOUND THE MAGAZINE A YEAR AGO, WHEN SHE WAS STILL HALF-CRAZY.
Ghastly Tales
MEN WOULD FOLLOW HER, OR FIGHT OVER WHO WAS BUYING HER NEXT DRINK.
OR ATTACK HER DATE, LIKE SAVAGES.
WHICH IS HOW SHE'D ENDED UP HIDING IN A BASEMENT THAT NIGHT...
...AND FINDING A STACK OF MAGAZINES, WAITING TO BE USED FOR KINDLING.
WHILE SHE WAITED FOR MORNING, SHE READ.

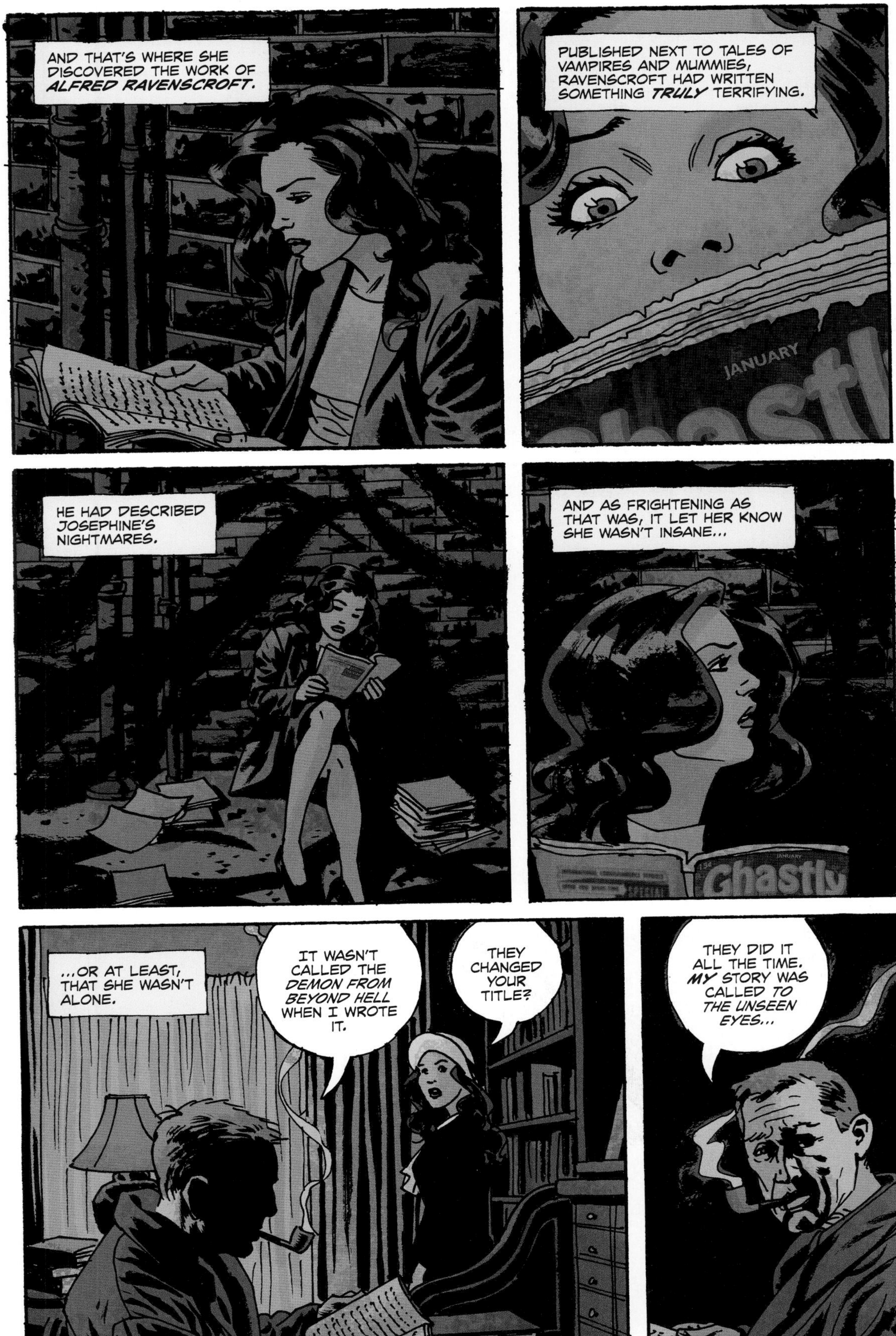
AND THAT'S WHERE SHE DISCOVERED THE WORK OF ALFRED RAVENSCROFT.
PUBLISHED NEXT TO TALES OF VAMPIRES AND MUMMIES, RAVENSCROFT HAD WRITTEN SOMETHING TRULY TERRIFYING.
JANUARY
HE HAD DESCRIBED JOSEPHINE'S NIGHTMARES.
AND AS FRIGHTENING AS THAT WAS, IT LET HER KNOW SHE WASN'T INSANE...
Ghastly
...OR AT LEAST, THAT SHE WASN'T ALONE.
IT WASN'T CALLED THE DEMON FROM BEYOND HELL WHEN I WROTE IT.
THEY CHANGED YOUR TITLE?
THEY DID IT ALL THE TIME. MY STORY WAS CALLED TO THE UNSEEN EYES...

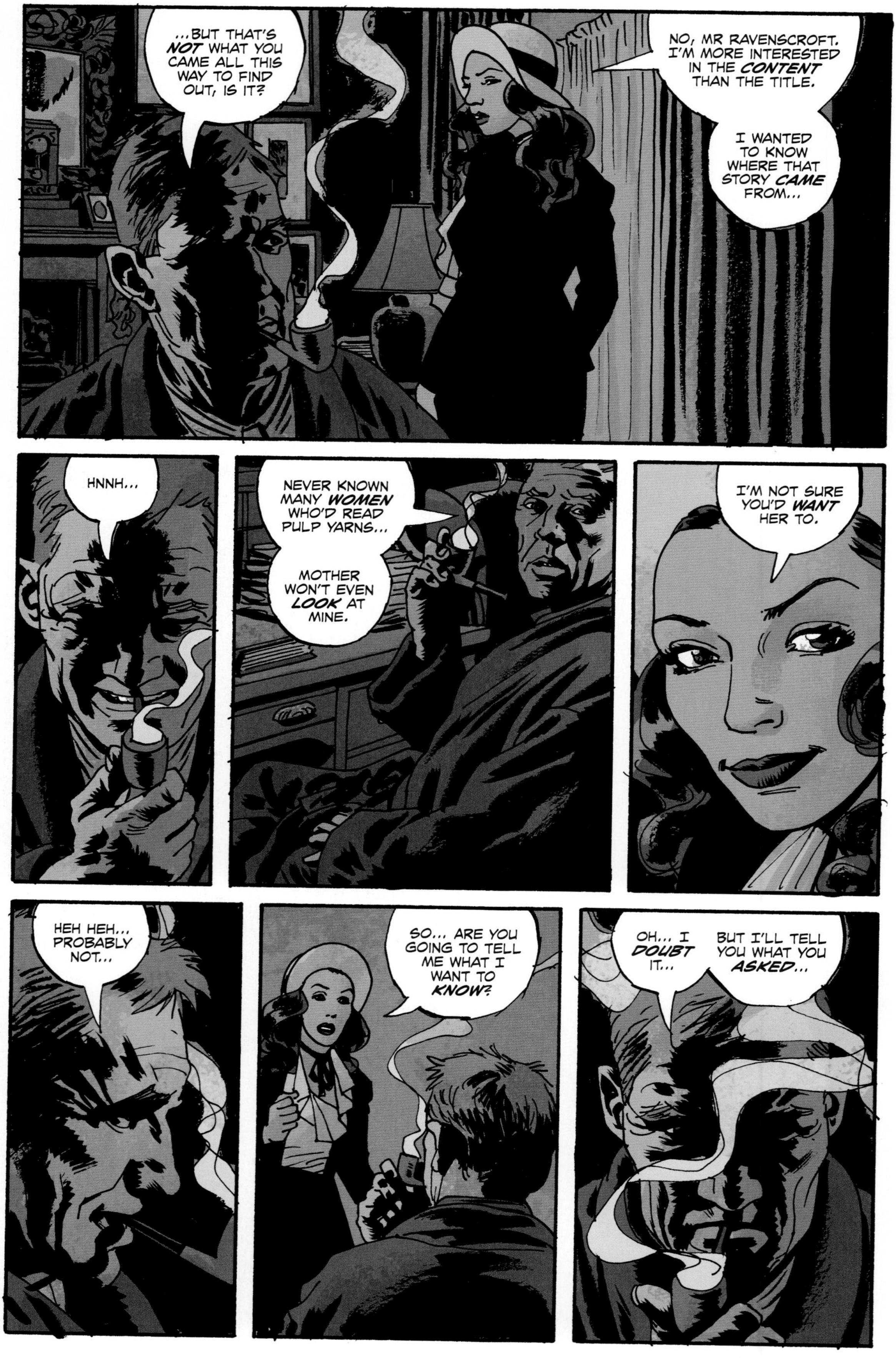
...BUT THAT'S NOT WHAT YOU CAME ALL THIS WAY TO FIND OUT, IS IT?
NO, MR RAVENSCROFT. I'M MORE INTERESTED IN THE CONTENT THAN THE TITLE.
I WANTED TO KNOW WHERE THAT STORY CAME FROM...
HNNH...
NEVER KNOWN MANY WOMEN WHO'D READ PULP YARNS...
MOTHER WON'T EVEN LOOK AT MINE.
I'M NOT SURE YOU'D WANT HER TO.
HEH HEH... PROBABLY NOT...
SO... ARE YOU GOING TO TELL ME WHAT I WANT TO KNOW?
OH... I DOUBT IT...
BUT I'LL TELL YOU WHAT YOU ASKED...

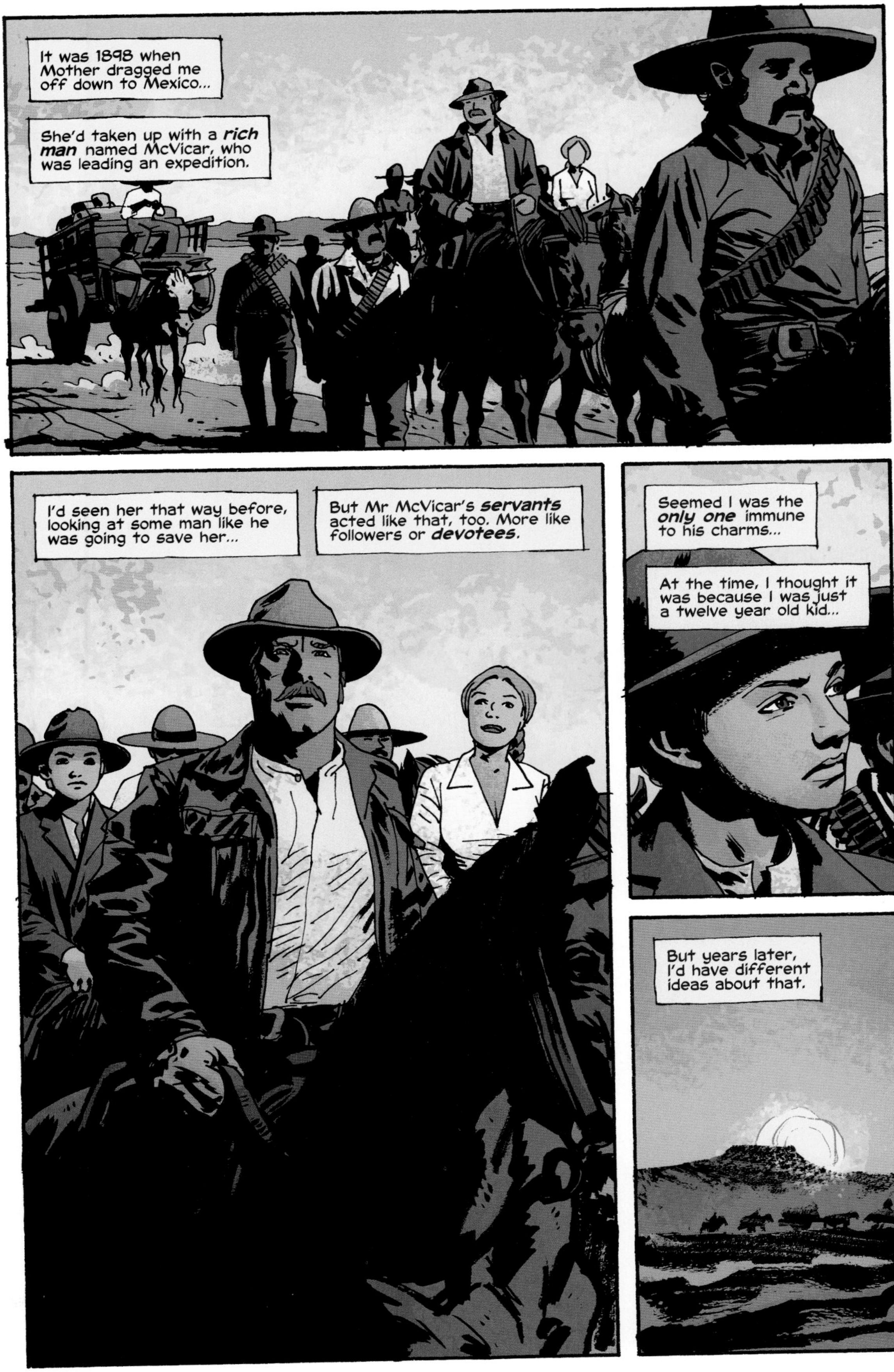
It was 1898 when Mother dragged me off down to Mexico...
She'd taken up with a *rich man* named McVicar, who was leading an expedition.
I'd seen her that way before, looking at some man like he was going to save her...
But Mr McVicar's *servants* acted like that, too. More like followers or *devotees*.
Seemed I was the *only one* immune to his charms...
At the time, I thought it was because I was just a twelve year old kid...
But years later, I'd have different ideas about that.

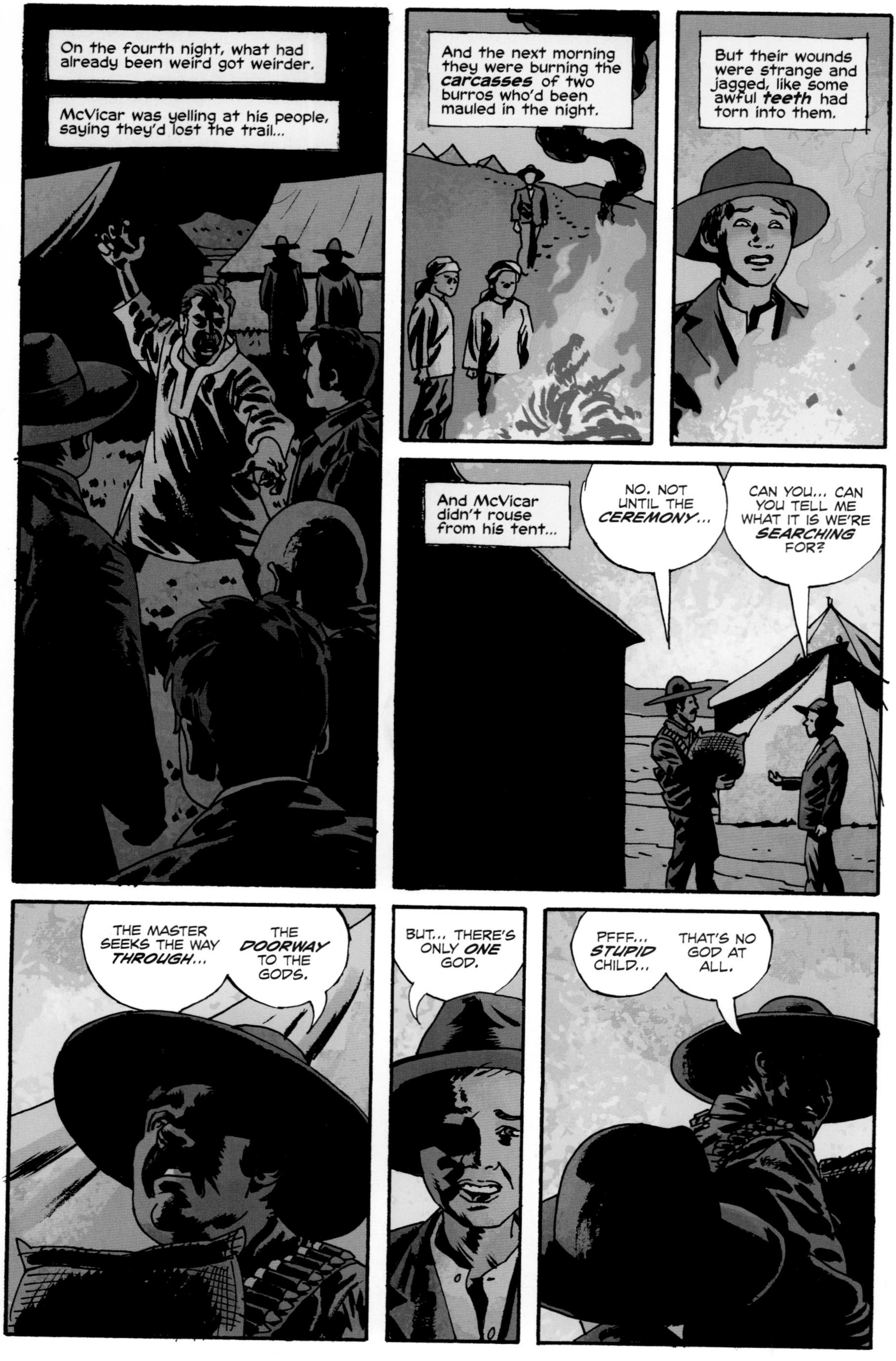
On the fourth night, what had already been weird got weirder.
McVicar was yelling at his people, saying they'd lost the trail...
And the next morning they were burning the carcasses of two burros who'd been mauled in the night.
But their wounds were strange and jagged, like some awful teeth had torn into them.
And McVicar didn't rouse from his tent...
NO. NOT UNTIL THE CEREMONY...
CAN YOU... CAN YOU TELL ME WHAT IT IS WE'RE SEARCHING FOR?
THE MASTER SEEKS THE WAY THROUGH...
THE DOORWAY TO THE GODS.
BUT... THERE'S ONLY ONE GOD.
PFFF... STUPID CHILD...
THAT'S NO GOD AT ALL.

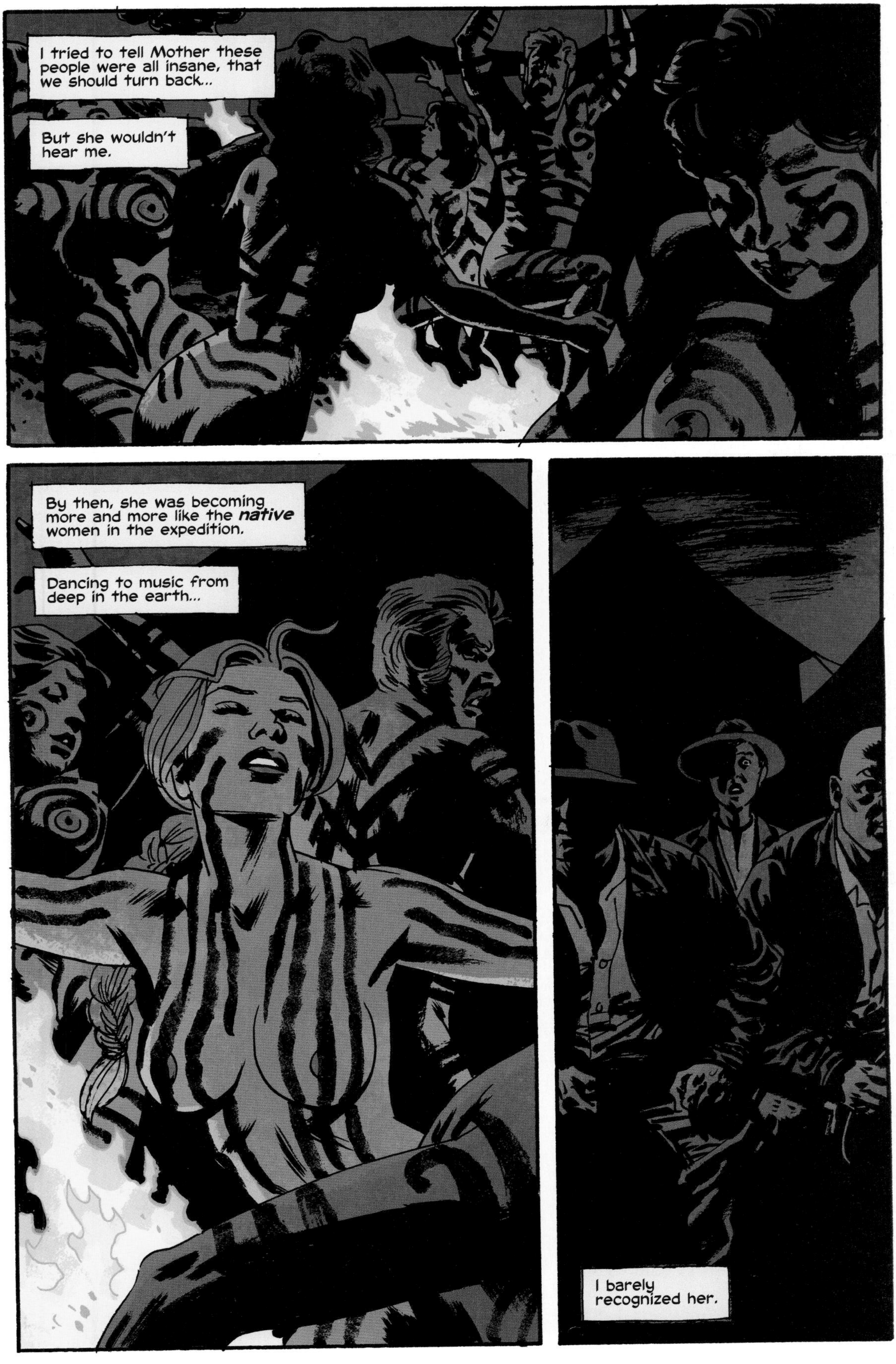
I tried to tell Mother these people were all insane, that we should turn back...
But she wouldn't hear me.
By then, she was becoming more and more like the *native* women in the expedition.
Dancing to music from deep in the earth...
I barely recognized her.

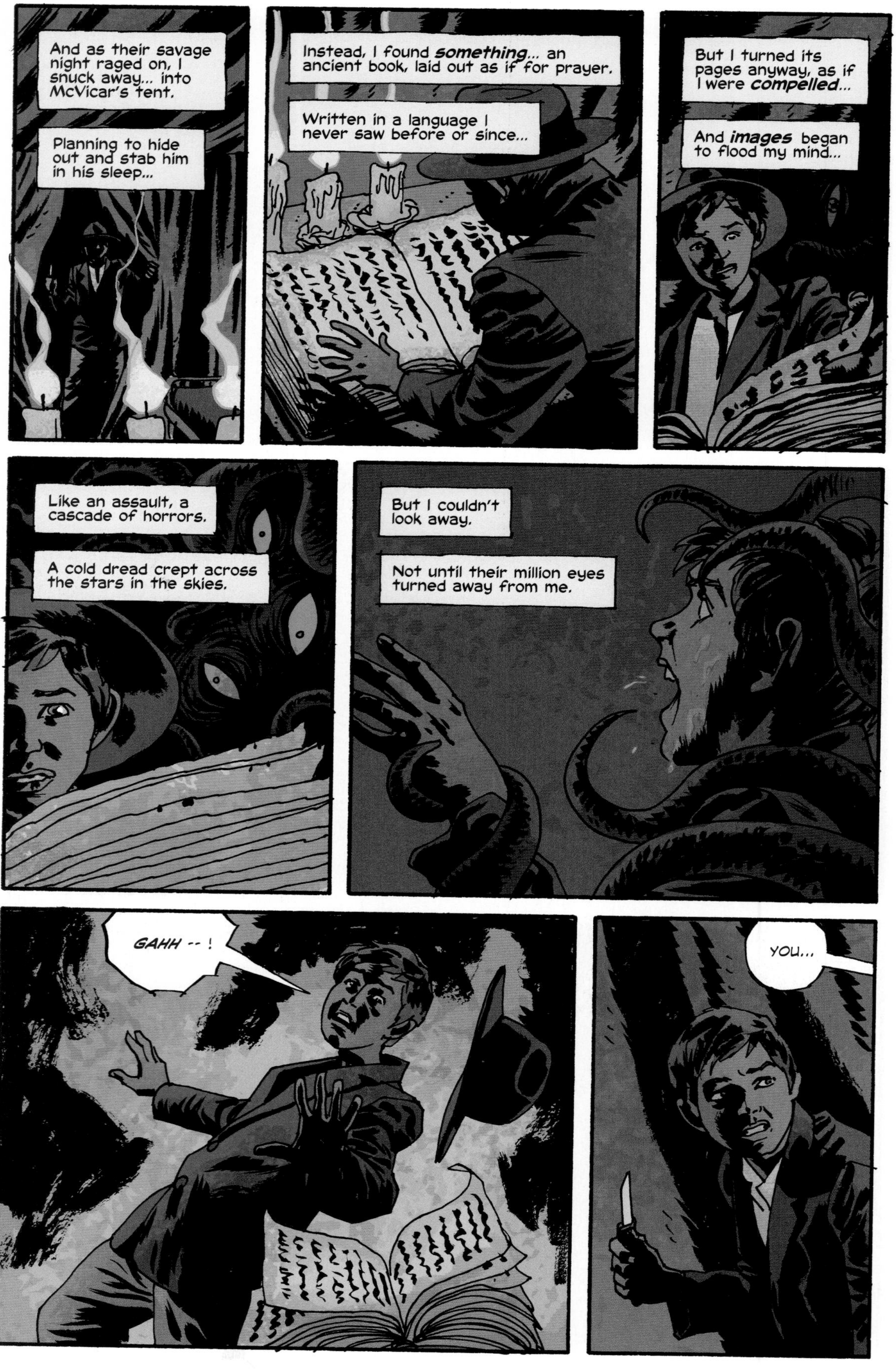
And as their savage night raged on, I snuck away... into McVicar's tent.
Planning to hide out and stab him in his sleep...
Instead, I found *something*... an ancient book, laid out as if for prayer.
Written in a language I never saw before or since...
But I turned its pages anyway, as if I were *compelled*...
And *images* began to flood my mind...
Like an assault, a cascade of horrors.
A cold dread crept across the stars in the skies.
But I couldn't look away.
Not until their million eyes turned away from me.
GAHH -- !
YOU...

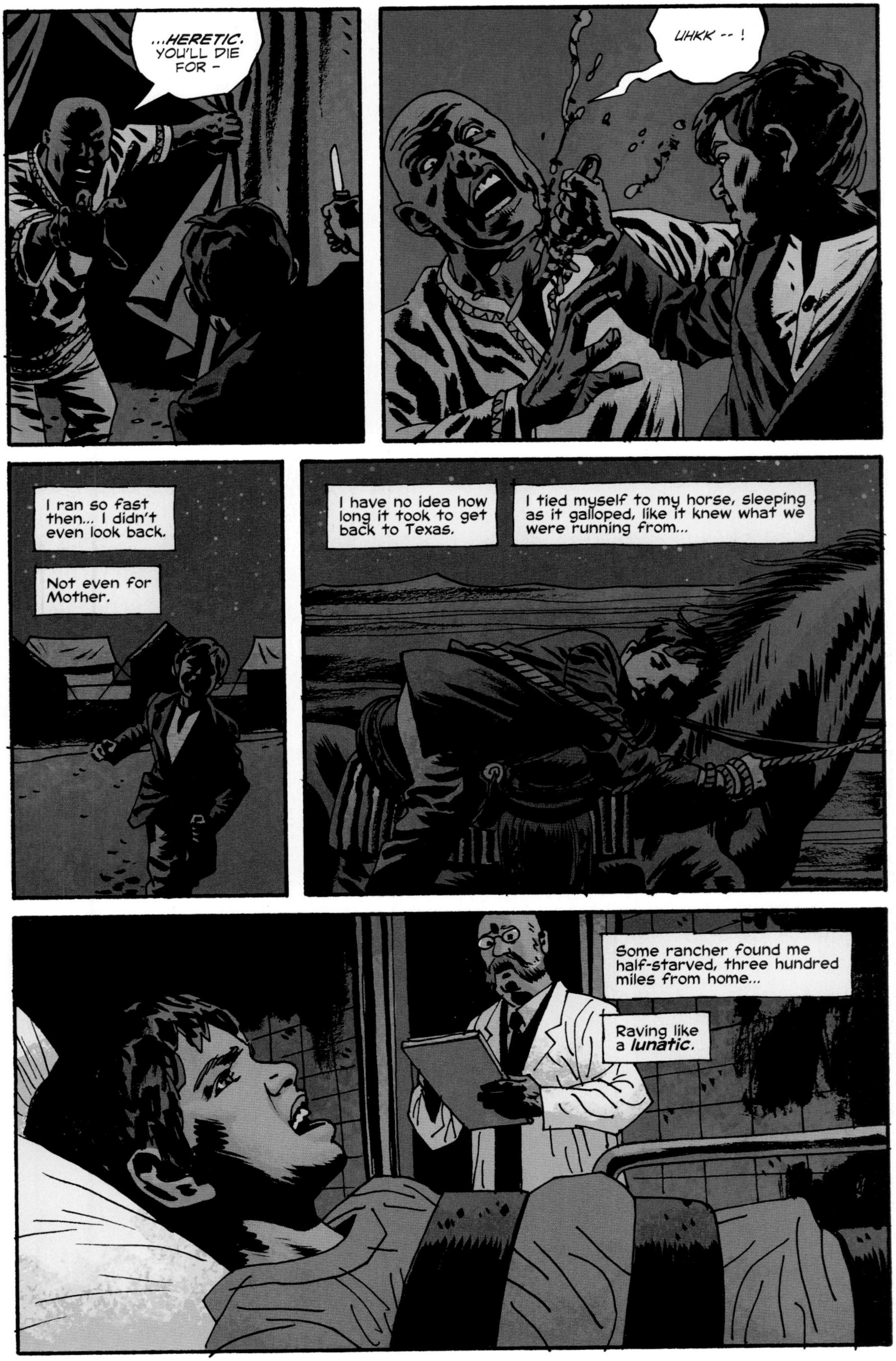
...HERETIC. YOU'LL DIE FOR -
UHKK -- !
I ran so fast then... I didn't even look back.
Not even for Mother.
I have no idea how long it took to get back to Texas.
I tied myself to my horse, sleeping as it galloped, like it knew what we were running from...
Some rancher found me half-starved, three hundred miles from home...
Raving like a lunatic.

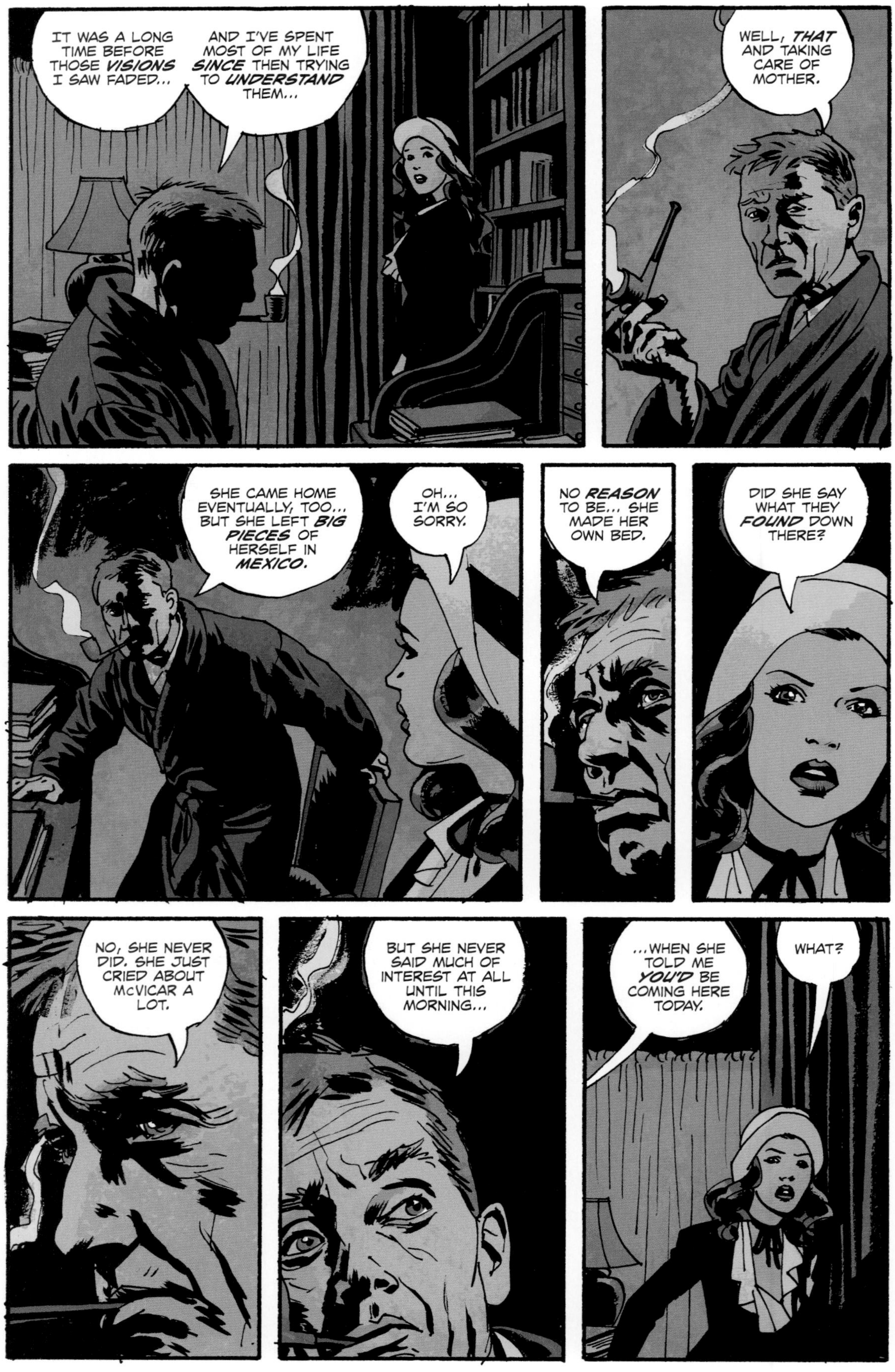
IT WAS A LONG TIME BEFORE THOSE VISIONS I SAW FADED...
AND I'VE SPENT MOST OF MY LIFE SINCE THEN TRYING TO UNDERSTAND THEM...
WELL, THAT AND TAKING CARE OF MOTHER.
SHE CAME HOME EVENTUALLY, TOO... BUT SHE LEFT BIG PIECES OF HERSELF IN MEXICO.
OH... I'M SO SORRY.
NO REASON TO BE... SHE MADE HER OWN BED.
DID SHE SAY WHAT THEY FOUND DOWN THERE?
NO, SHE NEVER DID. SHE JUST CRIED ABOUT McVICAR A LOT.
BUT SHE NEVER SAID MUCH OF INTEREST AT ALL UNTIL THIS MORNING...
...WHEN SHE TOLD ME YOU'D BE COMING HERE TODAY.
WHAT?

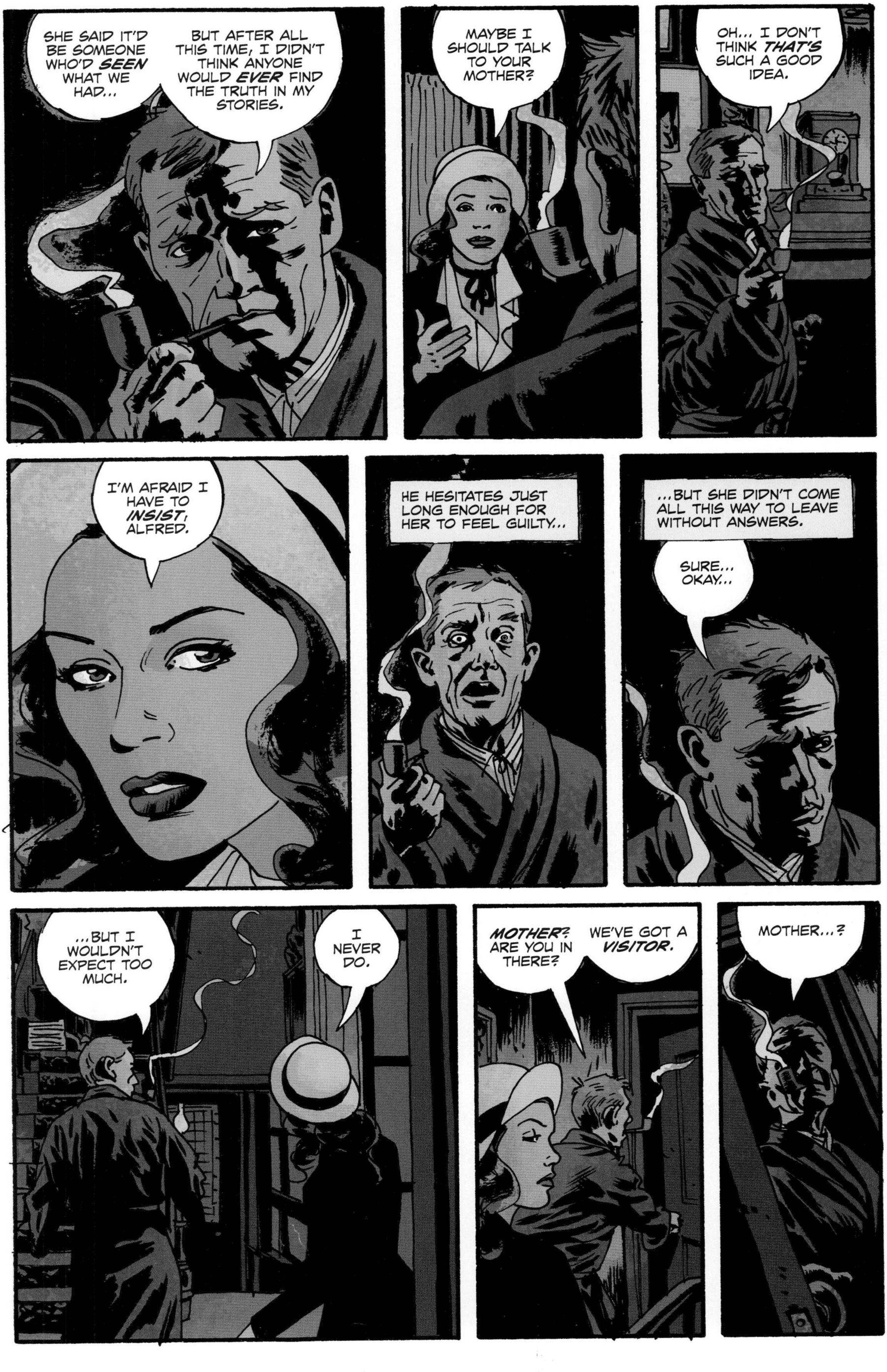

SHE SAID IT'D BE SOMEONE WHO'D SEEN WHAT WE HAD...
BUT AFTER ALL THIS TIME, I DIDN'T THINK ANYONE WOULD EVER FIND THE TRUTH IN MY STORIES.
MAYBE I SHOULD TALK TO YOUR MOTHER?
OH... I DON'T THINK THAT'S SUCH A GOOD IDEA.
I'M AFRAID I HAVE TO INSIST, ALFRED.
HE HESITATES JUST LONG ENOUGH FOR HER TO FEEL GUILTY...
...BUT SHE DIDN'T COME ALL THIS WAY TO LEAVE WITHOUT ANSWERS.
SURE... OKAY...
...BUT I WOULDN'T EXPECT TOO MUCH.
I NEVER DO.
MOTHER? ARE YOU IN THERE?
WE'VE GOT A VISITOR.
MOTHER...?

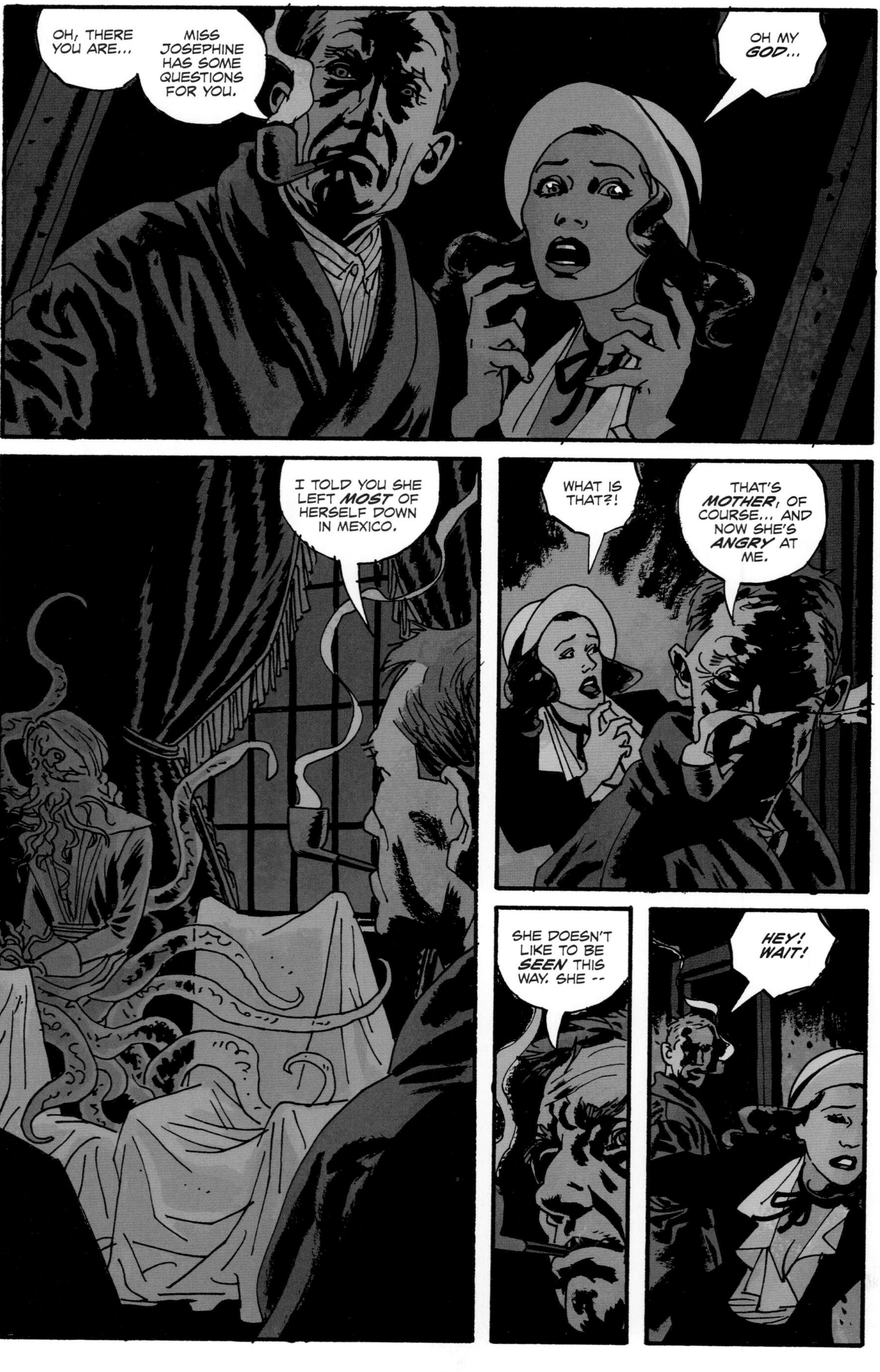
OH, THERE YOU ARE...
MISS JOSEPHINE HAS SOME QUESTIONS FOR YOU.
OH MY GOD...
I TOLD YOU SHE LEFT MOST OF HERSELF DOWN IN MEXICO.
WHAT IS THAT?!
THAT'S MOTHER, OF COURSE... AND NOW SHE'S ANGRY AT ME.
SHE DOESN'T LIKE TO BE SEEN THIS WAY. SHE --
HEY! WAIT!

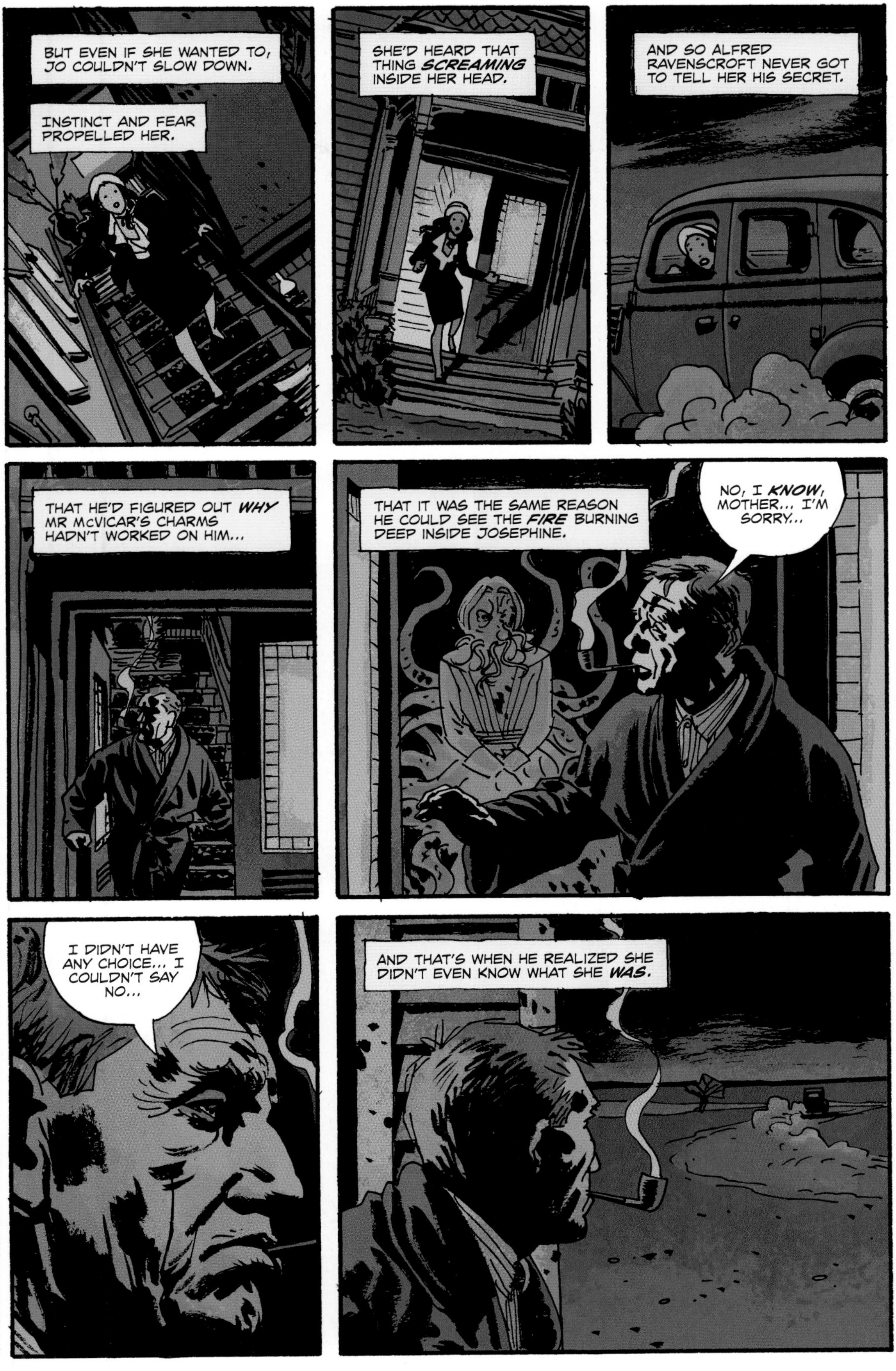
BUT EVEN IF SHE WANTED TO, JO COULDN'T SLOW DOWN.
INSTINCT AND FEAR PROPELLED HER.
SHE'D HEARD THAT THING *SCREAMING* INSIDE HER HEAD.
AND SO ALFRED RAVENSCROFT NEVER GOT TO TELL HER HIS SECRET.
THAT HE'D FIGURED OUT *WHY* MR McVICAR'S CHARMS HADN'T WORKED ON HIM...
THAT IT WAS THE SAME REASON HE COULD SEE THE *FIRE* BURNING DEEP INSIDE JOSEPHINE.
NO, I *KNOW*, MOTHER... I'M SORRY...
I DIDN'T HAVE ANY CHOICE... I COULDN'T SAY NO...
AND THAT'S WHEN HE REALIZED SHE DIDN'T EVEN KNOW WHAT SHE *WAS*.

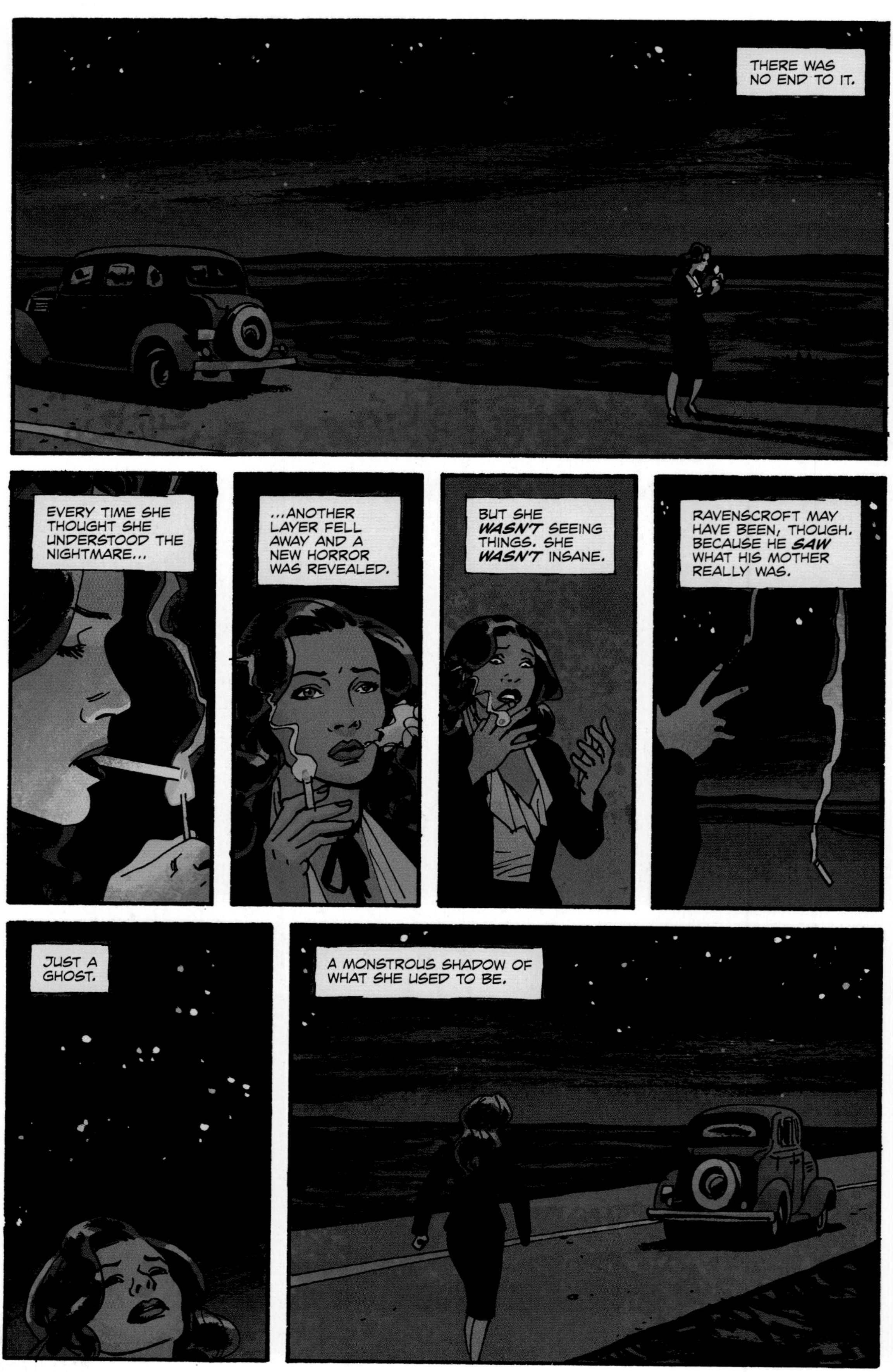
THERE WAS NO END TO IT.
EVERY TIME SHE THOUGHT SHE UNDERSTOOD THE NIGHTMARE...
...ANOTHER LAYER FELL AWAY AND A NEW HORROR WAS REVEALED.
BUT SHE WASN'T SEEING THINGS. SHE WASN'T INSANE.
RAVENSCROFT MAY HAVE BEEN, THOUGH. BECAUSE HE SAW WHAT HIS MOTHER REALLY WAS.
JUST A GHOST.
A MONSTROUS SHADOW OF WHAT SHE USED TO BE.

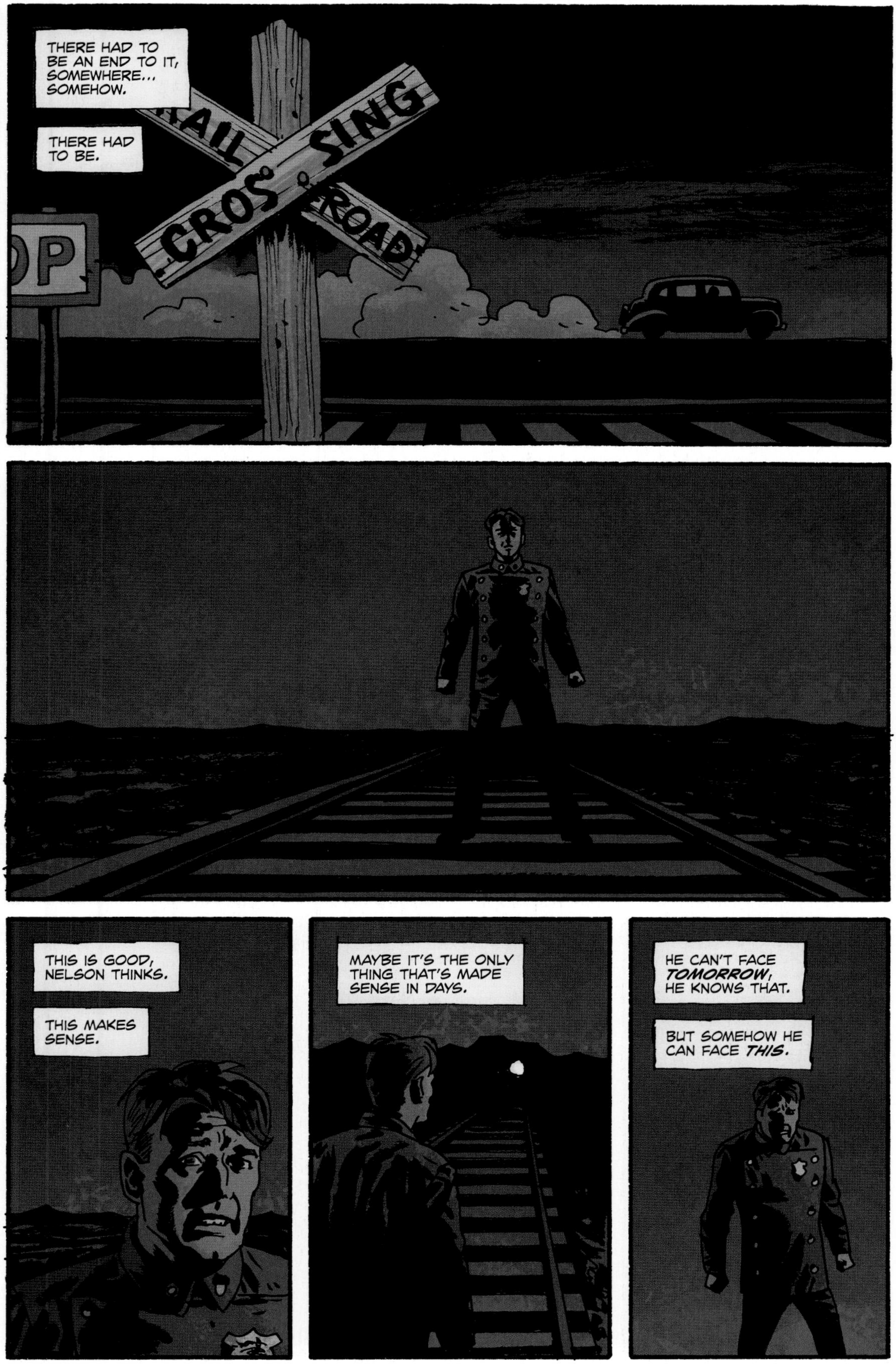
THERE HAD TO BE AN END TO IT, SOMEWHERE... SOMEHOW.
THERE HAD TO BE.
RAIL ROAD CROSSING
OP
THIS IS GOOD, NELSON THINKS.
THIS MAKES SENSE.
MAYBE IT'S THE ONLY THING THAT'S MADE SENSE IN DAYS.
HE CAN'T FACE *TOMORROW*, HE KNOWS THAT.
BUT SOMEHOW HE CAN FACE *THIS*.

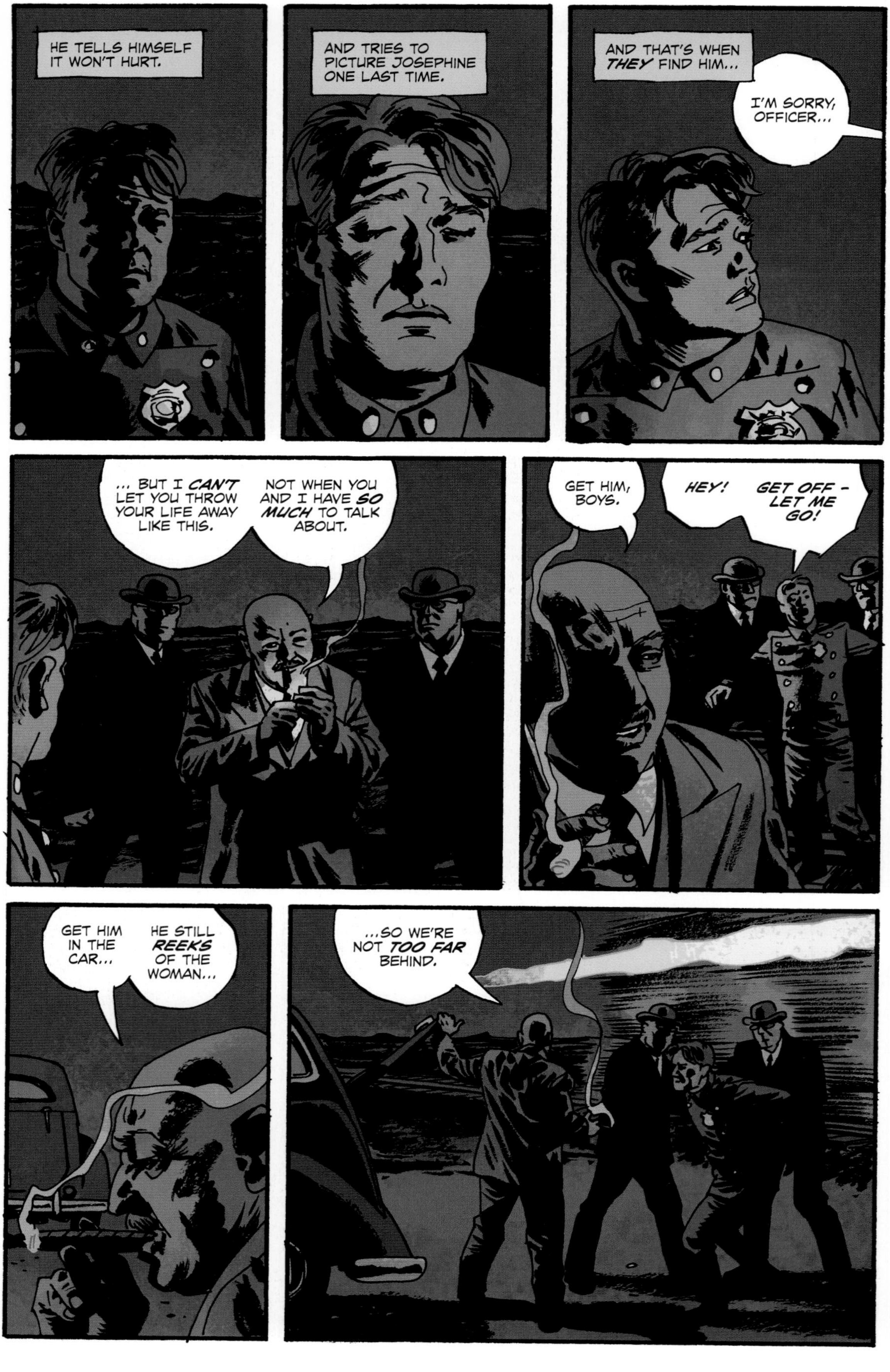
HE TELLS HIMSELF IT WON'T HURT.
AND TRIES TO PICTURE JOSEPHINE ONE LAST TIME.
AND THAT'S WHEN *THEY* FIND HIM...
I'M SORRY, OFFICER...
... BUT I *CAN'T* LET YOU THROW YOUR LIFE AWAY LIKE THIS.
NOT WHEN YOU AND I HAVE *SO MUCH* TO TALK ABOUT.
GET HIM, BOYS.
HEY!
GET OFF - LET ME GO!
GET HIM IN THE CAR...
HE STILL *REEKS* OF THE WOMAN...
...SO WE'RE NOT *TOO FAR* BEHIND.

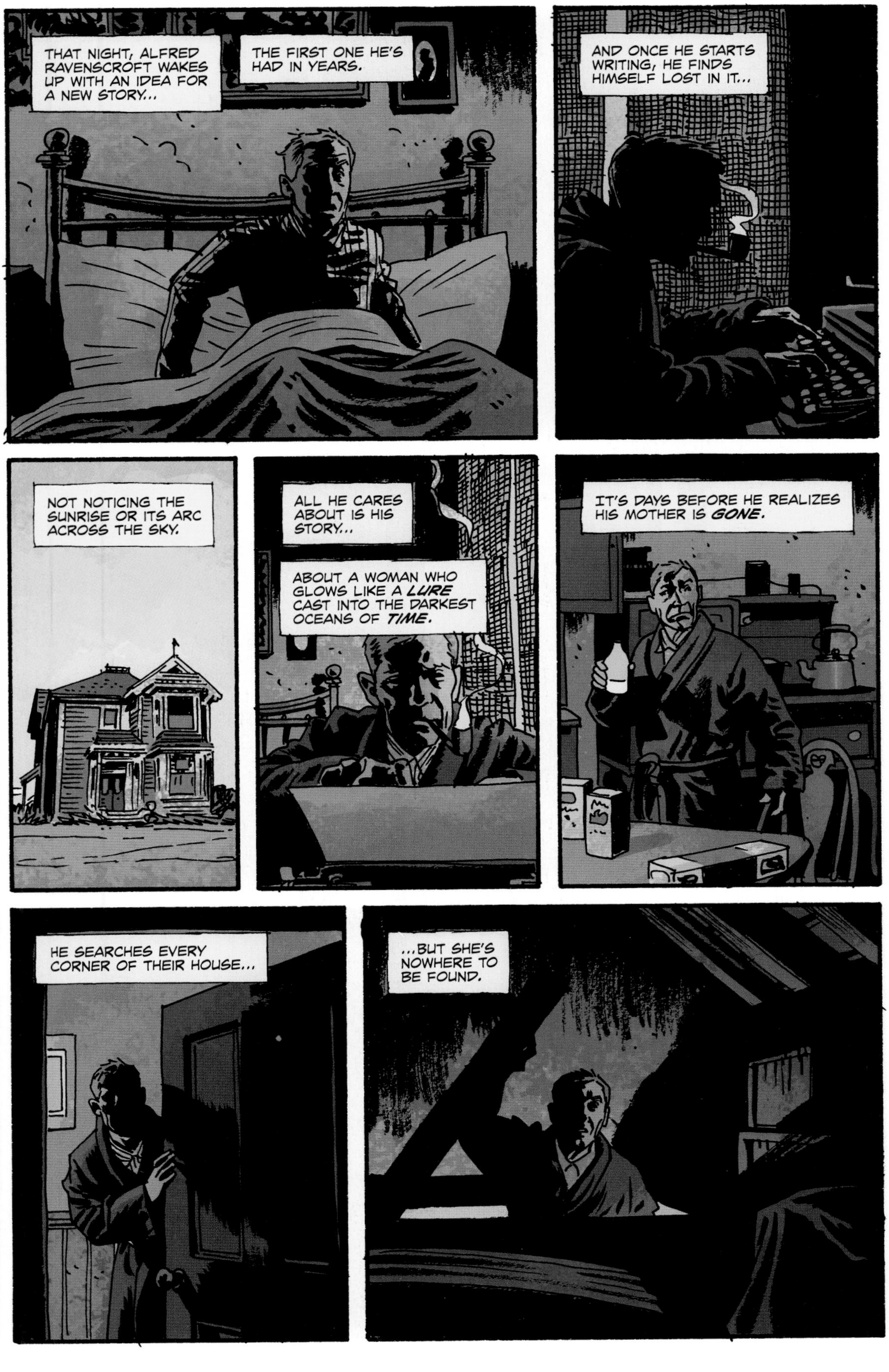
THAT NIGHT, ALFRED RAVENSCROFT WAKES UP WITH AN IDEA FOR A NEW STORY...
THE FIRST ONE HE'S HAD IN YEARS.
AND ONCE HE STARTS WRITING, HE FINDS HIMSELF LOST IN IT...
NOT NOTICING THE SUNRISE OR ITS ARC ACROSS THE SKY.
ALL HE CARES ABOUT IS HIS STORY...
ABOUT A WOMAN WHO GLOWS LIKE A LURE CAST INTO THE DARKEST OCEANS OF TIME.
IT'S DAYS BEFORE HE REALIZES HIS MOTHER IS GONE.
HE SEARCHES EVERY CORNER OF THEIR HOUSE...
...BUT SHE'S NOWHERE TO BE FOUND.

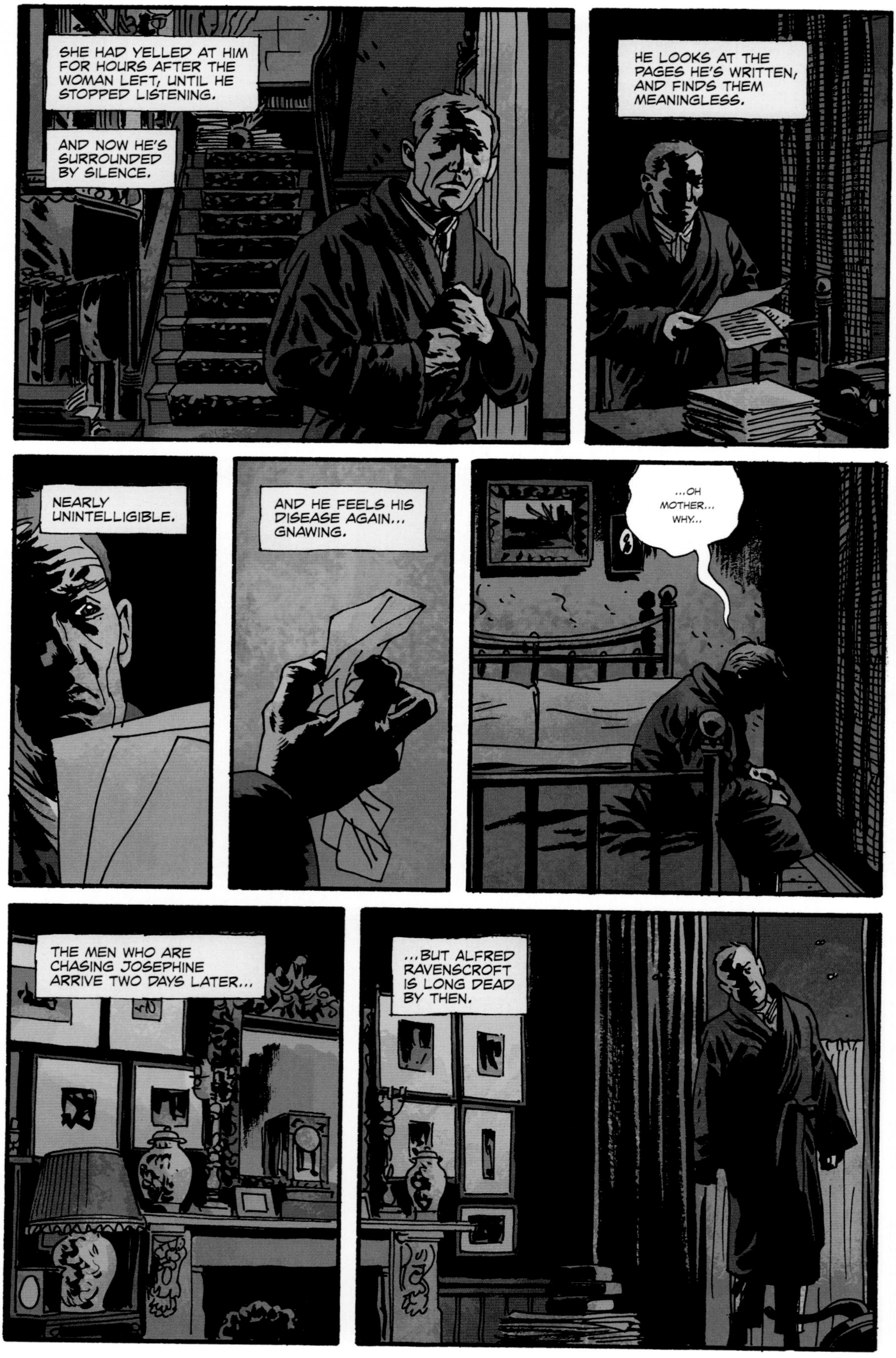

SHE HAD YELLED AT HIM FOR HOURS AFTER THE WOMAN LEFT, UNTIL HE STOPPED LISTENING.
AND NOW HE'S SURROUNDED BY SILENCE.
HE LOOKS AT THE PAGES HE'S WRITTEN, AND FINDS THEM MEANINGLESS.
NEARLY UNINTELLIGIBLE.
AND HE FEELS HIS DISEASE AGAIN... GNAWING.
...OH MOTHER... WHY...
THE MEN WHO ARE CHASING JOSEPHINE ARRIVE TWO DAYS LATER...
...BUT ALFRED RAVENSCROFT IS LONG DEAD BY THEN.

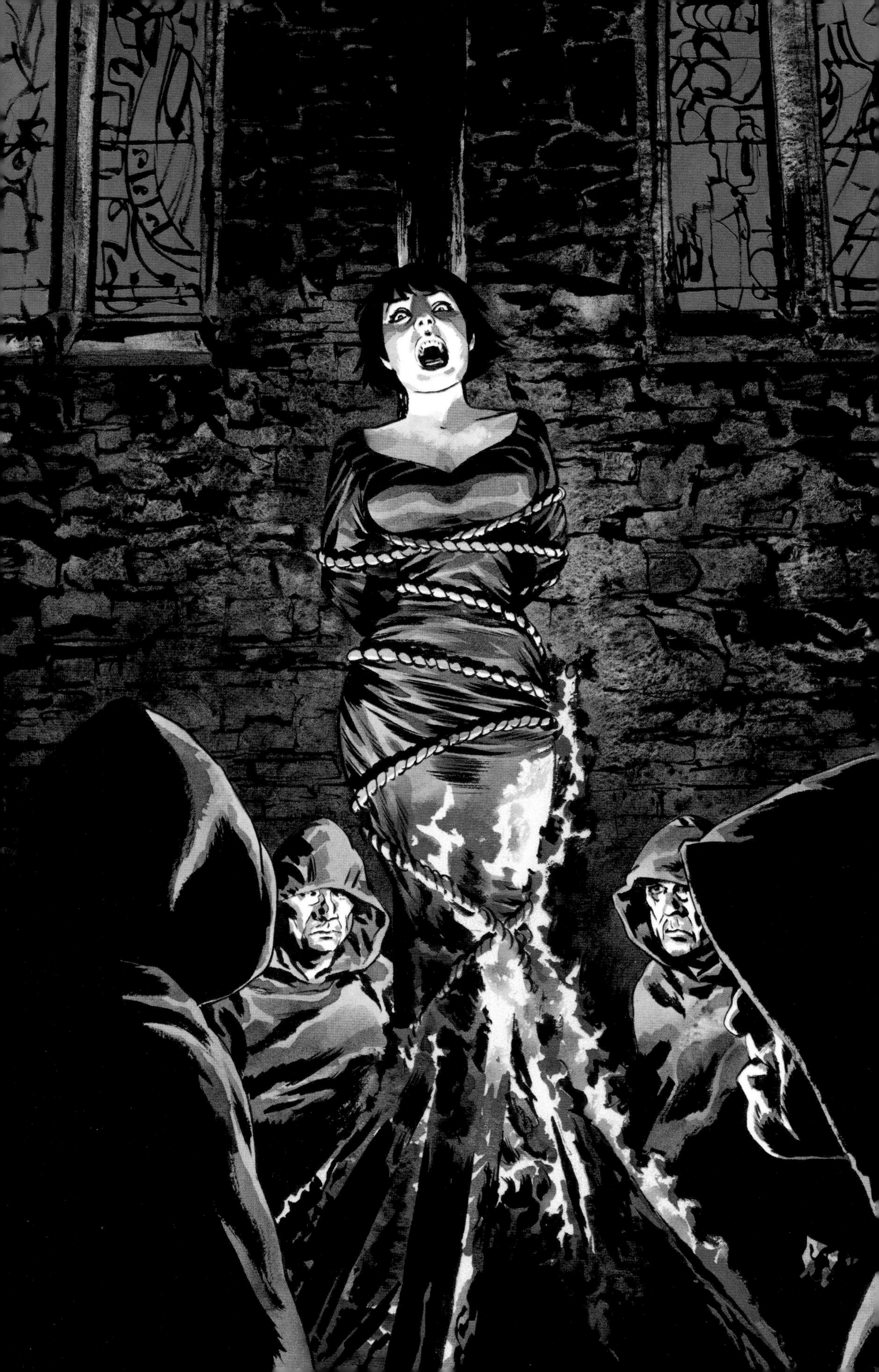

A Lovely Sort Of Death

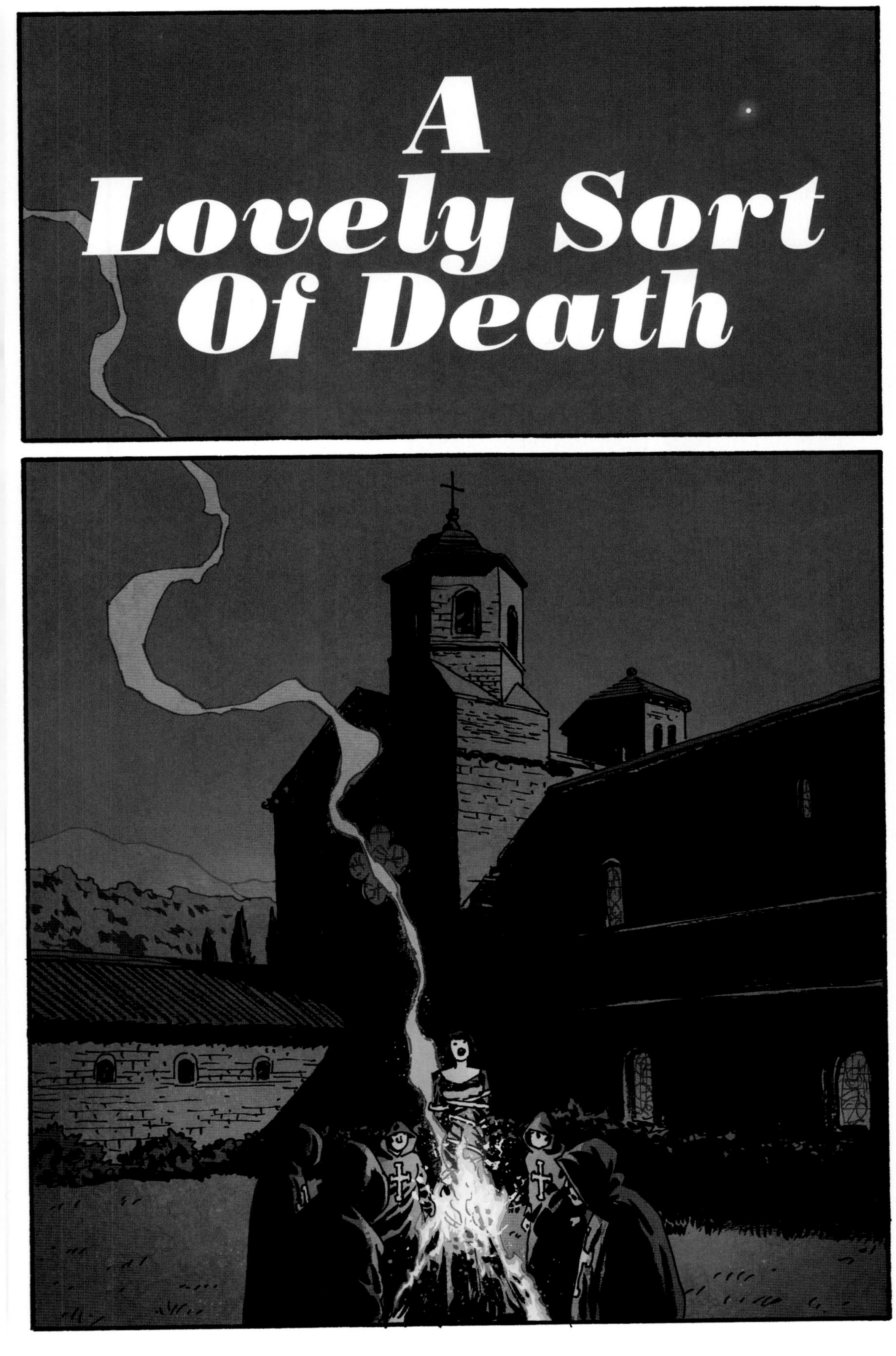

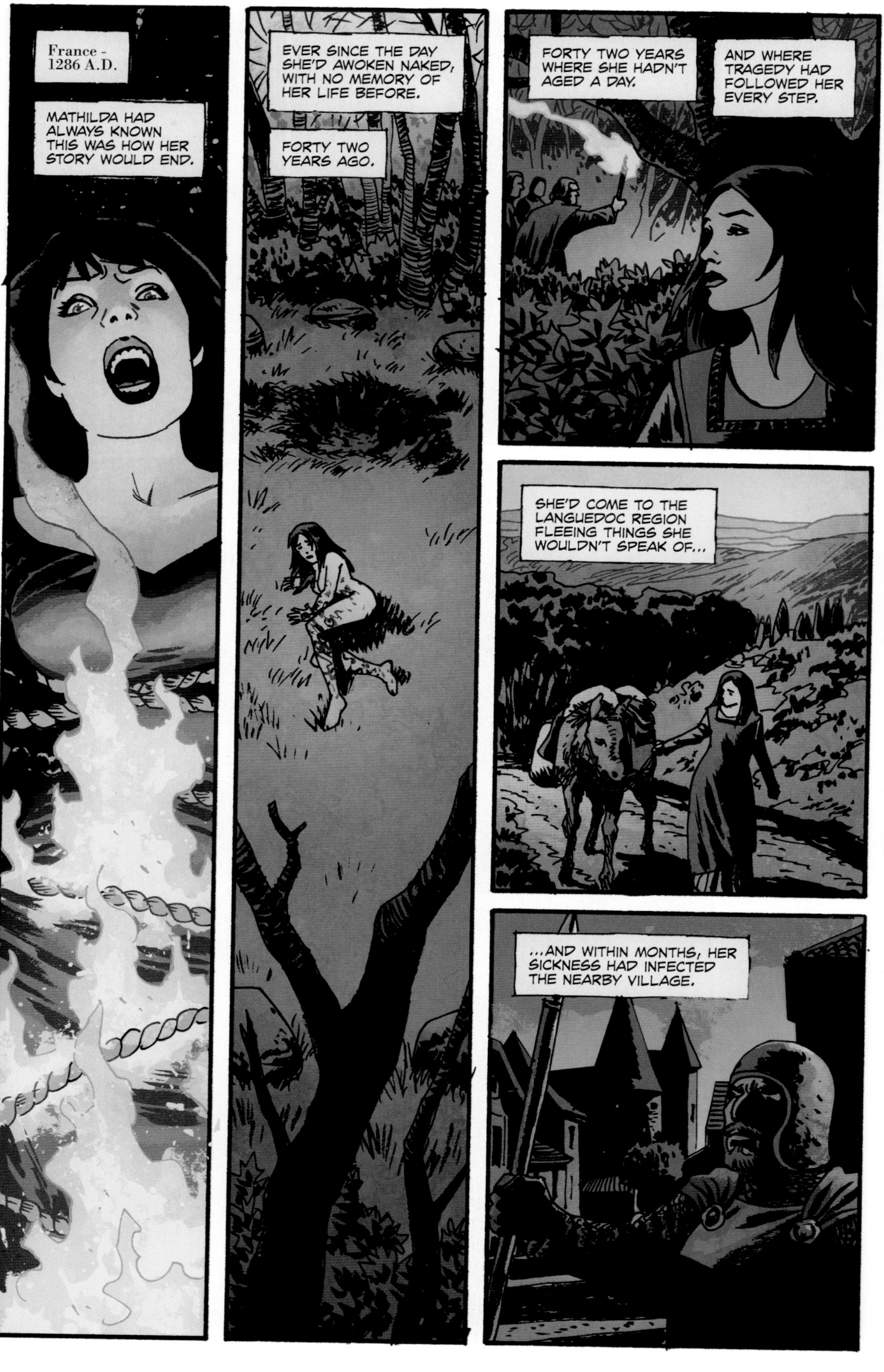
France - 1286 A.D.
MATHILDA HAD ALWAYS KNOWN THIS WAS HOW HER STORY WOULD END.
EVER SINCE THE DAY SHE'D AWOKEN NAKED, WITH NO MEMORY OF HER LIFE BEFORE.
FORTY TWO YEARS AGO.
FORTY TWO YEARS WHERE SHE HADN'T AGED A DAY.
AND WHERE TRAGEDY HAD FOLLOWED HER EVERY STEP.
SHE'D COME TO THE LANGUEDOC REGION FLEEING THINGS SHE WOULDN'T SPEAK OF...
...AND WITHIN MONTHS, HER SICKNESS HAD INFECTED THE NEARBY VILLAGE.

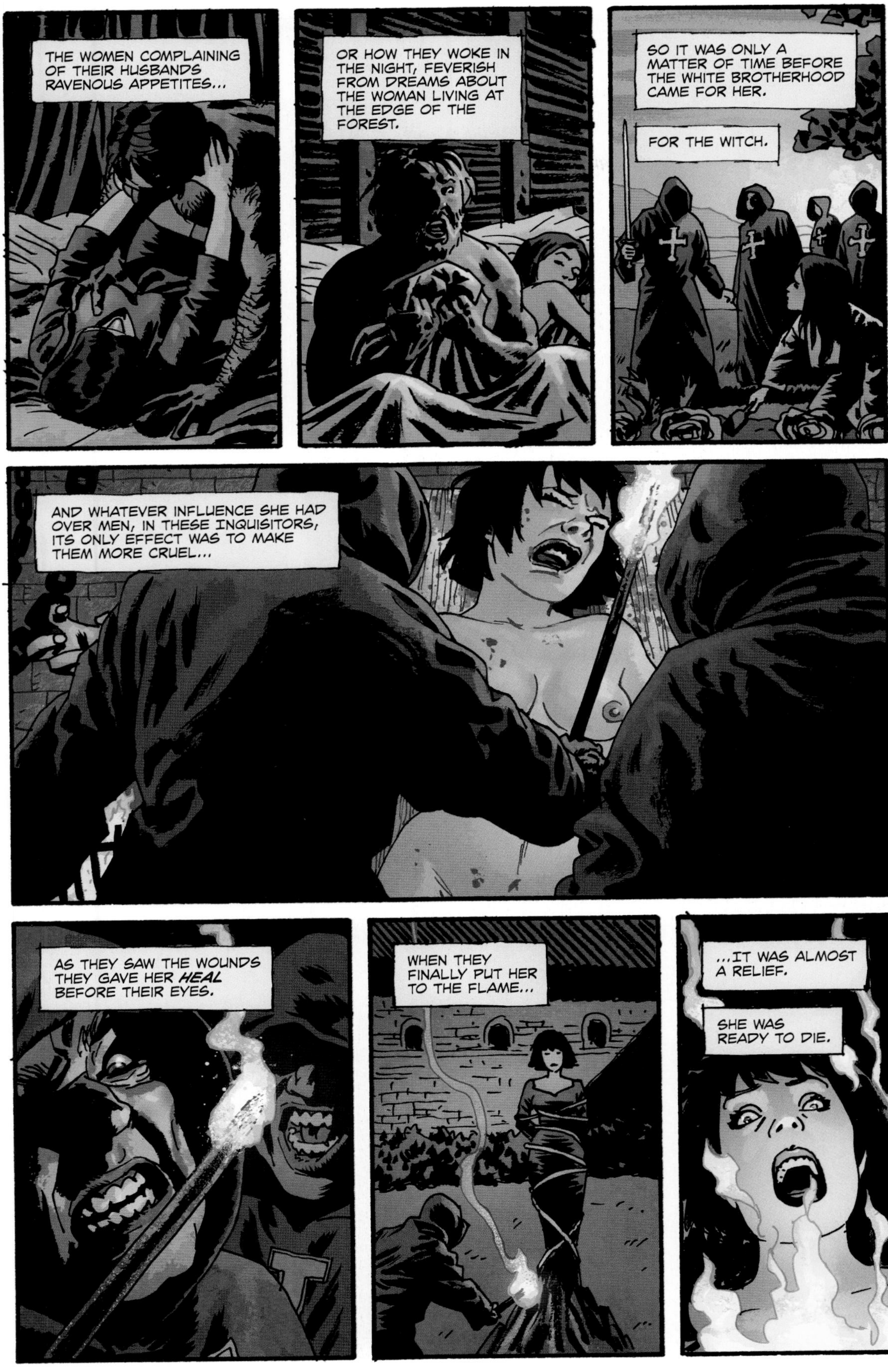
THE WOMEN COMPLAINING OF THEIR HUSBANDS RAVENOUS APPETITES...
OR HOW THEY WOKE IN THE NIGHT, FEVERISH FROM DREAMS ABOUT THE WOMAN LIVING AT THE EDGE OF THE FOREST.
SO IT WAS ONLY A MATTER OF TIME BEFORE THE WHITE BROTHERHOOD CAME FOR HER.
FOR THE WITCH.
AND WHATEVER INFLUENCE SHE HAD OVER MEN, IN THESE INQUISITORS, ITS ONLY EFFECT WAS TO MAKE THEM MORE CRUEL...
AS THEY SAW THE WOUNDS THEY GAVE HER *HEAL* BEFORE THEIR EYES.
WHEN THEY FINALLY PUT HER TO THE FLAME...
...IT WAS ALMOST A RELIEF.
SHE WAS READY TO DIE.

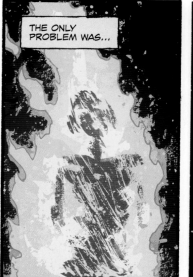

THE ONLY PROBLEM WAS...

...THIS *WASN'T* THE END OF HER STORY.

...WHAT... WHAT IS...

GAAAAHHH -- !

NO! NO! STOP!

NNNHH -- !

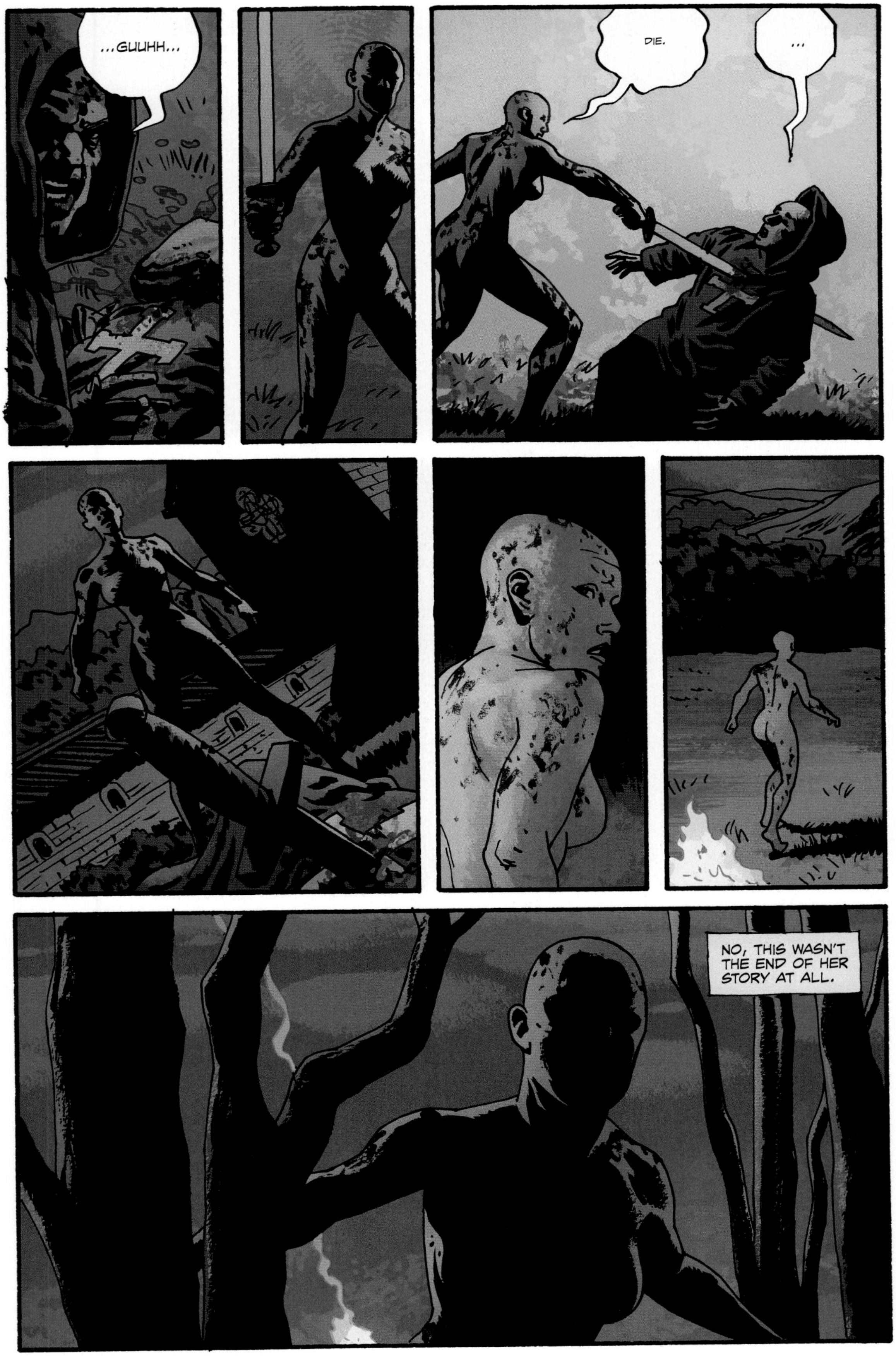
...GUUHH...
DIE.
...
NO, THIS WASN'T THE END OF HER STORY AT ALL.

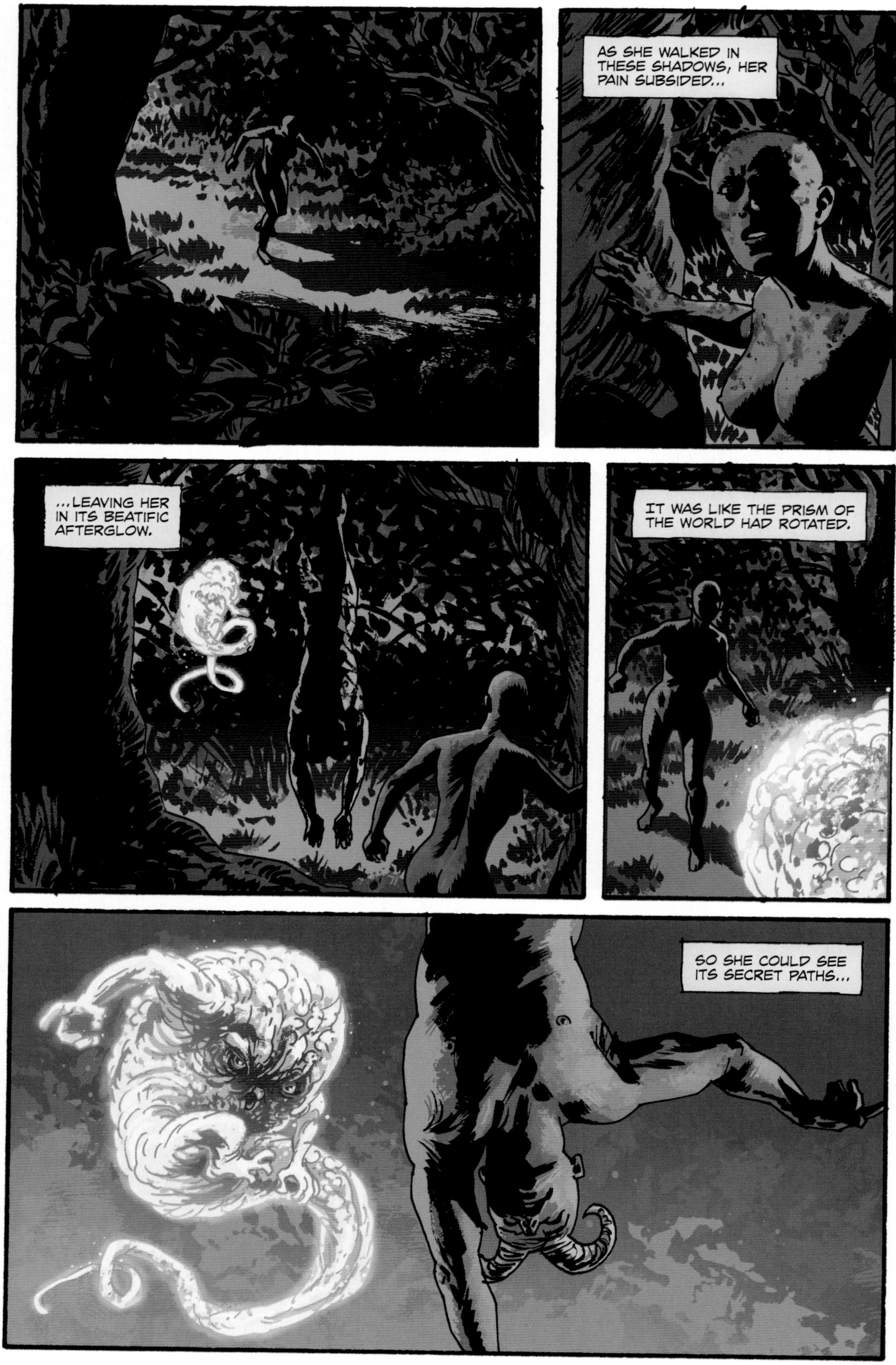
AS SHE WALKED IN THESE SHADOWS, HER PAIN SUBSIDED...
...LEAVING HER IN ITS BEATIFIC AFTERGLOW.
IT WAS LIKE THE PRISM OF THE WORLD HAD ROTATED.
SO SHE COULD SEE ITS SECRET PATHS...

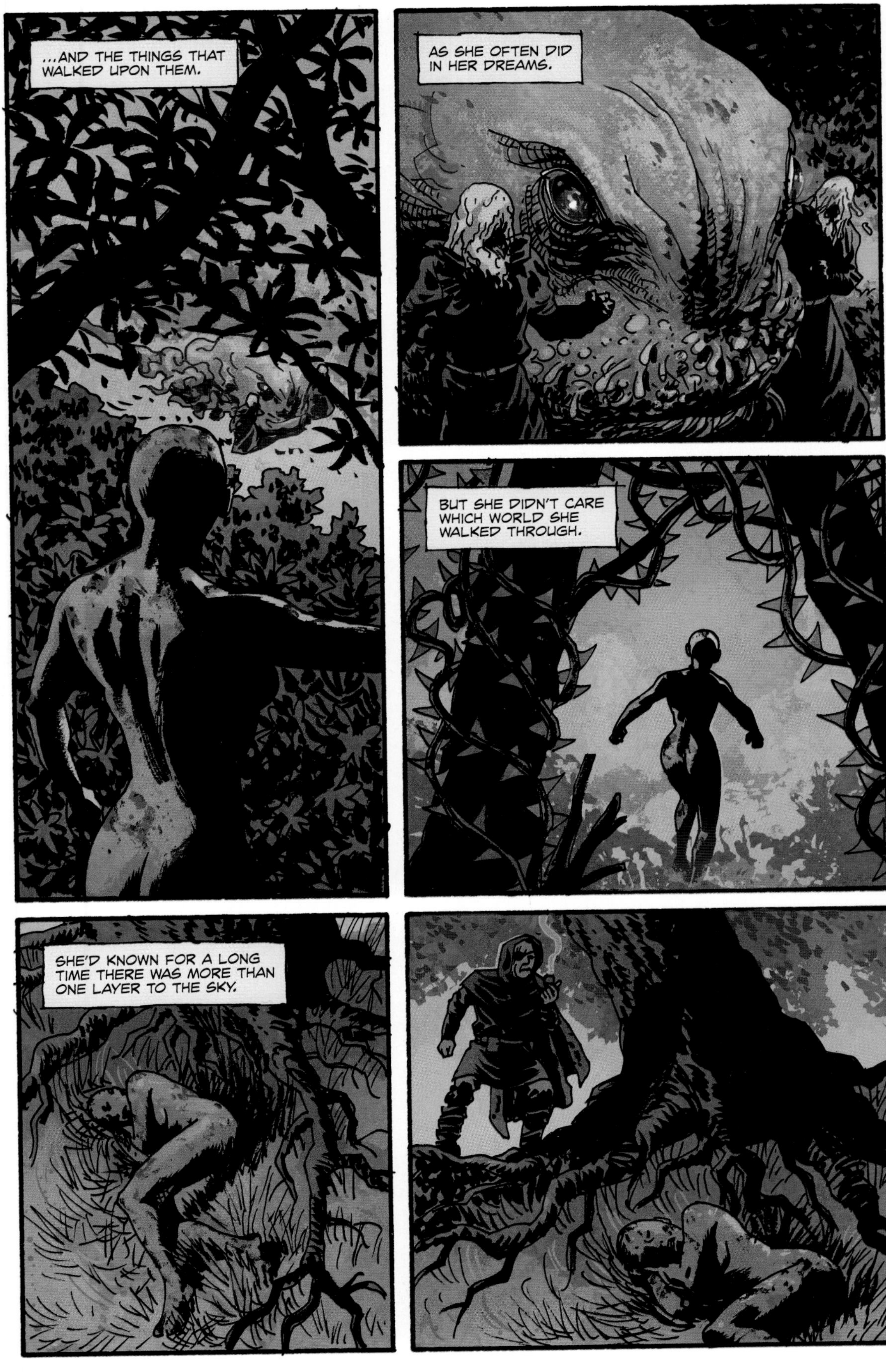
...AND THE THINGS THAT WALKED UPON THEM.
AS SHE OFTEN DID IN HER DREAMS.
BUT SHE DIDN'T CARE WHICH WORLD SHE WALKED THROUGH.
SHE'D KNOWN FOR A LONG TIME THERE WAS MORE THAN ONE LAYER TO THE SKY.

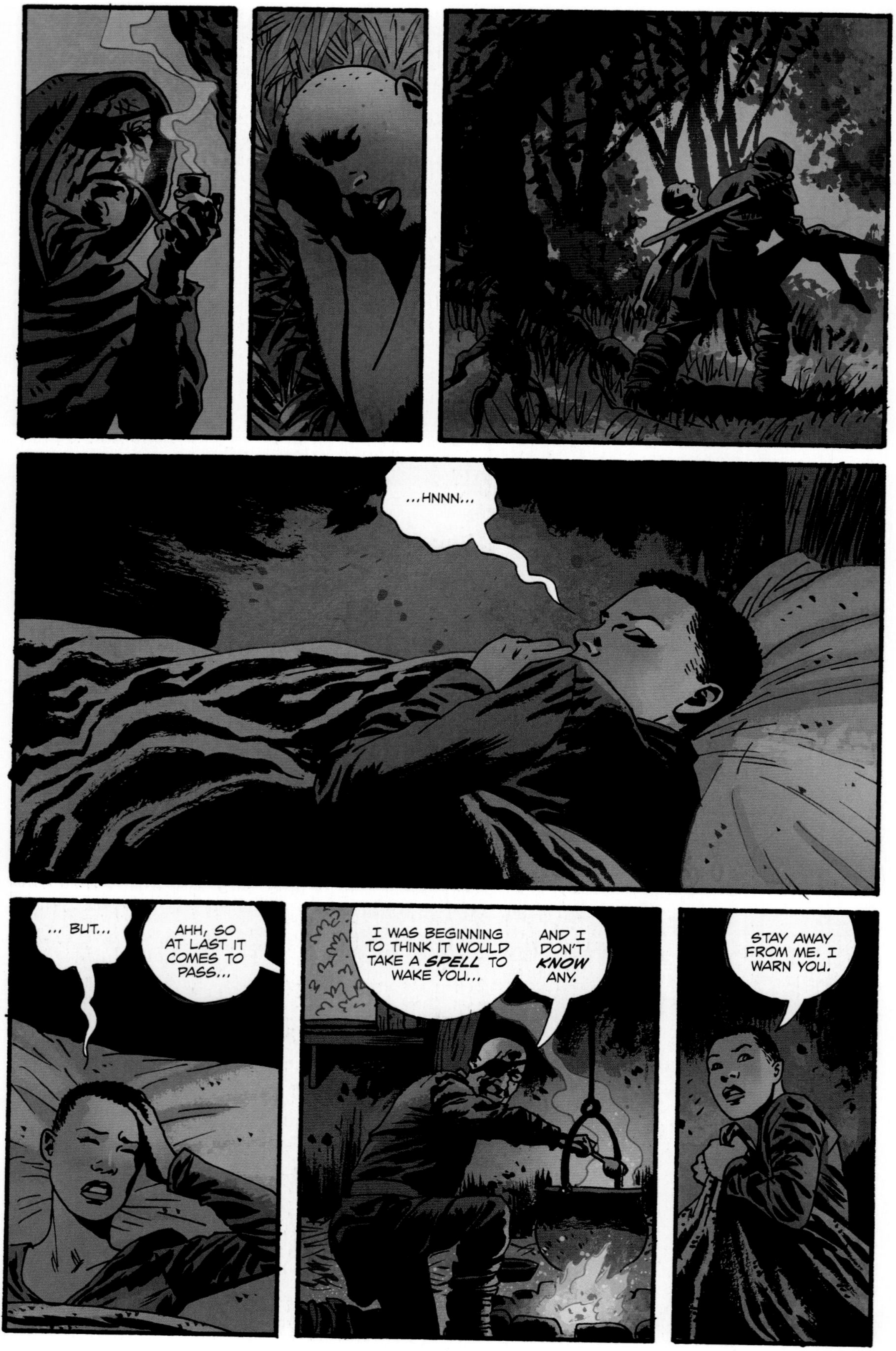
...HNNN...
... BUT...
AHH, SO AT LAST IT COMES TO PASS...
I WAS BEGINNING TO THINK IT WOULD TAKE A *SPELL* TO WAKE YOU...
AND I DON'T *KNOW* ANY.
STAY AWAY FROM ME. I WARN YOU.

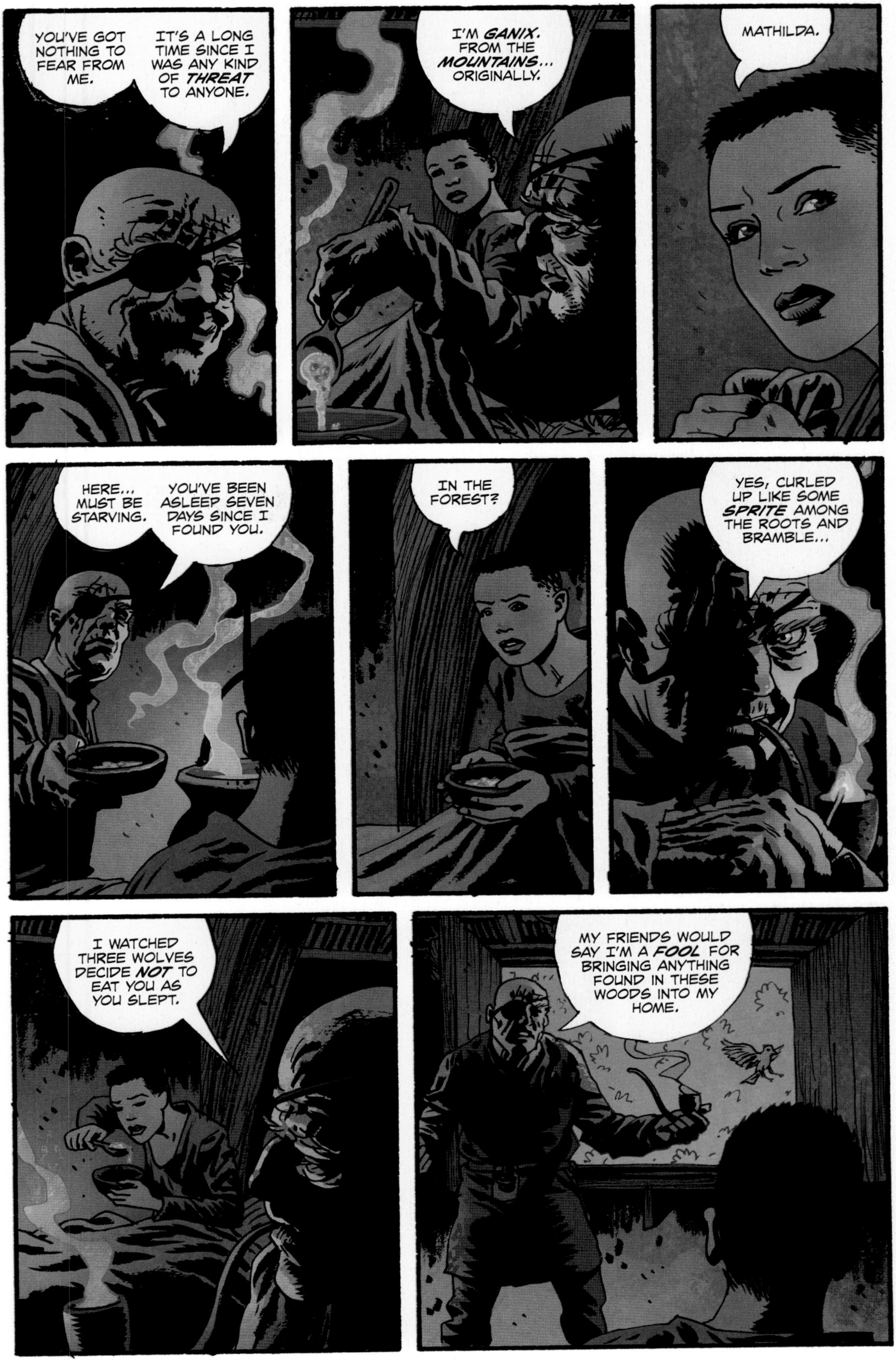
YOU'VE GOT NOTHING TO FEAR FROM ME.
IT'S A LONG TIME SINCE I WAS ANY KIND OF THREAT TO ANYONE.
I'M GANIX. FROM THE MOUNTAINS... ORIGINALLY.
MATHILDA.
HERE... MUST BE STARVING.
YOU'VE BEEN ASLEEP SEVEN DAYS SINCE I FOUND YOU.
IN THE FOREST?
YES, CURLED UP LIKE SOME SPRITE AMONG THE ROOTS AND BRAMBLE...
I WATCHED THREE WOLVES DECIDE NOT TO EAT YOU AS YOU SLEPT.
MY FRIENDS WOULD SAY I'M A FOOL FOR BRINGING ANYTHING FOUND IN THESE WOODS INTO MY HOME.

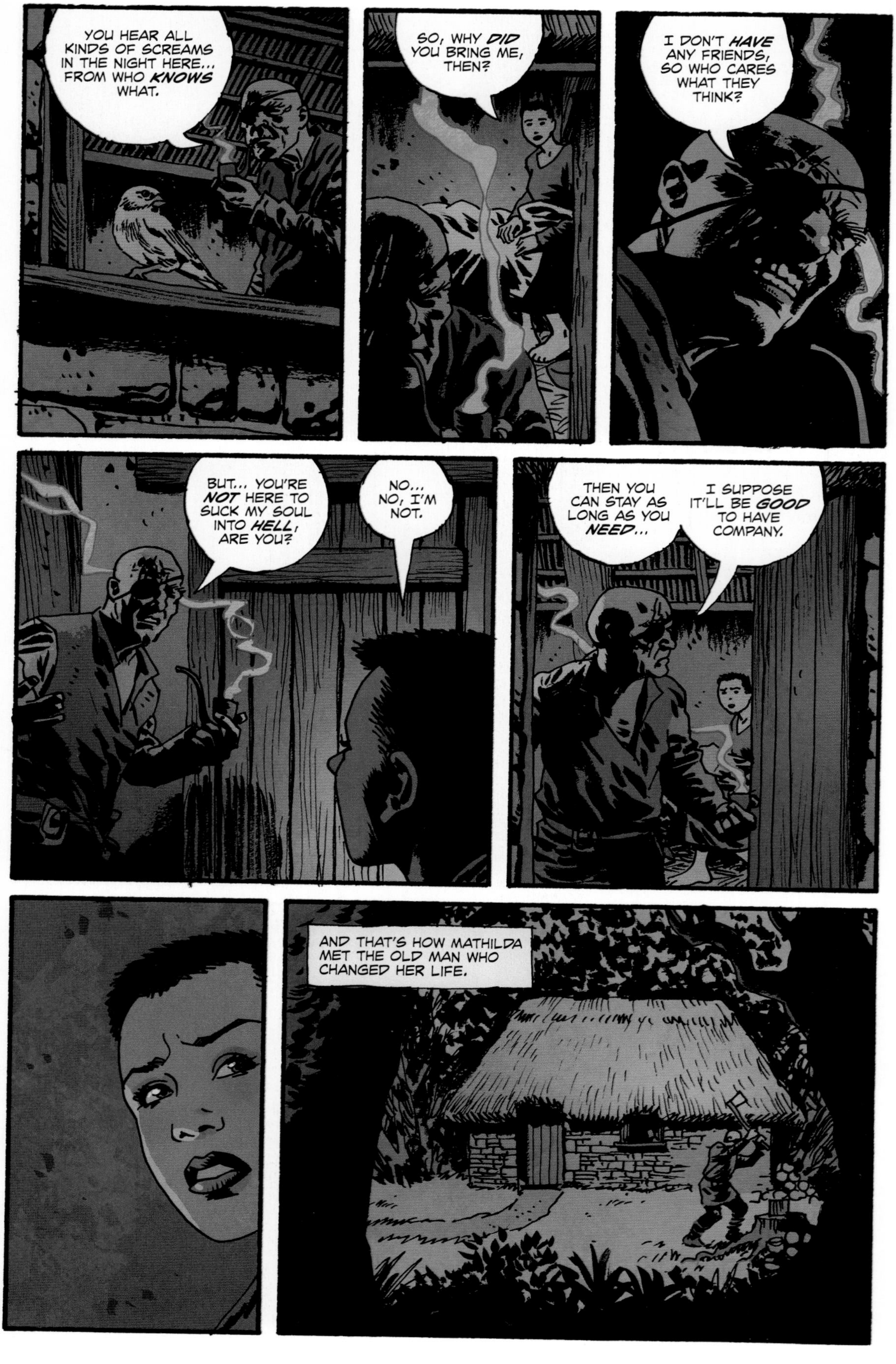
YOU HEAR ALL KINDS OF SCREAMS IN THE NIGHT HERE... FROM WHO KNOWS WHAT.
SO, WHY DID YOU BRING ME, THEN?
I DON'T HAVE ANY FRIENDS, SO WHO CARES WHAT THEY THINK?
BUT... YOU'RE NOT HERE TO SUCK MY SOUL INTO HELL, ARE YOU?
NO... NO, I'M NOT.
THEN YOU CAN STAY AS LONG AS YOU NEED...
I SUPPOSE IT'LL BE GOOD TO HAVE COMPANY.
AND THAT'S HOW MATHILDA MET THE OLD MAN WHO CHANGED HER LIFE.

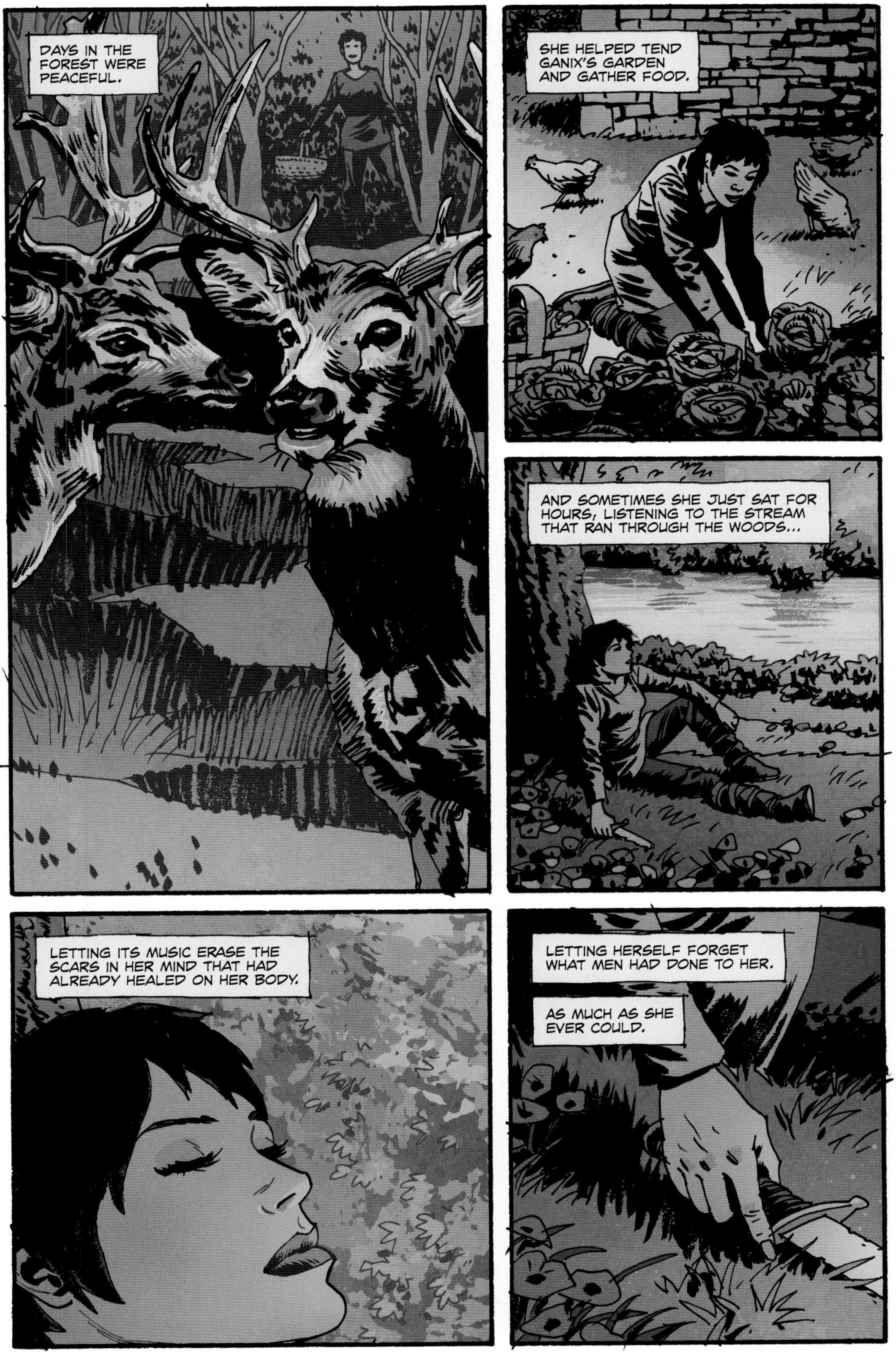
DAYS IN THE FOREST WERE PEACEFUL.
SHE HELPED TEND GANIX'S GARDEN AND GATHER FOOD.
AND SOMETIMES SHE JUST SAT FOR HOURS, LISTENING TO THE STREAM THAT RAN THROUGH THE WOODS...
LETTING ITS MUSIC ERASE THE SCARS IN HER MIND THAT HAD ALREADY HEALED ON HER BODY.
LETTING HERSELF FORGET WHAT MEN HAD DONE TO HER.
AS MUCH AS SHE EVER COULD.

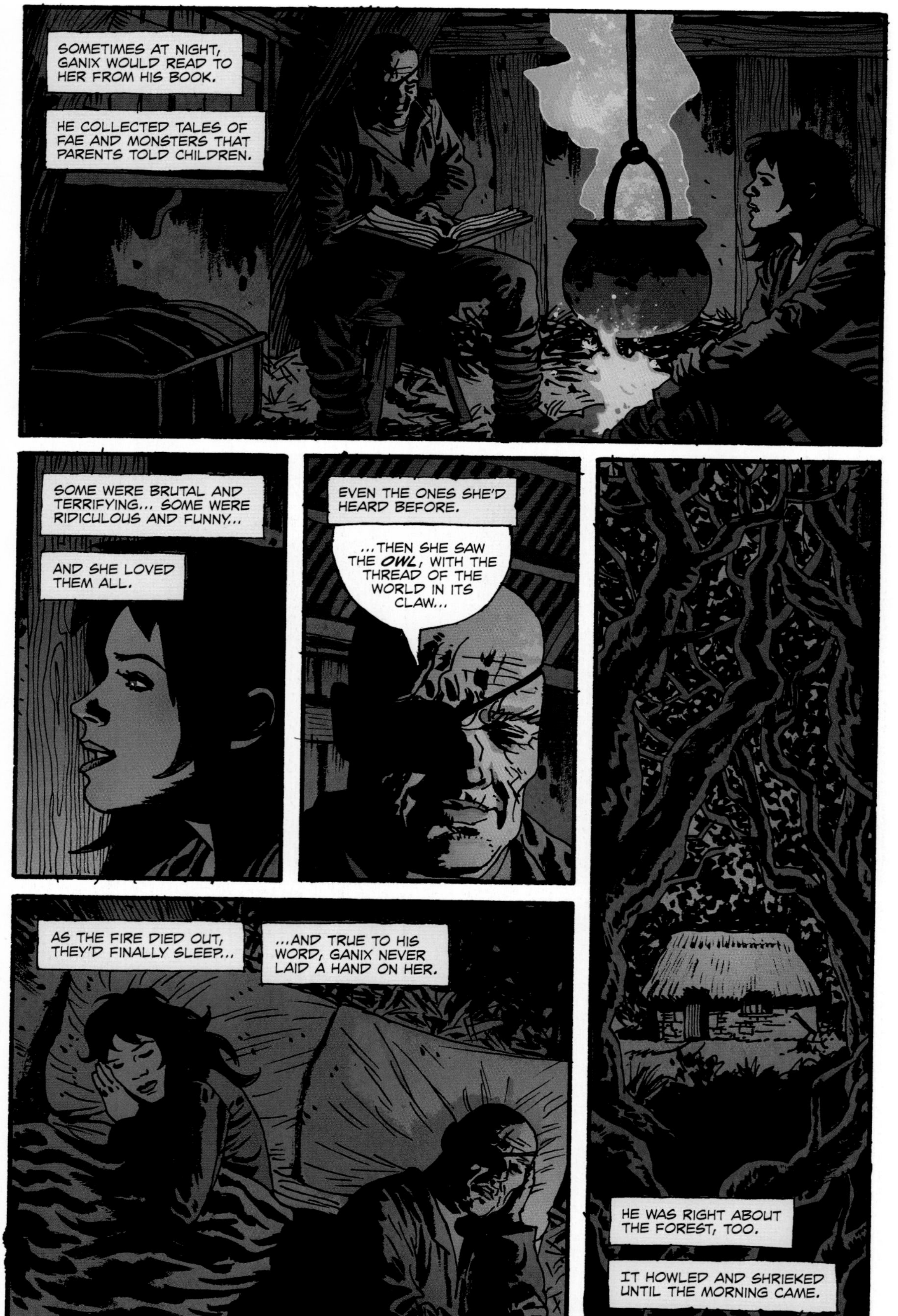
SOMETIMES AT NIGHT, GANIX WOULD READ TO HER FROM HIS BOOK.
HE COLLECTED TALES OF FAE AND MONSTERS THAT PARENTS TOLD CHILDREN.
SOME WERE BRUTAL AND TERRIFYING... SOME WERE RIDICULOUS AND FUNNY...
AND SHE LOVED THEM ALL.
EVEN THE ONES SHE'D HEARD BEFORE.
...THEN SHE SAW THE OWL, WITH THE THREAD OF THE WORLD IN ITS CLAW...
AS THE FIRE DIED OUT, THEY'D FINALLY SLEEP...
...AND TRUE TO HIS WORD, GANIX NEVER LAID A HAND ON HER.
HE WAS RIGHT ABOUT THE FOREST, TOO.
IT HOWLED AND SHRIEKED UNTIL THE MORNING CAME.

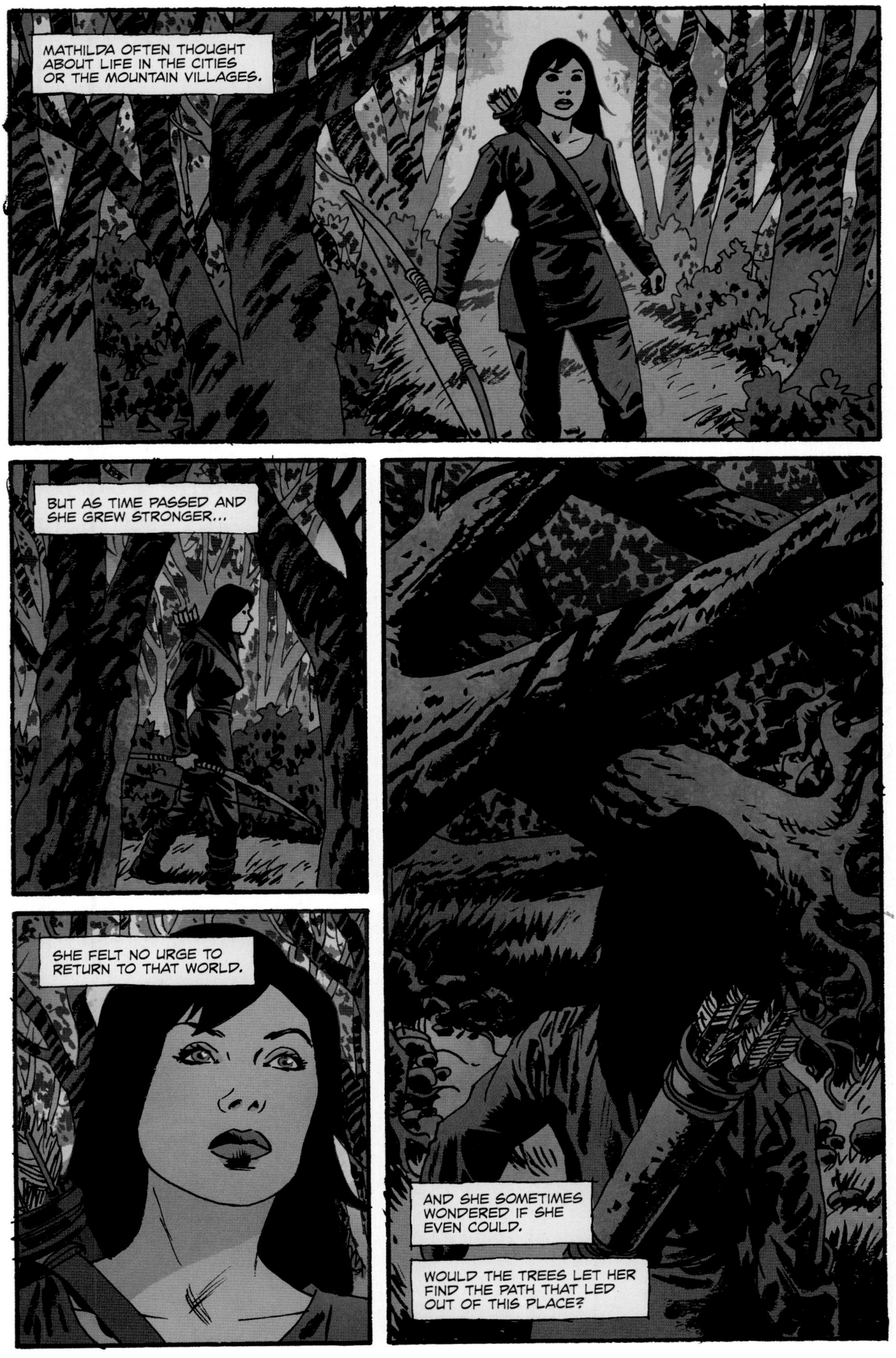
MATHILDA OFTEN THOUGHT ABOUT LIFE IN THE CITIES OR THE MOUNTAIN VILLAGES.
BUT AS TIME PASSED AND SHE GREW STRONGER...
SHE FELT NO URGE TO RETURN TO THAT WORLD.
AND SHE SOMETIMES WONDERED IF SHE EVEN COULD.
WOULD THE TREES LET HER FIND THE PATH THAT LED OUT OF THIS PLACE?

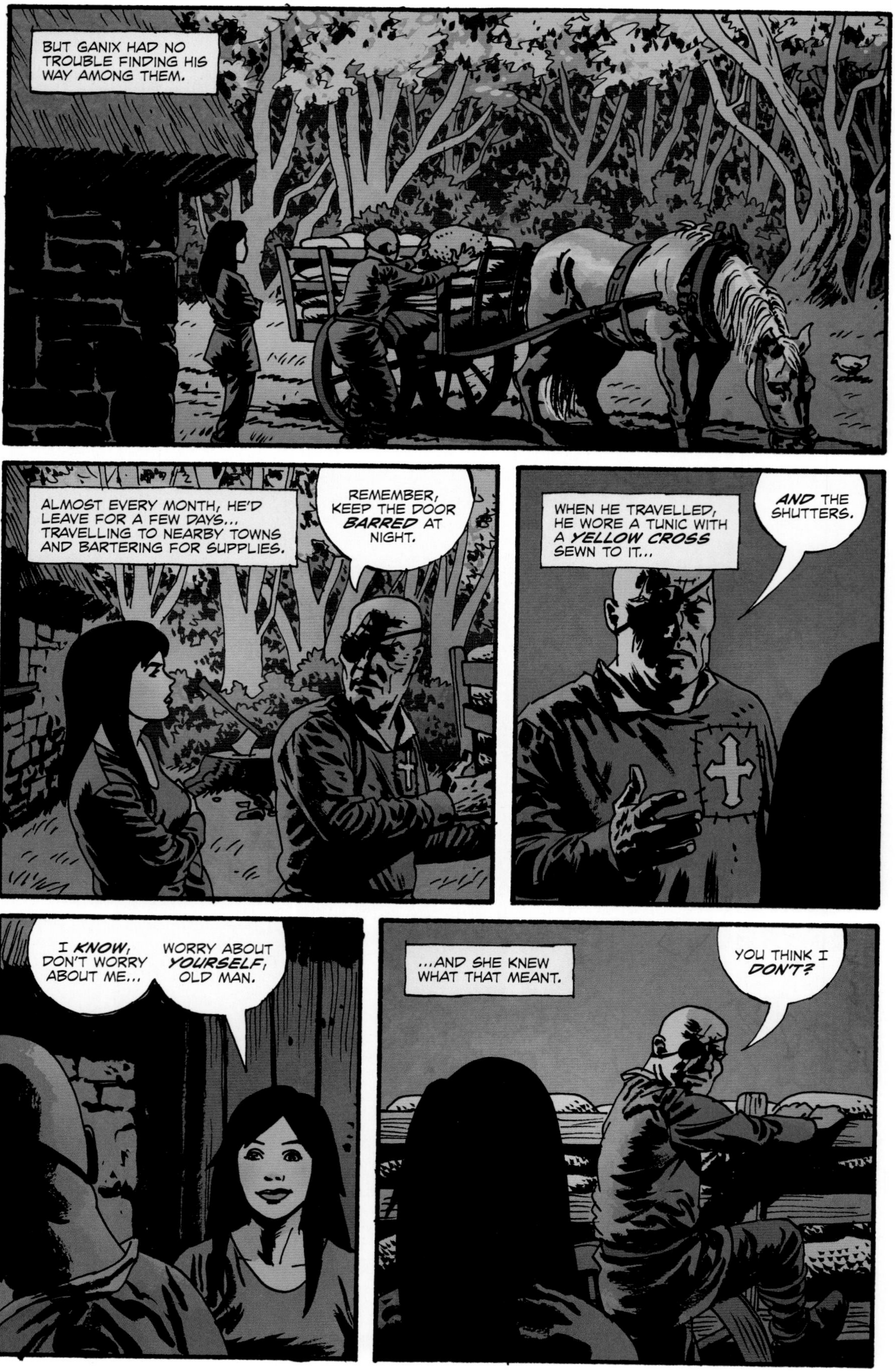
BUT GANIX HAD NO TROUBLE FINDING HIS WAY AMONG THEM.
ALMOST EVERY MONTH, HE'D LEAVE FOR A FEW DAYS... TRAVELLING TO NEARBY TOWNS AND BARTERING FOR SUPPLIES.
REMEMBER, KEEP THE DOOR *BARRED* AT NIGHT.
WHEN HE TRAVELLED, HE WORE A TUNIC WITH A *YELLOW CROSS* SEWN TO IT...
AND THE SHUTTERS.
I *KNOW*, DON'T WORRY ABOUT ME...
WORRY ABOUT *YOURSELF*, OLD MAN.
...AND SHE KNEW WHAT THAT MEANT.
YOU THINK I *DON'T?*

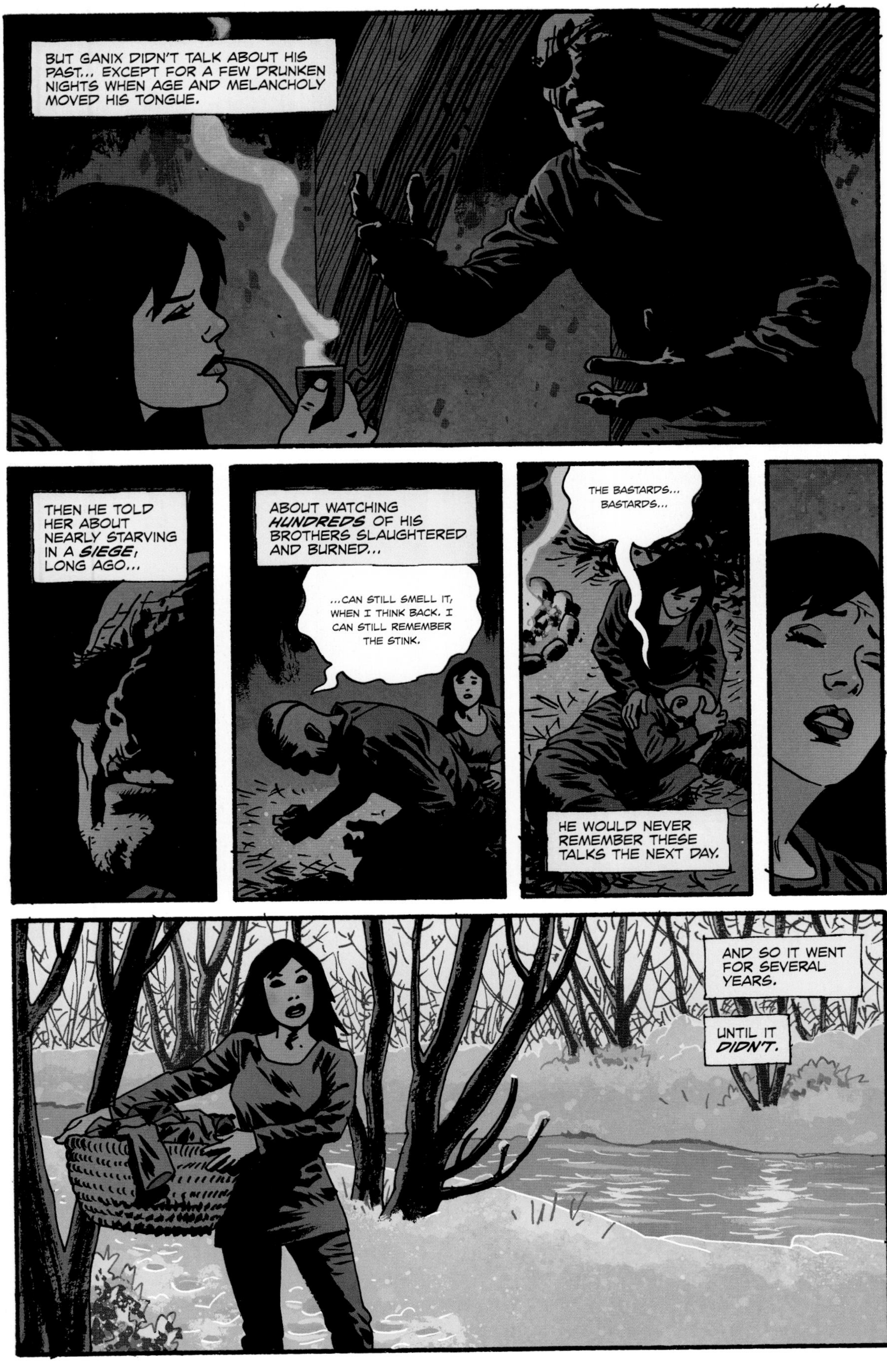
BUT GANIX DIDN'T TALK ABOUT HIS PAST... EXCEPT FOR A FEW DRUNKEN NIGHTS WHEN AGE AND MELANCHOLY MOVED HIS TONGUE.
THEN HE TOLD HER ABOUT NEARLY STARVING IN A *SIEGE*, LONG AGO...
ABOUT WATCHING *HUNDREDS* OF HIS BROTHERS SLAUGHTERED AND BURNED...
...CAN STILL SMELL IT, WHEN I THINK BACK. I CAN STILL REMEMBER THE STINK.
THE BASTARDS... BASTARDS...
HE WOULD NEVER REMEMBER THESE TALKS THE NEXT DAY.
AND SO IT WENT FOR SEVERAL YEARS.
UNTIL IT *DIDN'T*.

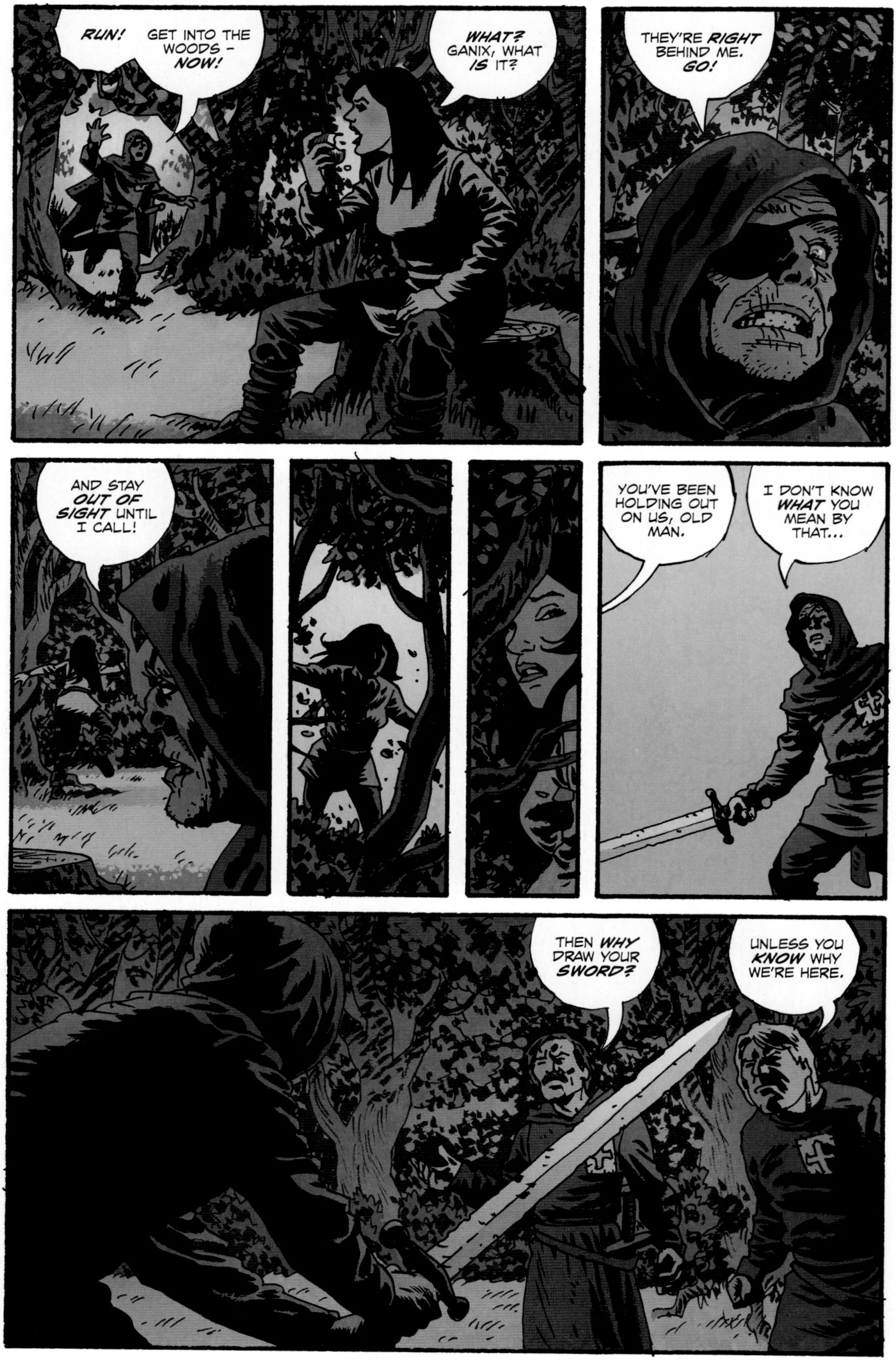
RUN! GET INTO THE WOODS - NOW!
WHAT? GANIX, WHAT IS IT?
THEY'RE RIGHT BEHIND ME. GO!
AND STAY OUT OF SIGHT UNTIL I CALL!
YOU'VE BEEN HOLDING OUT ON US, OLD MAN.
I DON'T KNOW WHAT YOU MEAN BY THAT...
THEN WHY DRAW YOUR SWORD?
UNLESS YOU KNOW WHY WE'RE HERE.

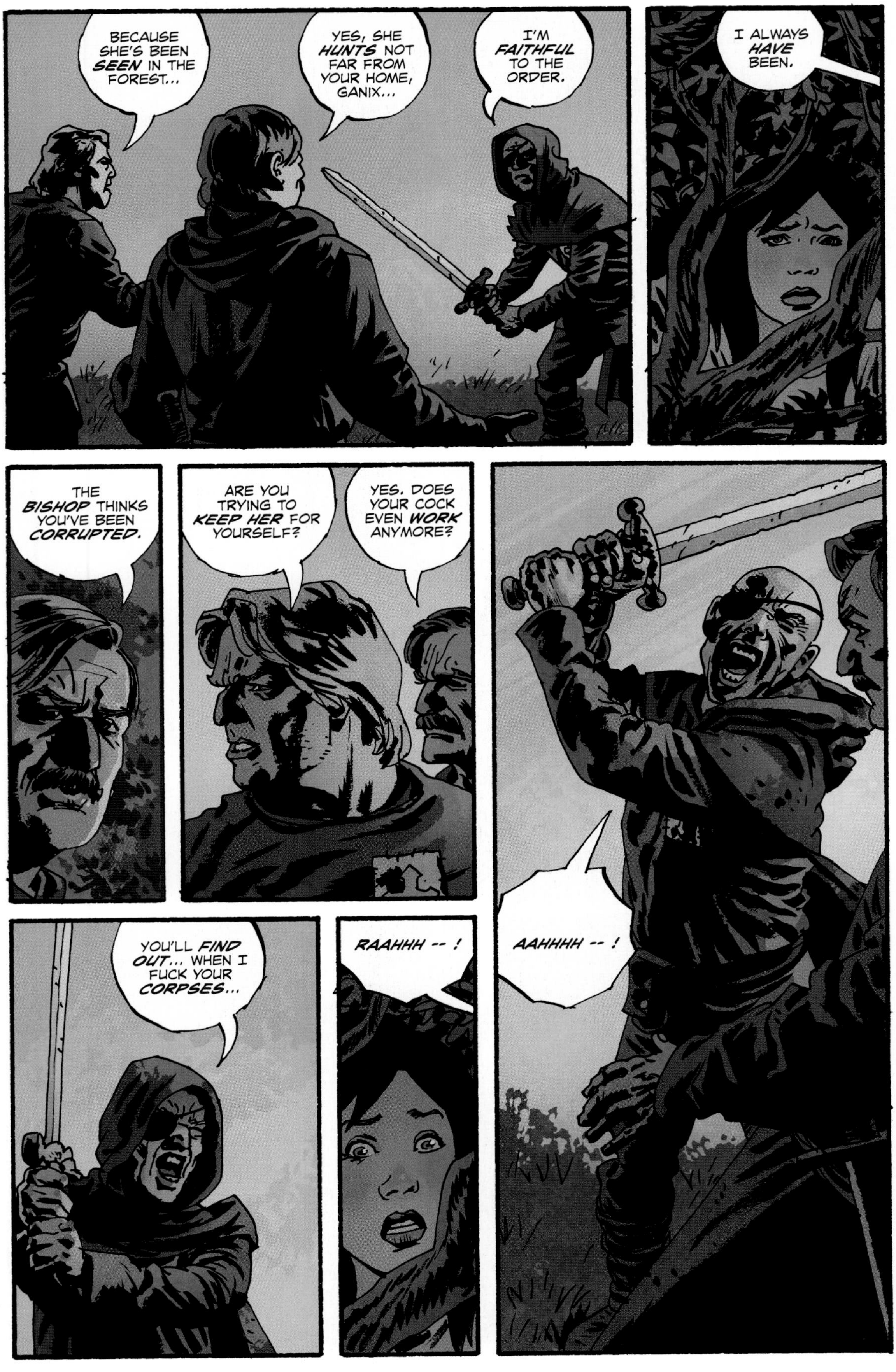
BECAUSE SHE'S BEEN SEEN IN THE FOREST...
YES, SHE HUNTS NOT FAR FROM YOUR HOME, GANIX...
I'M FAITHFUL TO THE ORDER.
I ALWAYS HAVE BEEN.
THE BISHOP THINKS YOU'VE BEEN CORRUPTED.
ARE YOU TRYING TO KEEP HER FOR YOURSELF?
YES. DOES YOUR COCK EVEN WORK ANYMORE?
YOU'LL FIND OUT... WHEN I FUCK YOUR CORPSES...
RAAHHH -- !
AAHHHH -- !

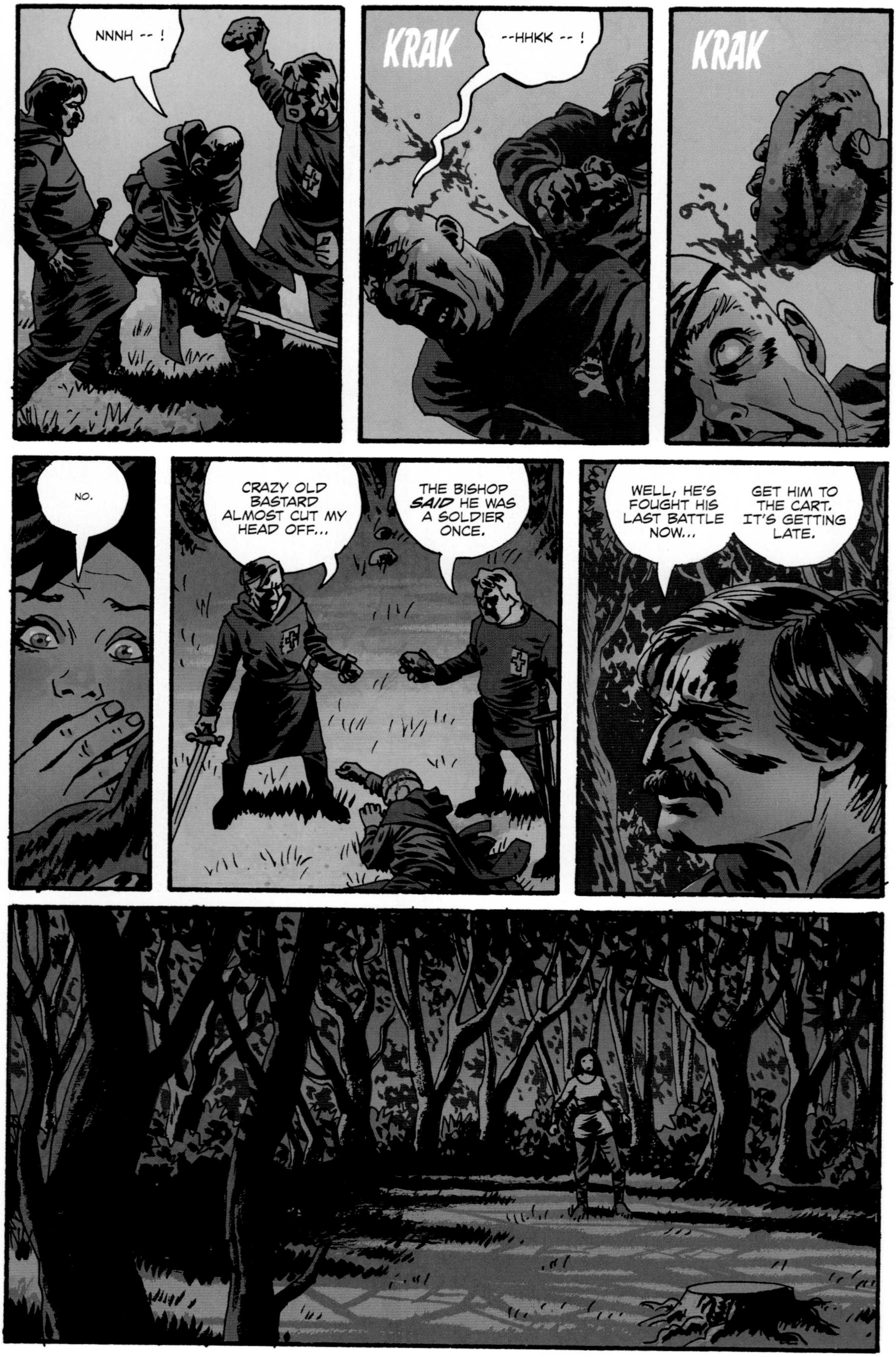
NNNH -- !
KRAK
--HHKK -- !
KRAK
NO.
CRAZY OLD BASTARD ALMOST CUT MY HEAD OFF...
THE BISHOP SAID HE WAS A SOLDIER ONCE.
WELL, HE'S FOUGHT HIS LAST BATTLE NOW...
GET HIM TO THE CART. IT'S GETTING LATE.

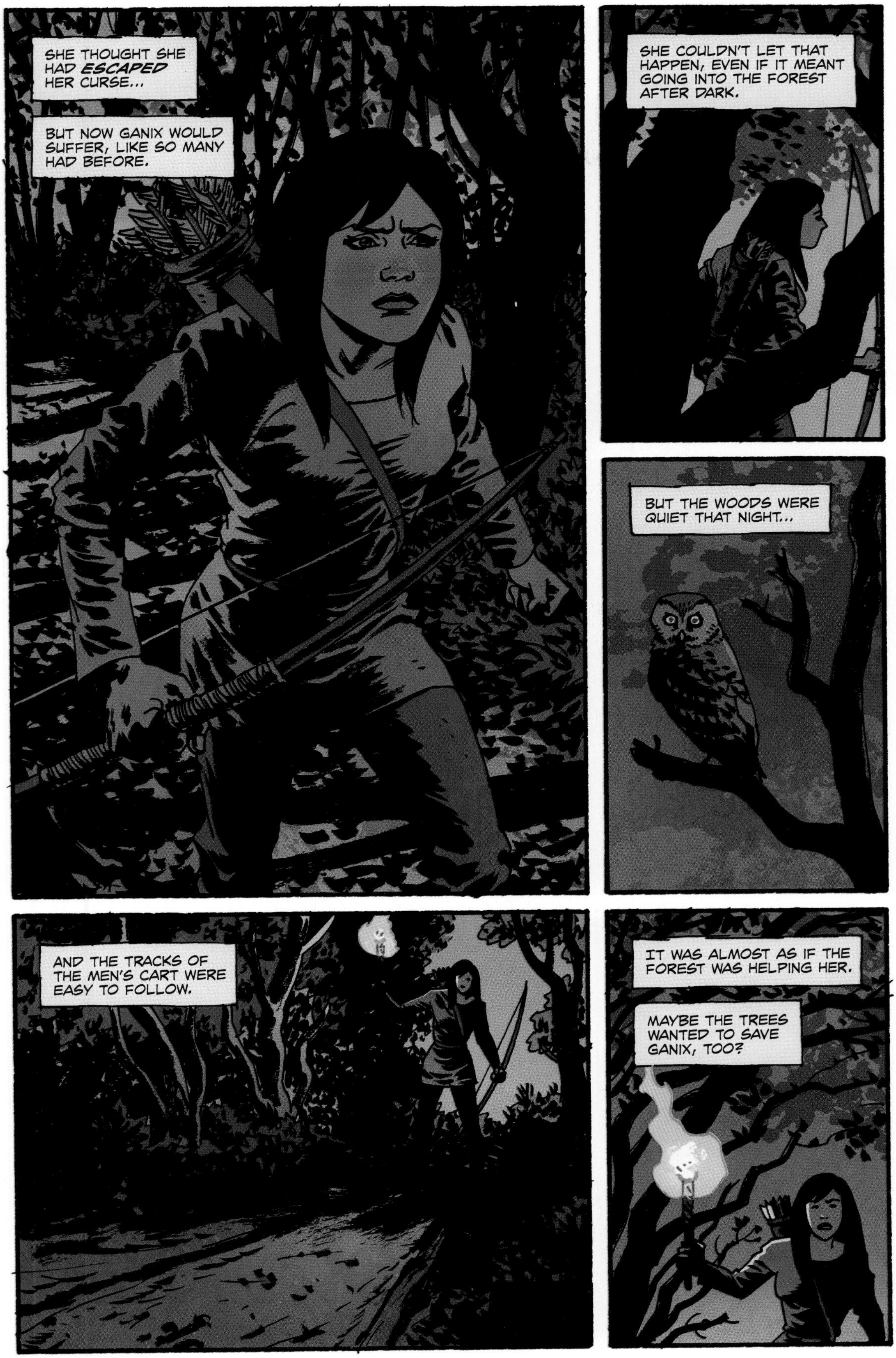
SHE THOUGHT SHE HAD ESCAPED HER CURSE...
BUT NOW GANIX WOULD SUFFER, LIKE SO MANY HAD BEFORE.
SHE COULDN'T LET THAT HAPPEN, EVEN IF IT MEANT GOING INTO THE FOREST AFTER DARK.
BUT THE WOODS WERE QUIET THAT NIGHT...
AND THE TRACKS OF THE MEN'S CART WERE EASY TO FOLLOW.
IT WAS ALMOST AS IF THE FOREST WAS HELPING HER.
MAYBE THE TREES WANTED TO SAVE GANIX, TOO?

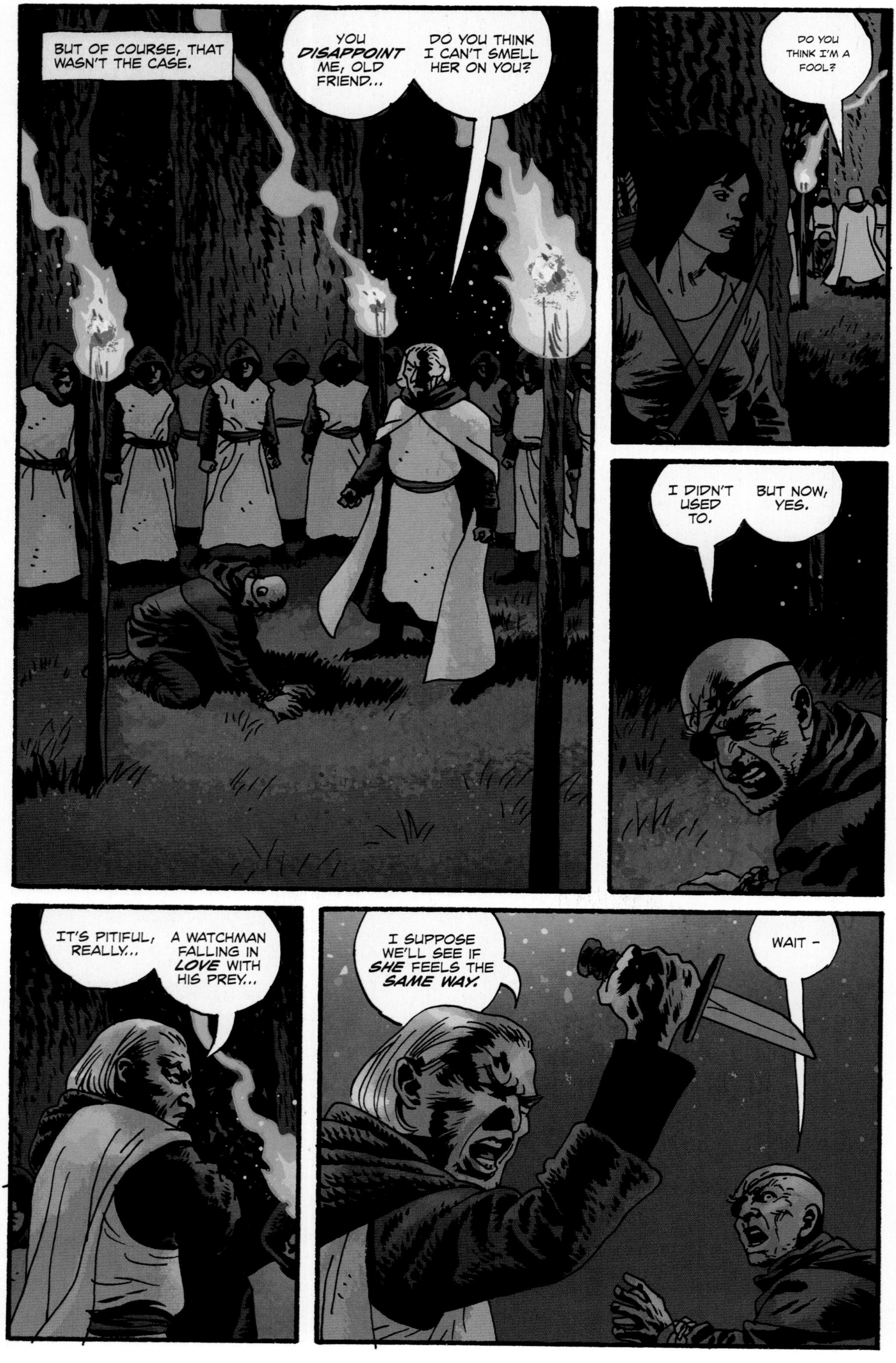
BUT OF COURSE, THAT WASN'T THE CASE.
YOU *DISAPPOINT* ME, OLD FRIEND...
DO YOU THINK I CAN'T SMELL HER ON YOU?
DO YOU THINK I'M A FOOL?
I DIDN'T USED TO.
BUT NOW, YES.
IT'S PITIFUL, REALLY...
A WATCHMAN FALLING IN *LOVE* WITH HIS PREY...
I SUPPOSE WE'LL SEE IF *SHE* FEELS THE *SAME WAY.*
WAIT -

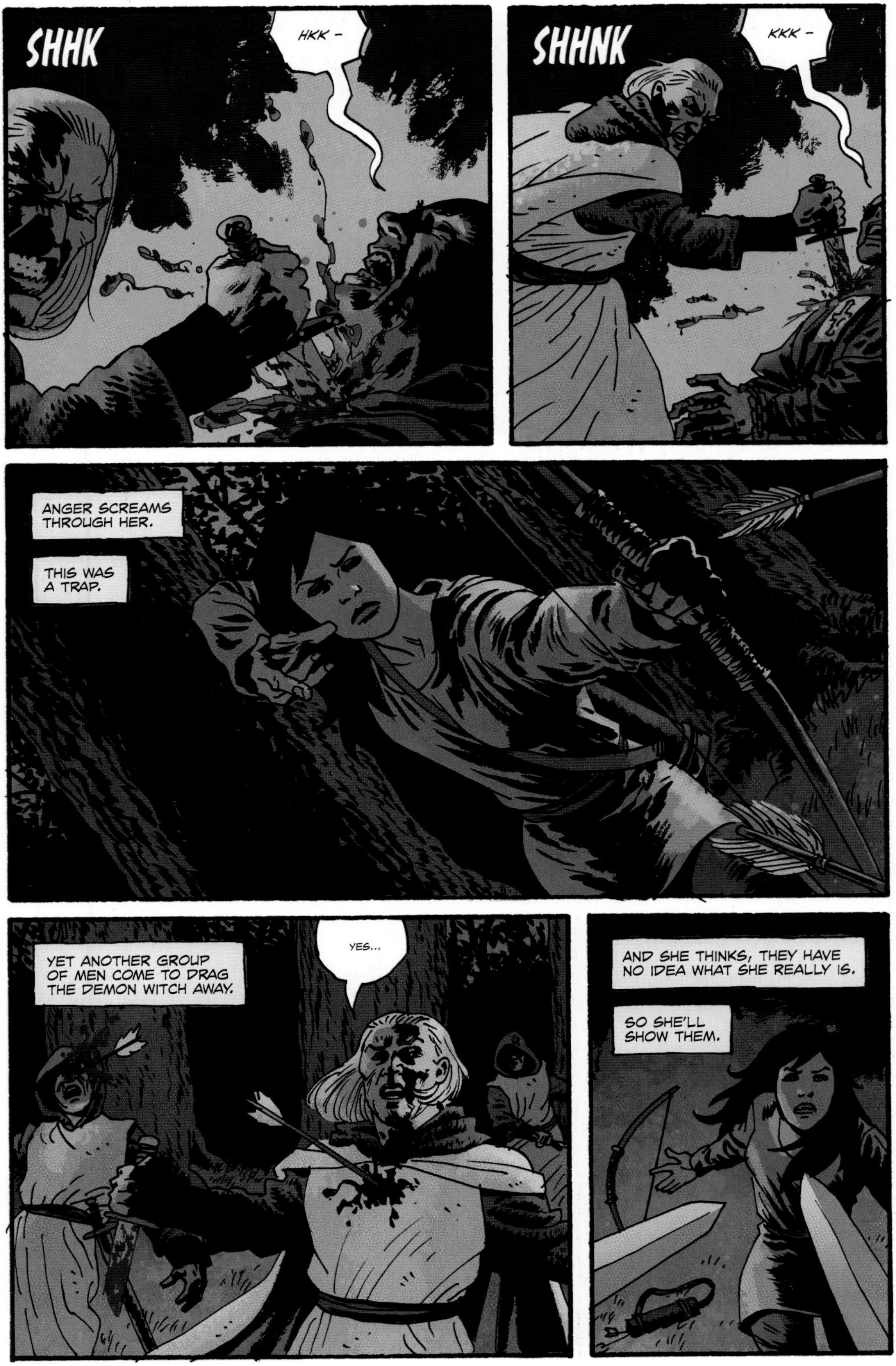
SHHK
HKK –
SHHNK
KKK –
ANGER SCREAMS THROUGH HER.
THIS WAS A TRAP.
YET ANOTHER GROUP OF MEN COME TO DRAG THE DEMON WITCH AWAY.
YES...
AND SHE THINKS, THEY HAVE NO IDEA WHAT SHE REALLY IS.
SO SHE'LL SHOW THEM.

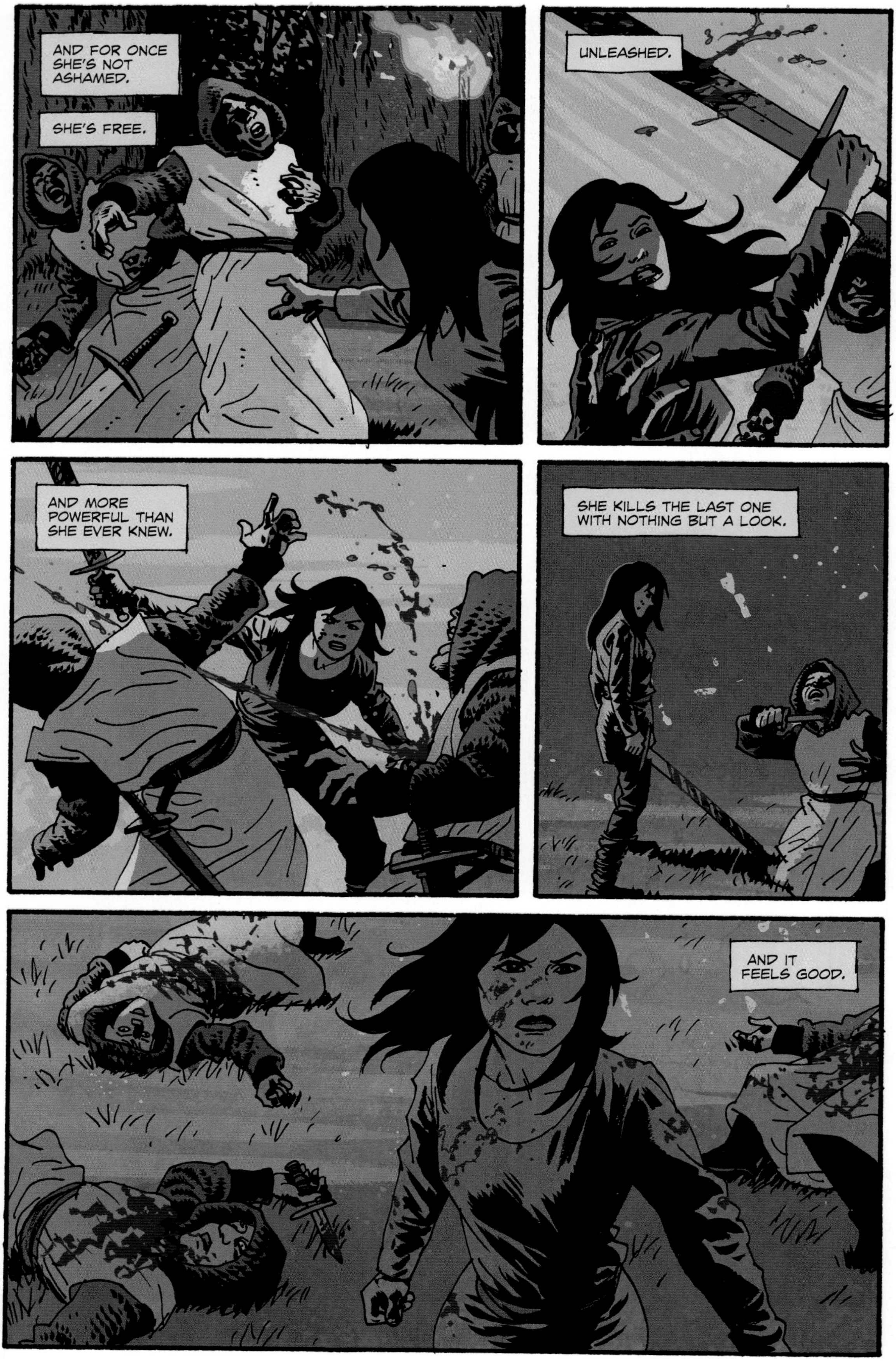
AND FOR ONCE SHE'S NOT ASHAMED.
SHE'S FREE.
UNLEASHED.
AND MORE POWERFUL THAN SHE EVER KNEW.
SHE KILLS THE LAST ONE WITH NOTHING BUT A LOOK.
AND IT FEELS GOOD.

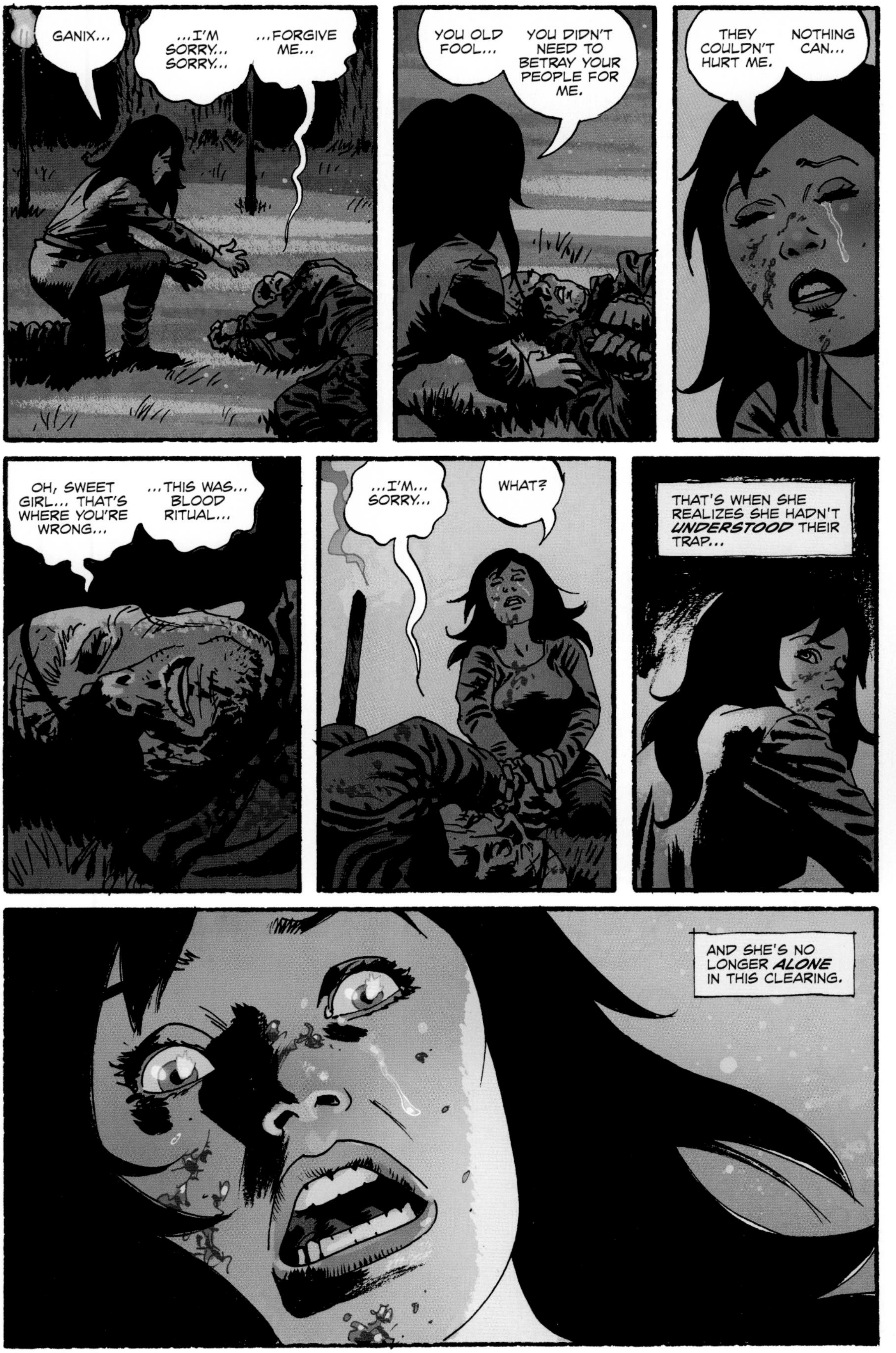
GANIX...
...I'M SORRY... SORRY...
...FORGIVE ME...
YOU OLD FOOL...
YOU DIDN'T NEED TO BETRAY YOUR PEOPLE FOR ME.
THEY COULDN'T HURT ME.
NOTHING CAN...
OH, SWEET GIRL... THAT'S WHERE YOU'RE WRONG...
...THIS WAS... BLOOD RITUAL...
...I'M... SORRY...
WHAT?
THAT'S WHEN SHE REALIZES SHE HADN'T UNDERSTOOD THEIR TRAP...
AND SHE'S NO LONGER ALONE IN THIS CLEARING.

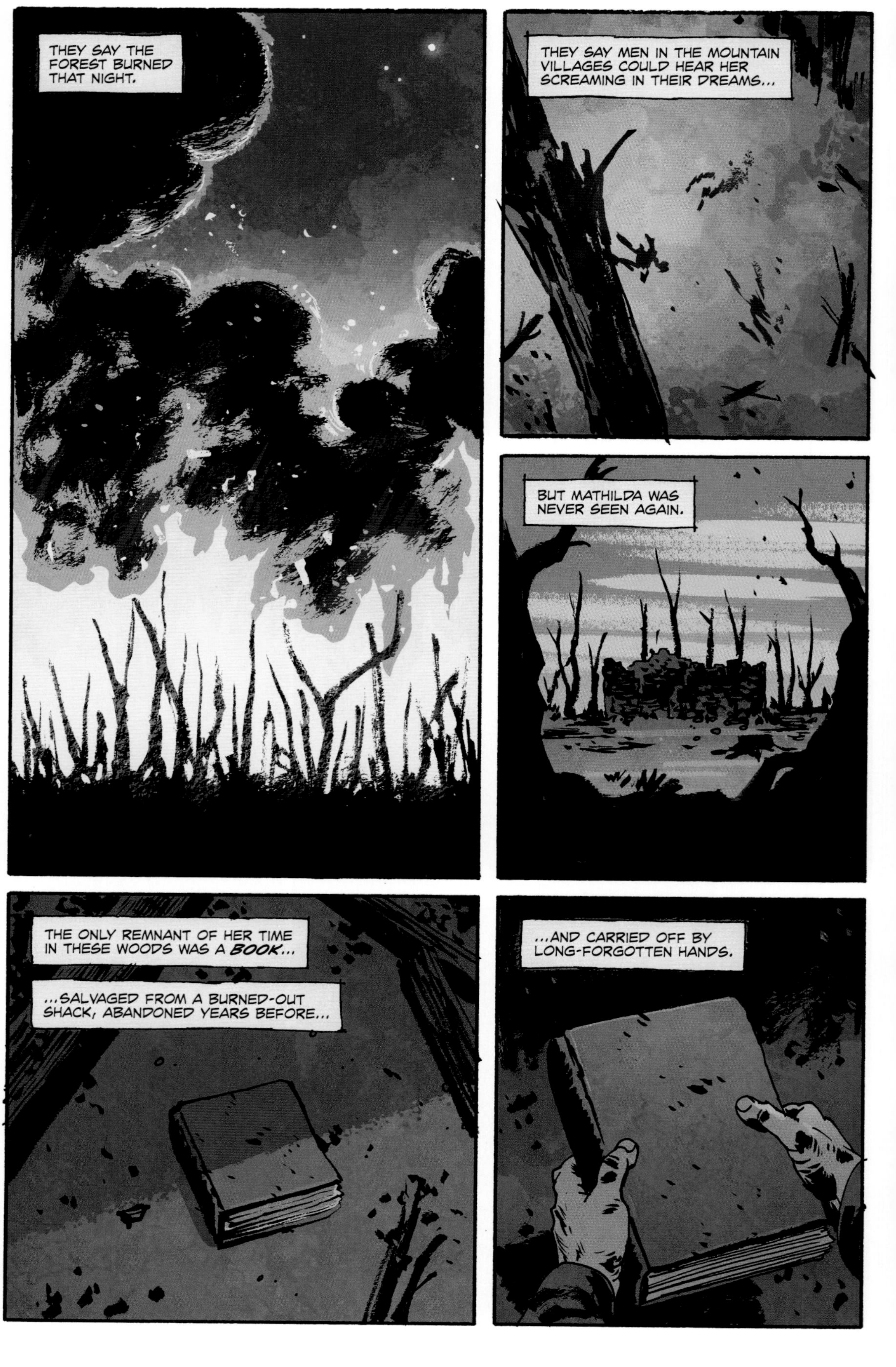
THEY SAY THE FOREST BURNED THAT NIGHT.
THEY SAY MEN IN THE MOUNTAIN VILLAGES COULD HEAR HER SCREAMING IN THEIR DREAMS...
BUT MATHILDA WAS NEVER SEEN AGAIN.
THE ONLY REMNANT OF HER TIME IN THESE WOODS WAS A *BOOK*...
...SALVAGED FROM A BURNED-OUT SHACK, ABANDONED YEARS BEFORE...
...AND CARRIED OFF BY LONG-FORGOTTEN HANDS.

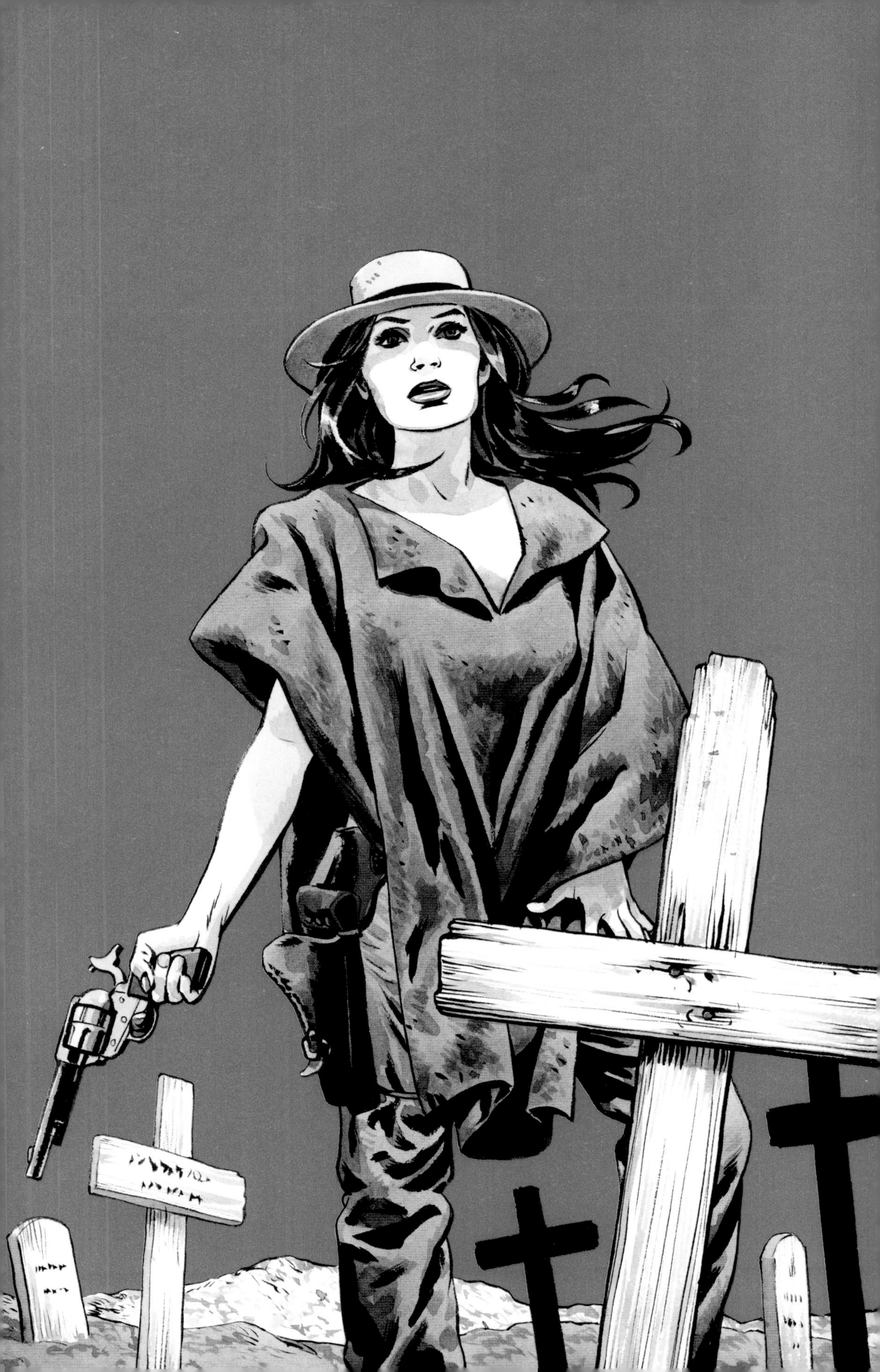

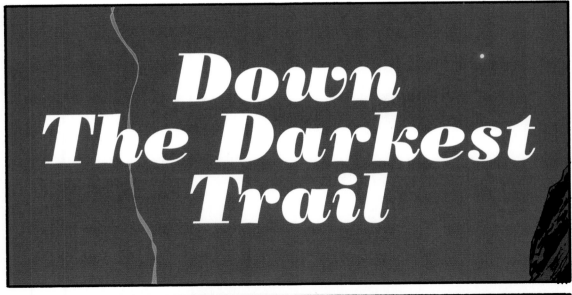

Down The Darkest Trail

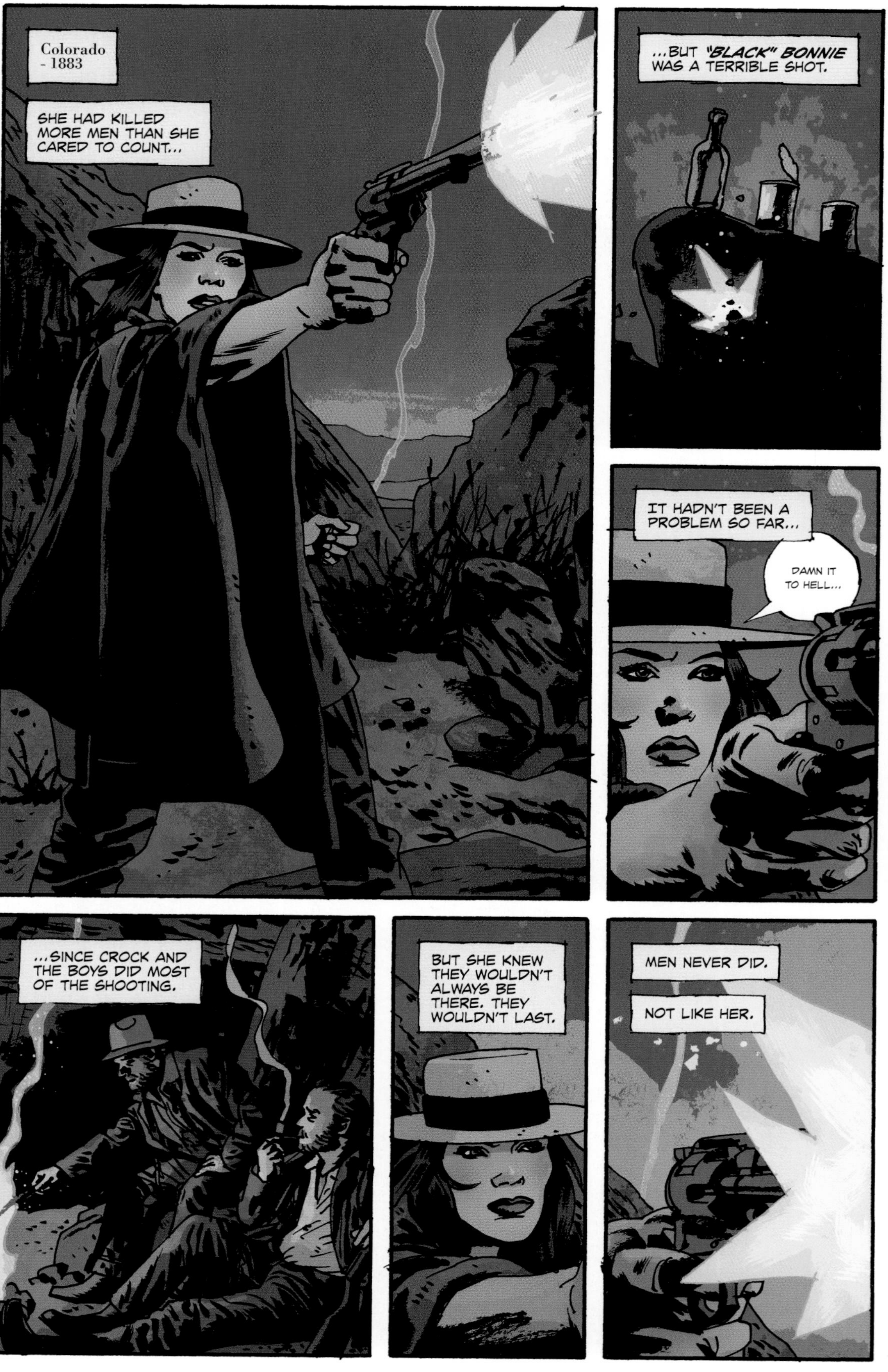
Colorado
- 1883
SHE HAD KILLED MORE MEN THAN SHE CARED TO COUNT...
...BUT "BLACK" BONNIE WAS A TERRIBLE SHOT.
IT HADN'T BEEN A PROBLEM SO FAR...
DAMN IT TO HELL...
...SINCE CROCK AND THE BOYS DID MOST OF THE SHOOTING.
BUT SHE KNEW THEY WOULDN'T ALWAYS BE THERE. THEY WOULDN'T LAST.
MEN NEVER DID.
NOT LIKE HER.

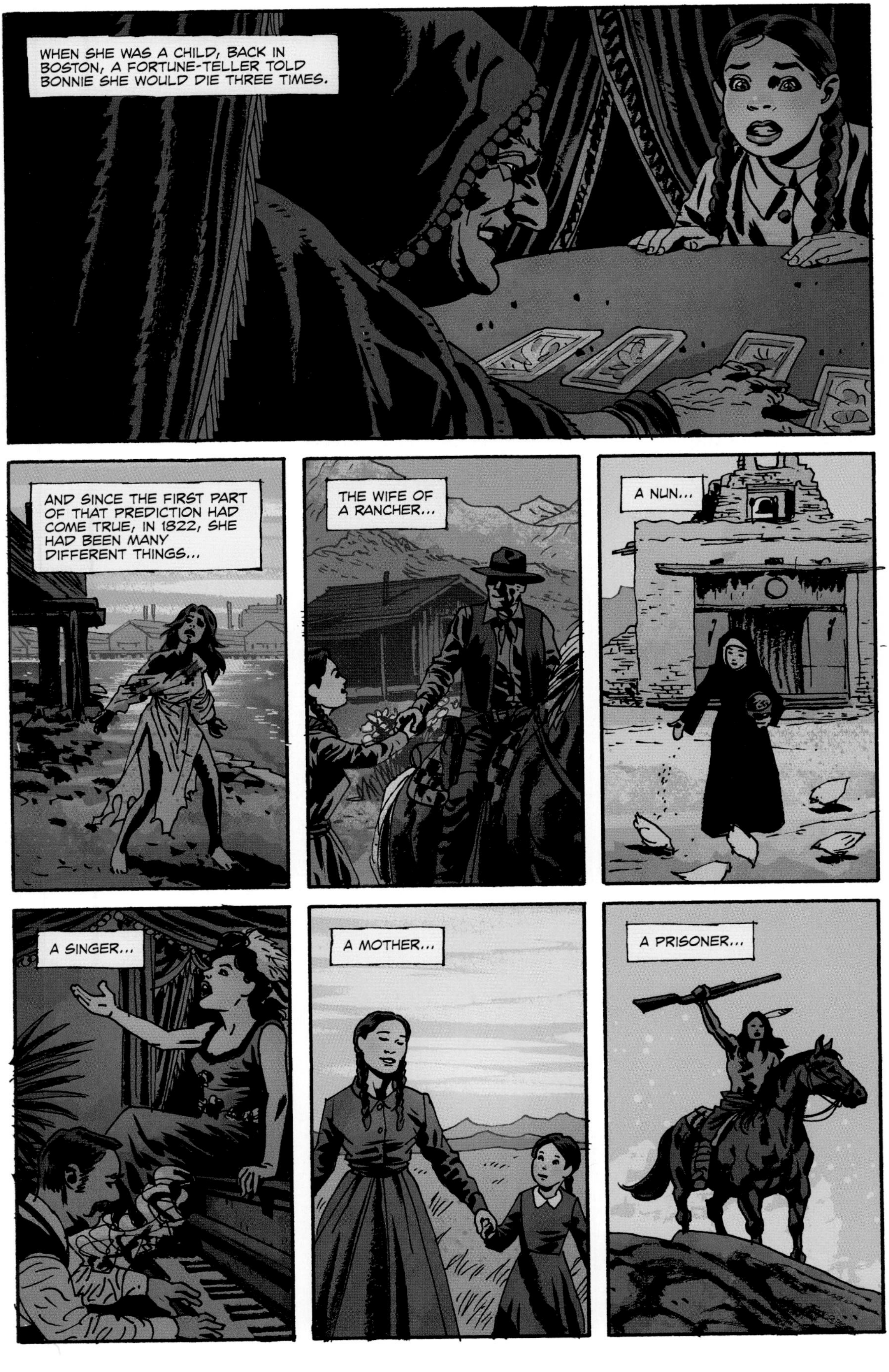
WHEN SHE WAS A CHILD, BACK IN BOSTON, A FORTUNE-TELLER TOLD BONNIE SHE WOULD DIE THREE TIMES.
AND SINCE THE FIRST PART OF THAT PREDICTION HAD COME TRUE, IN 1822, SHE HAD BEEN MANY DIFFERENT THINGS...
THE WIFE OF A RANCHER...
A NUN...
A SINGER...
A MOTHER...
A PRISONER...

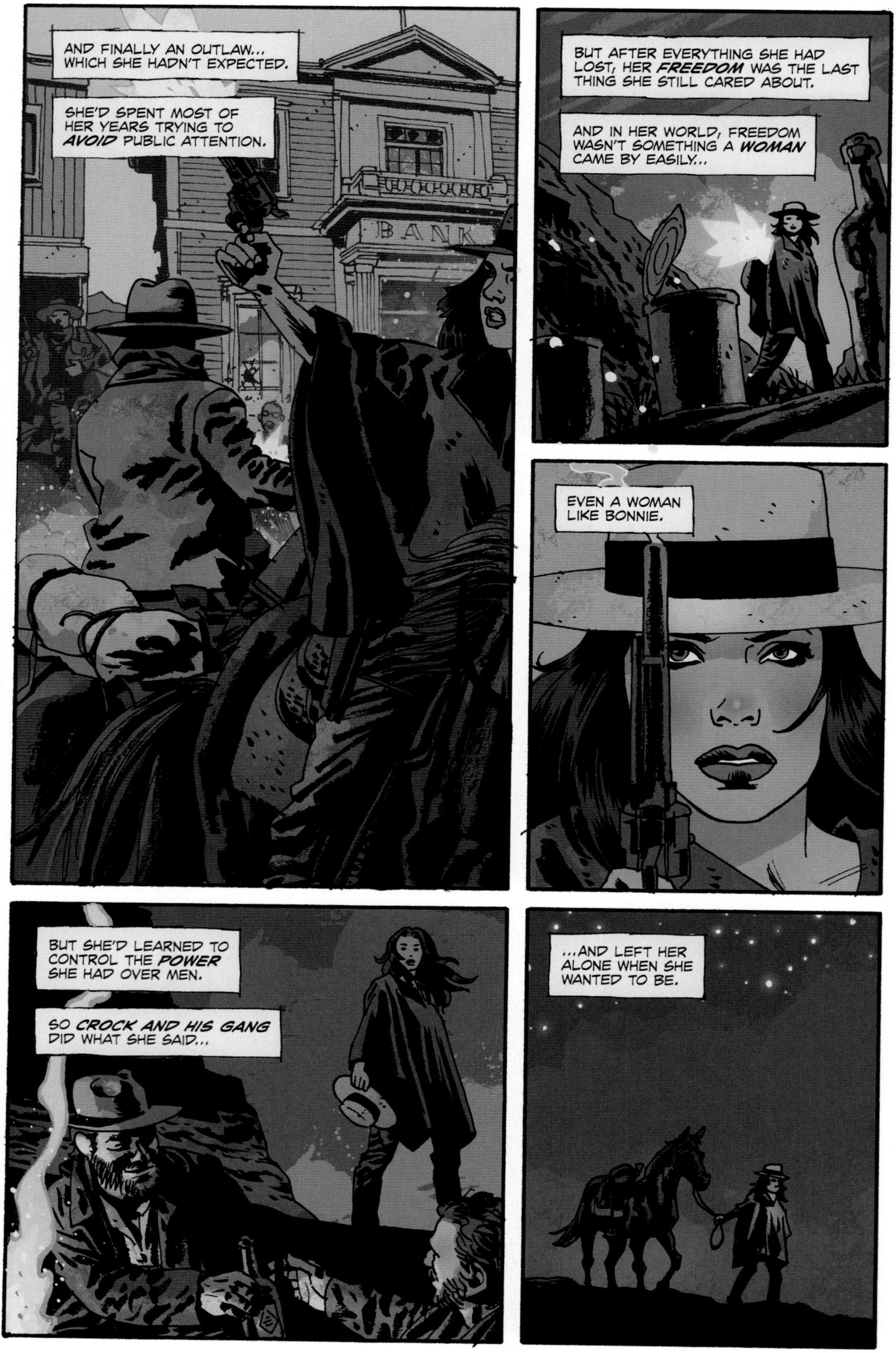
AND FINALLY AN OUTLAW... WHICH SHE HADN'T EXPECTED.
SHE'D SPENT MOST OF HER YEARS TRYING TO *AVOID* PUBLIC ATTENTION.
BANK
BUT AFTER EVERYTHING SHE HAD LOST, HER *FREEDOM* WAS THE LAST THING SHE STILL CARED ABOUT.
AND IN HER WORLD, FREEDOM WASN'T SOMETHING A *WOMAN* CAME BY EASILY...
EVEN A WOMAN LIKE BONNIE.
BUT SHE'D LEARNED TO CONTROL THE *POWER* SHE HAD OVER MEN.
SO *CROCK AND HIS GANG* DID WHAT SHE SAID...
...AND LEFT HER ALONE WHEN SHE WANTED TO BE.

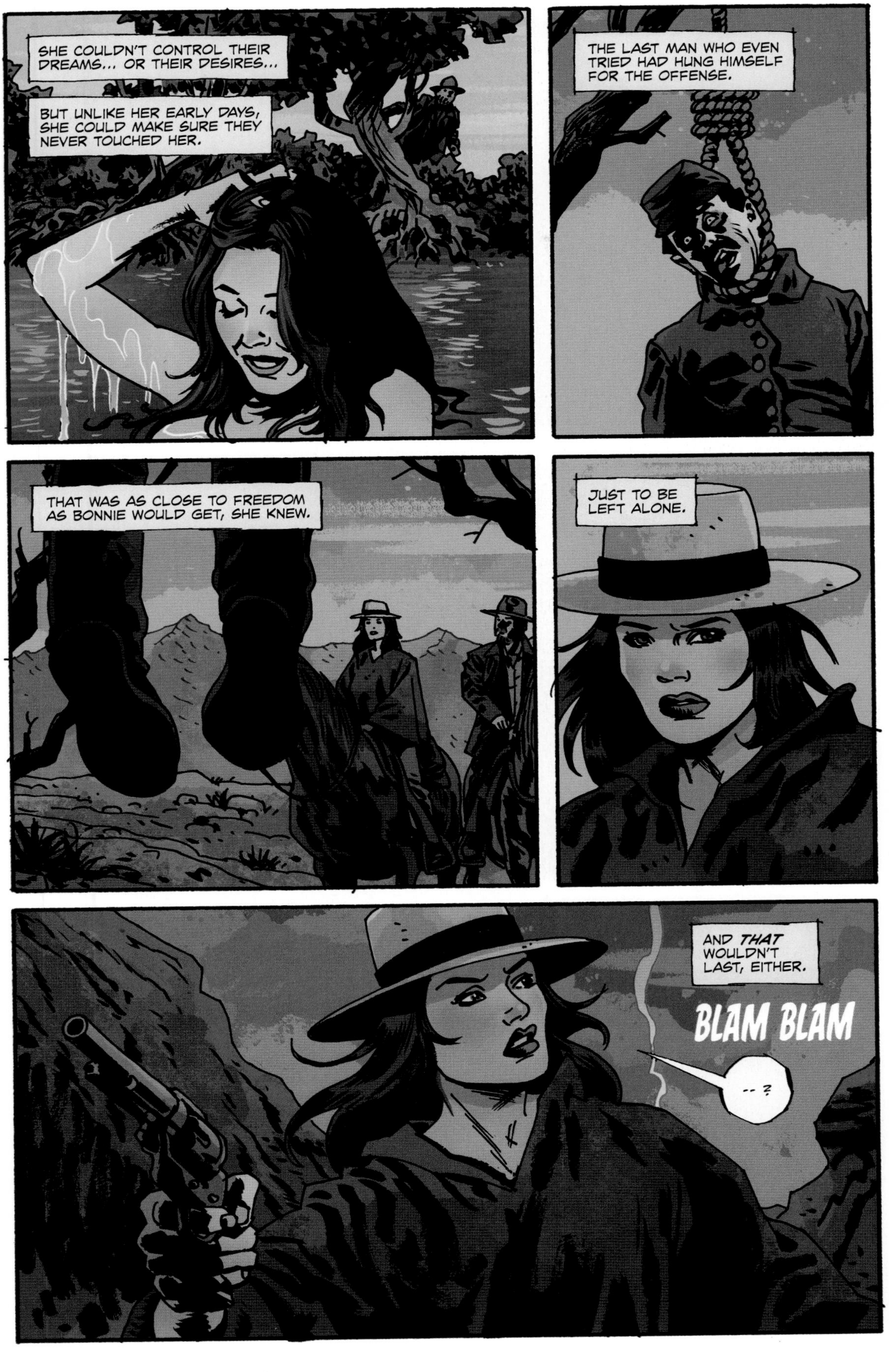
SHE COULDN'T CONTROL THEIR DREAMS... OR THEIR DESIRES...
BUT UNLIKE HER EARLY DAYS, SHE COULD MAKE SURE THEY NEVER TOUCHED HER.
THE LAST MAN WHO EVEN TRIED HAD HUNG HIMSELF FOR THE OFFENSE.
THAT WAS AS CLOSE TO FREEDOM AS BONNIE WOULD GET, SHE KNEW.
JUST TO BE LEFT ALONE.
AND *THAT* WOULDN'T LAST, EITHER.
BLAM BLAM
-- ?

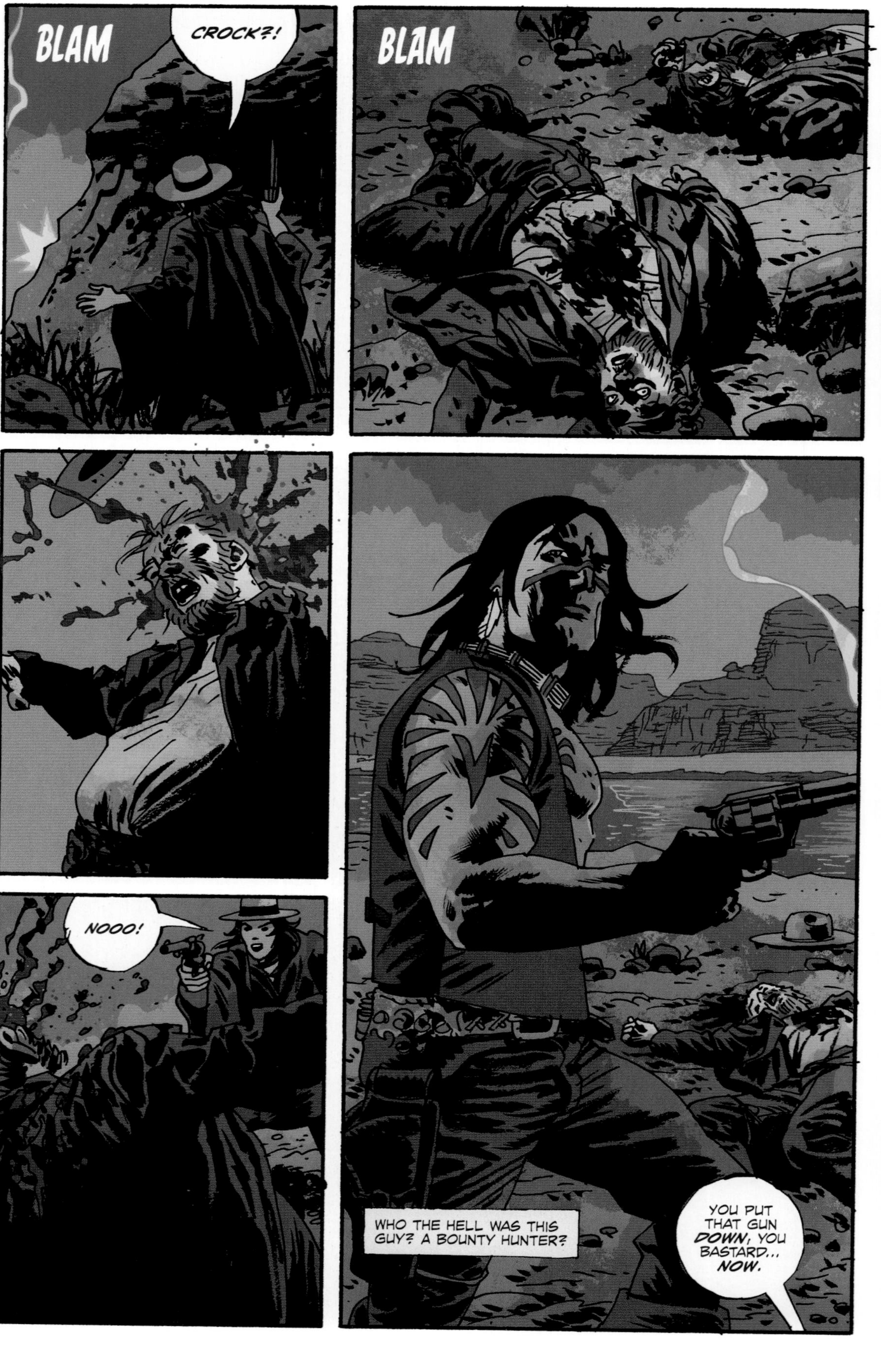
BLAM
CROCK?!
BLAM
NOOO!
WHO THE HELL WAS THIS GUY? A BOUNTY HUNTER?
YOU PUT THAT GUN *DOWN*, YOU BASTARD... *NOW.*

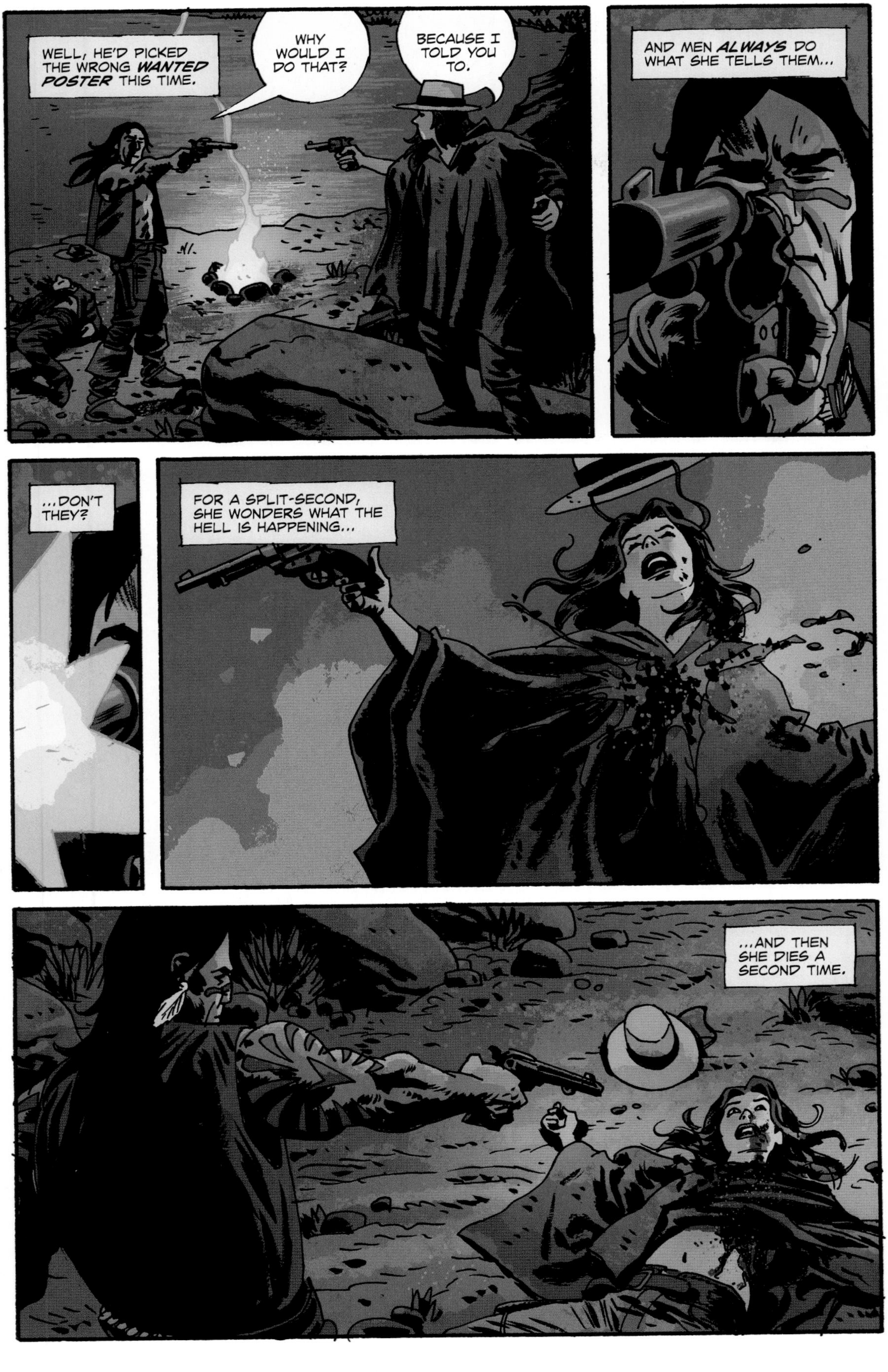
WELL, HE'D PICKED THE WRONG **WANTED POSTER** THIS TIME.
WHY WOULD I DO THAT?
BECAUSE I TOLD YOU TO.
AND MEN **ALWAYS** DO WHAT SHE TELLS THEM...
...DON'T THEY?
FOR A SPLIT-SECOND, SHE WONDERS WHAT THE HELL IS HAPPENING...
...AND THEN SHE DIES A SECOND TIME.

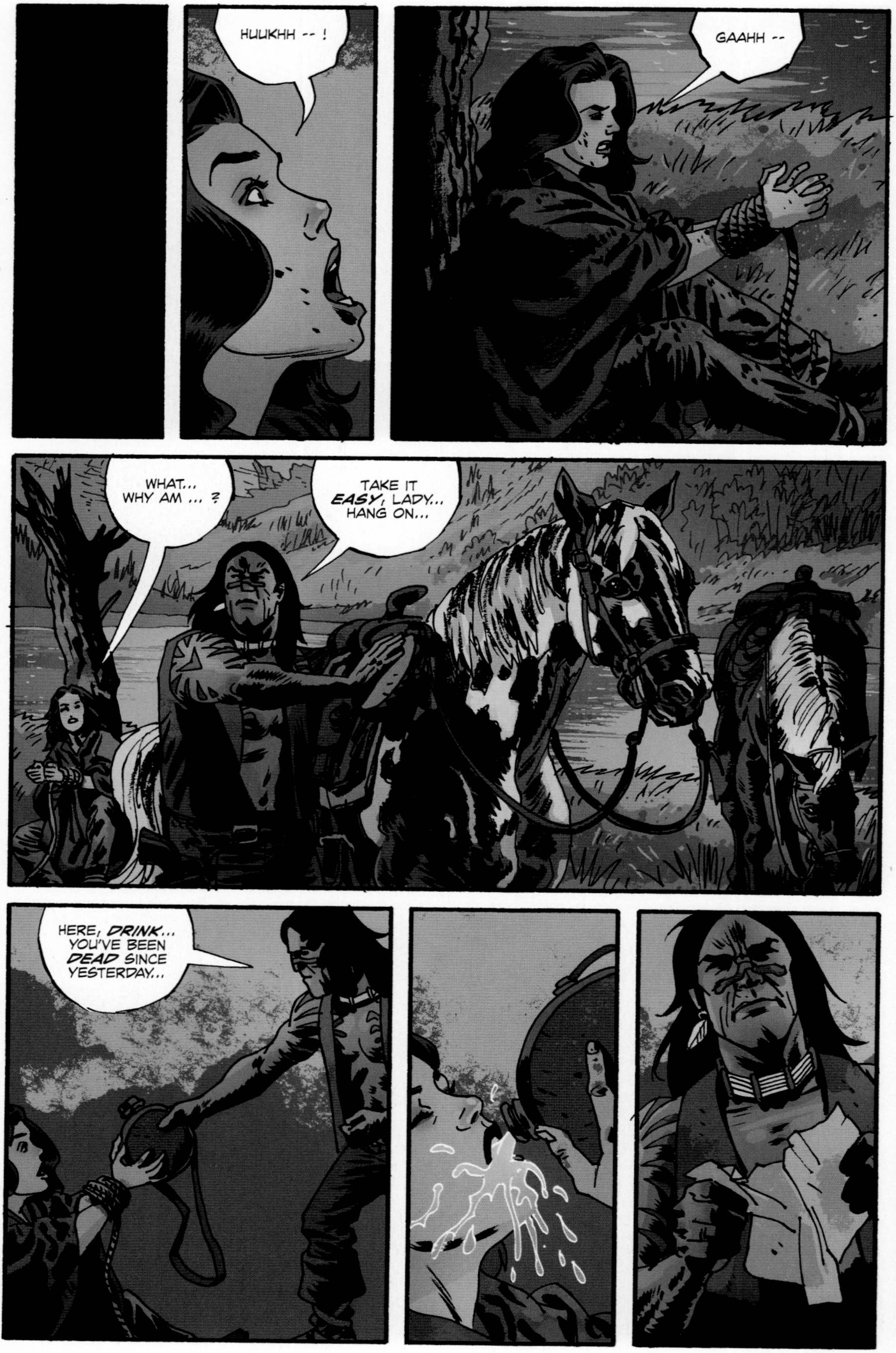
HUUKHH -- !
GAAHH --
WHAT... WHY AM ... ?
TAKE IT EASY, LADY... HANG ON...
HERE, DRINK... YOU'VE BEEN DEAD SINCE YESTERDAY...

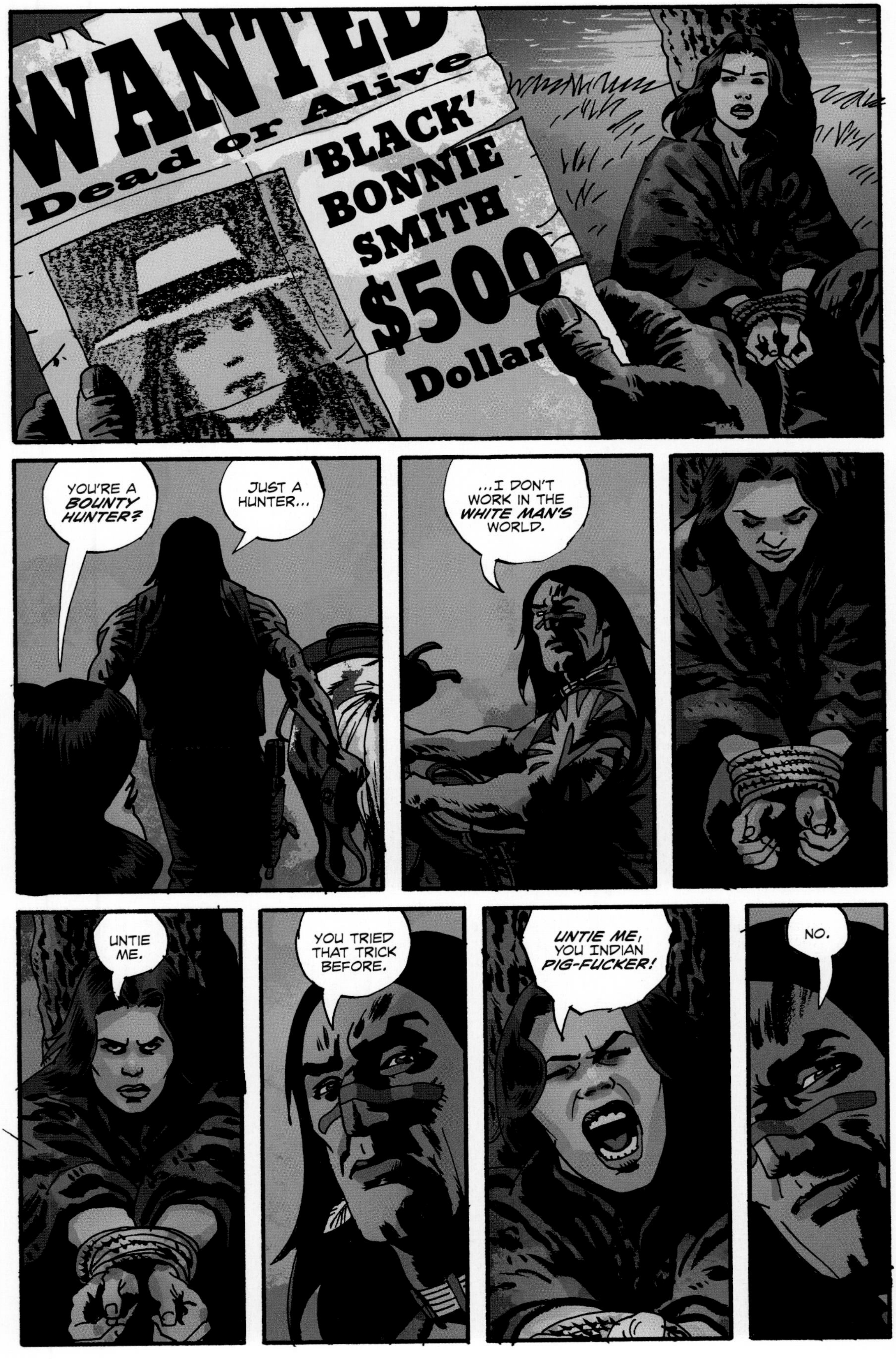
WANTED
Dead or Alive
'BLACK' BONNIE SMITH
$500
Dollar
YOU'RE A BOUNTY HUNTER?
JUST A HUNTER...
...I DON'T WORK IN THE WHITE MAN'S WORLD.
UNTIE ME.
YOU TRIED THAT TRICK BEFORE.
UNTIE ME, YOU INDIAN PIG-FUCKER!
NO.

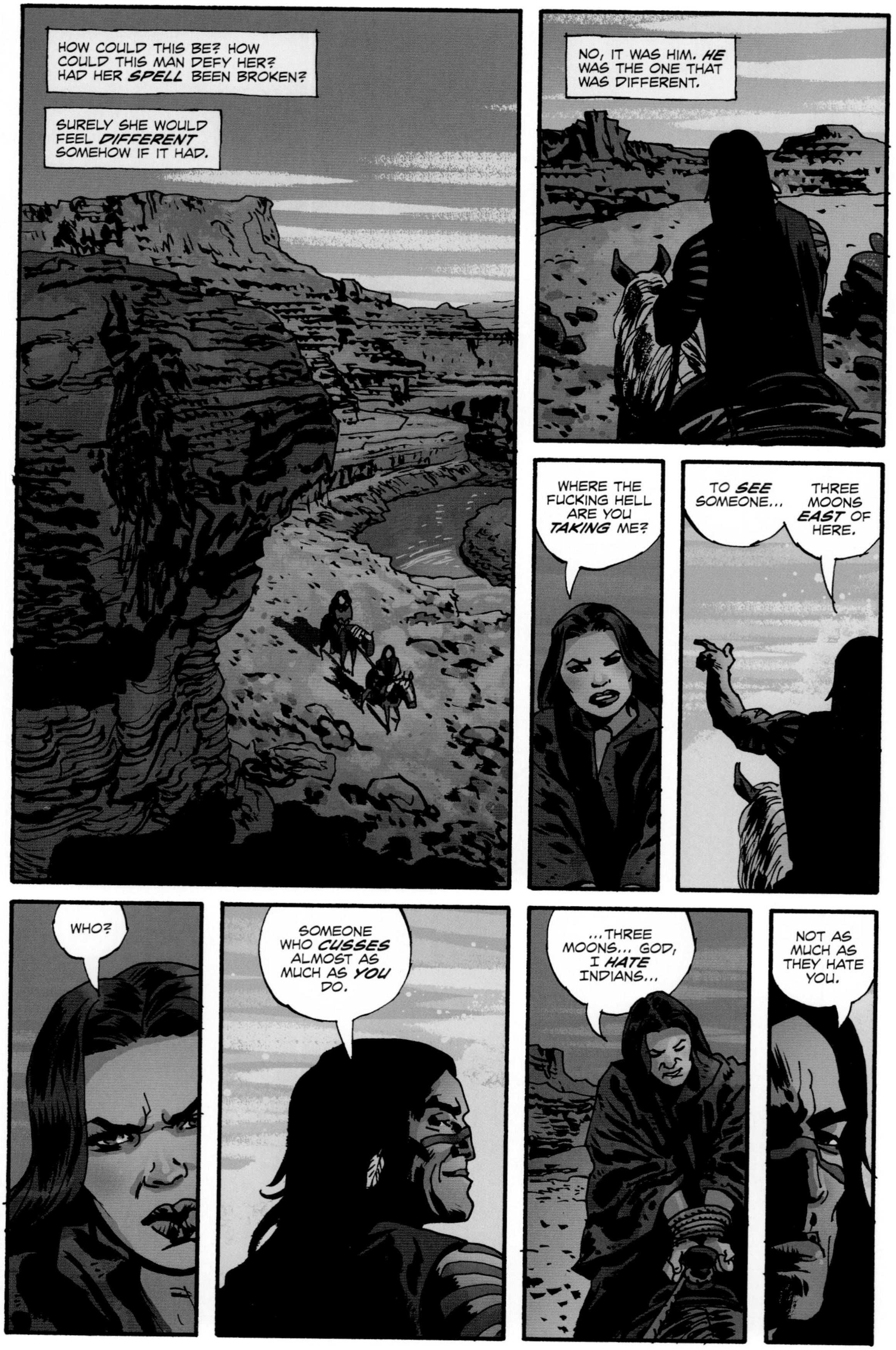
HOW COULD THIS BE? HOW COULD THIS MAN DEFY HER? HAD HER SPELL BEEN BROKEN?
SURELY SHE WOULD FEEL DIFFERENT SOMEHOW IF IT HAD.
NO, IT WAS HIM. HE WAS THE ONE THAT WAS DIFFERENT.
WHERE THE FUCKING HELL ARE YOU TAKING ME?
TO SEE SOMEONE...
THREE MOONS EAST OF HERE.
WHO?
SOMEONE WHO CUSSES ALMOST AS MUCH AS YOU DO.
...THREE MOONS... GOD, I HATE INDIANS...
NOT AS MUCH AS THEY HATE YOU.

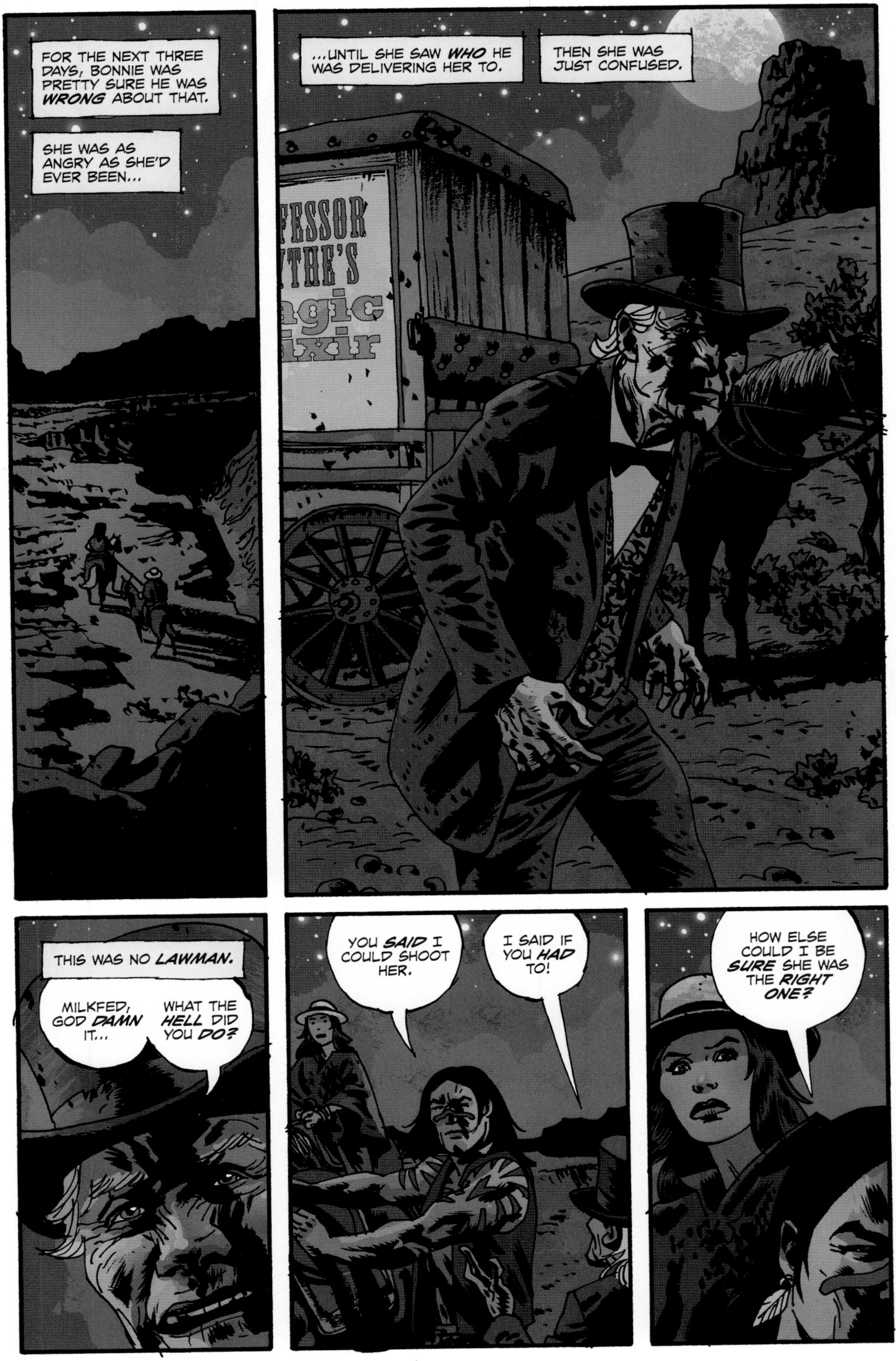
FOR THE NEXT THREE DAYS, BONNIE WAS PRETTY SURE HE WAS WRONG ABOUT THAT.
SHE WAS AS ANGRY AS SHE'D EVER BEEN...
...UNTIL SHE SAW WHO HE WAS DELIVERING HER TO.
THEN SHE WAS JUST CONFUSED.
FESSOR
YTHE'S
agic
ixir
THIS WAS NO LAWMAN.
MILKFED, GOD DAMN IT...
WHAT THE HELL DID YOU DO?
YOU SAID I COULD SHOOT HER.
I SAID IF YOU HAD TO!
HOW ELSE COULD I BE SURE SHE WAS THE RIGHT ONE?

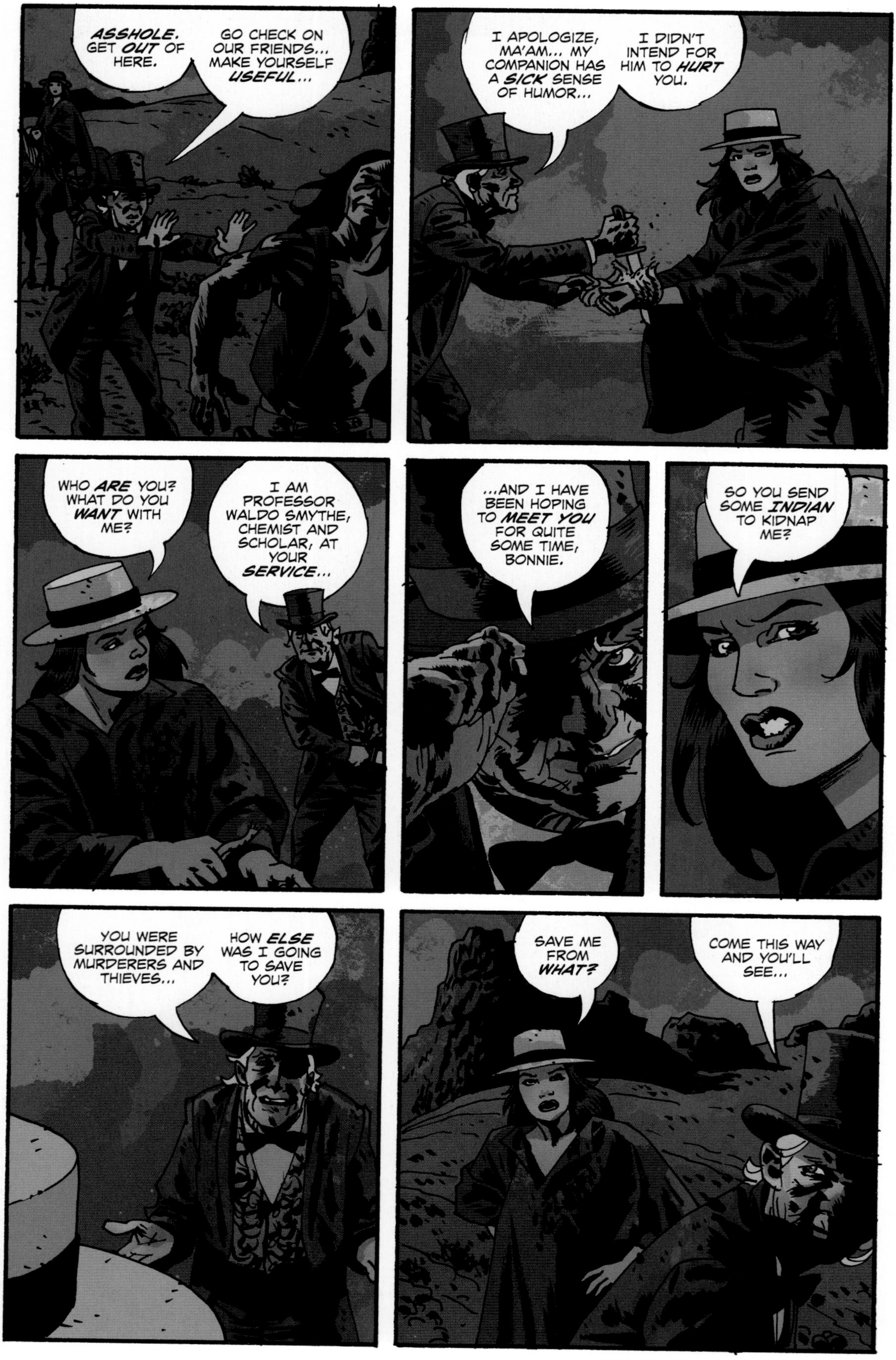
ASSHOLE. GET OUT OF HERE.
GO CHECK ON OUR FRIENDS... MAKE YOURSELF USEFUL...
I APOLOGIZE, MA'AM... MY COMPANION HAS A SICK SENSE OF HUMOR...
I DIDN'T INTEND FOR HIM TO HURT YOU.
WHO ARE YOU? WHAT DO YOU WANT WITH ME?
I AM PROFESSOR WALDO SMYTHE, CHEMIST AND SCHOLAR, AT YOUR SERVICE...
...AND I HAVE BEEN HOPING TO MEET YOU FOR QUITE SOME TIME, BONNIE.
SO YOU SEND SOME INDIAN TO KIDNAP ME?
YOU WERE SURROUNDED BY MURDERERS AND THIEVES...
HOW ELSE WAS I GOING TO SAVE YOU?
SAVE ME FROM WHAT?
COME THIS WAY AND YOU'LL SEE...

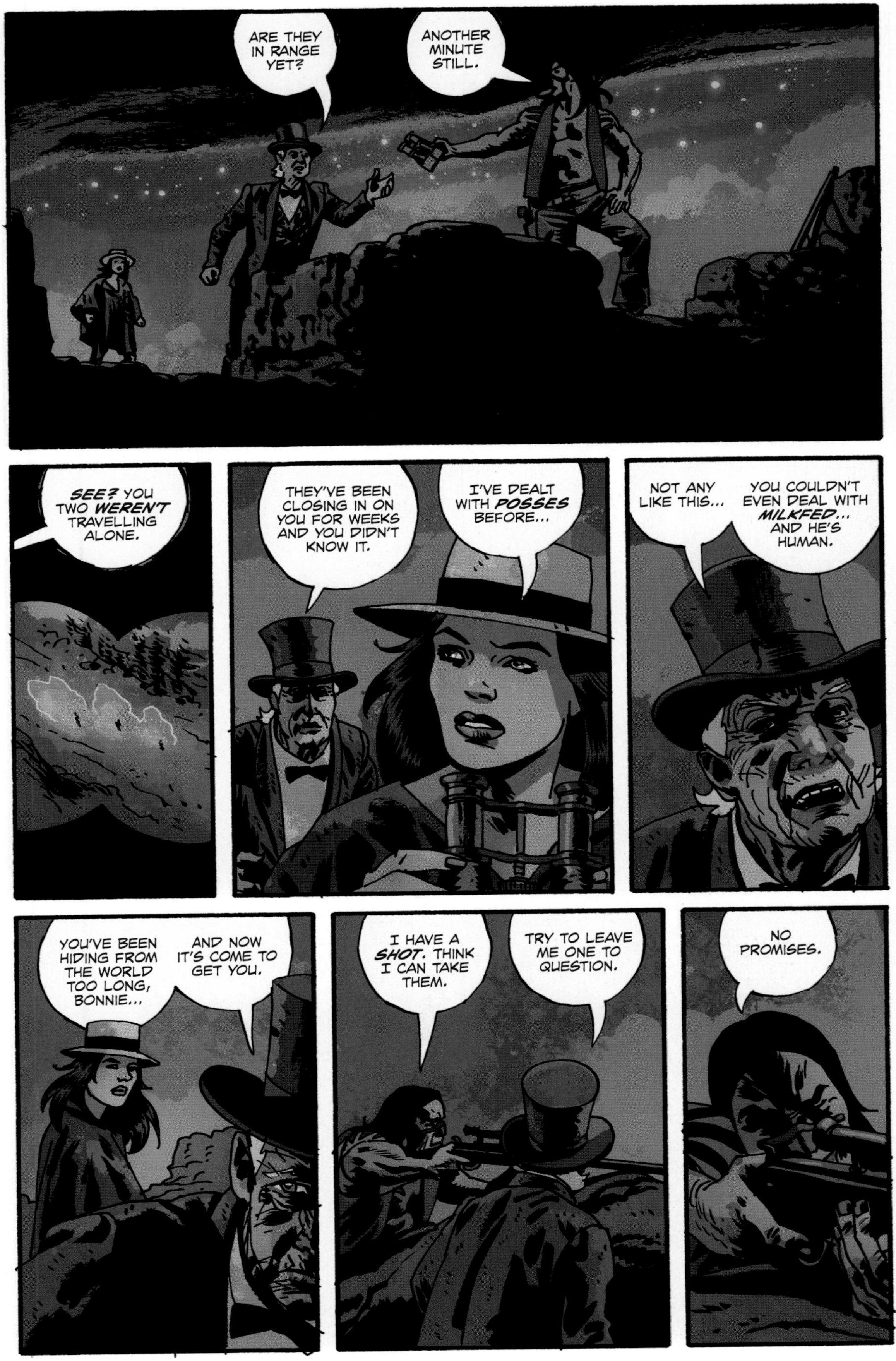
ARE THEY IN RANGE YET?
ANOTHER MINUTE STILL.
SEE? YOU TWO WEREN'T TRAVELLING ALONE.
THEY'VE BEEN CLOSING IN ON YOU FOR WEEKS AND YOU DIDN'T KNOW IT.
I'VE DEALT WITH POSSES BEFORE...
NOT ANY LIKE THIS...
YOU COULDN'T EVEN DEAL WITH MILKFED... AND HE'S HUMAN.
YOU'VE BEEN HIDING FROM THE WORLD TOO LONG, BONNIE...
AND NOW IT'S COME TO GET YOU.
I HAVE A SHOT. THINK I CAN TAKE THEM.
TRY TO LEAVE ME ONE TO QUESTION.
NO PROMISES.

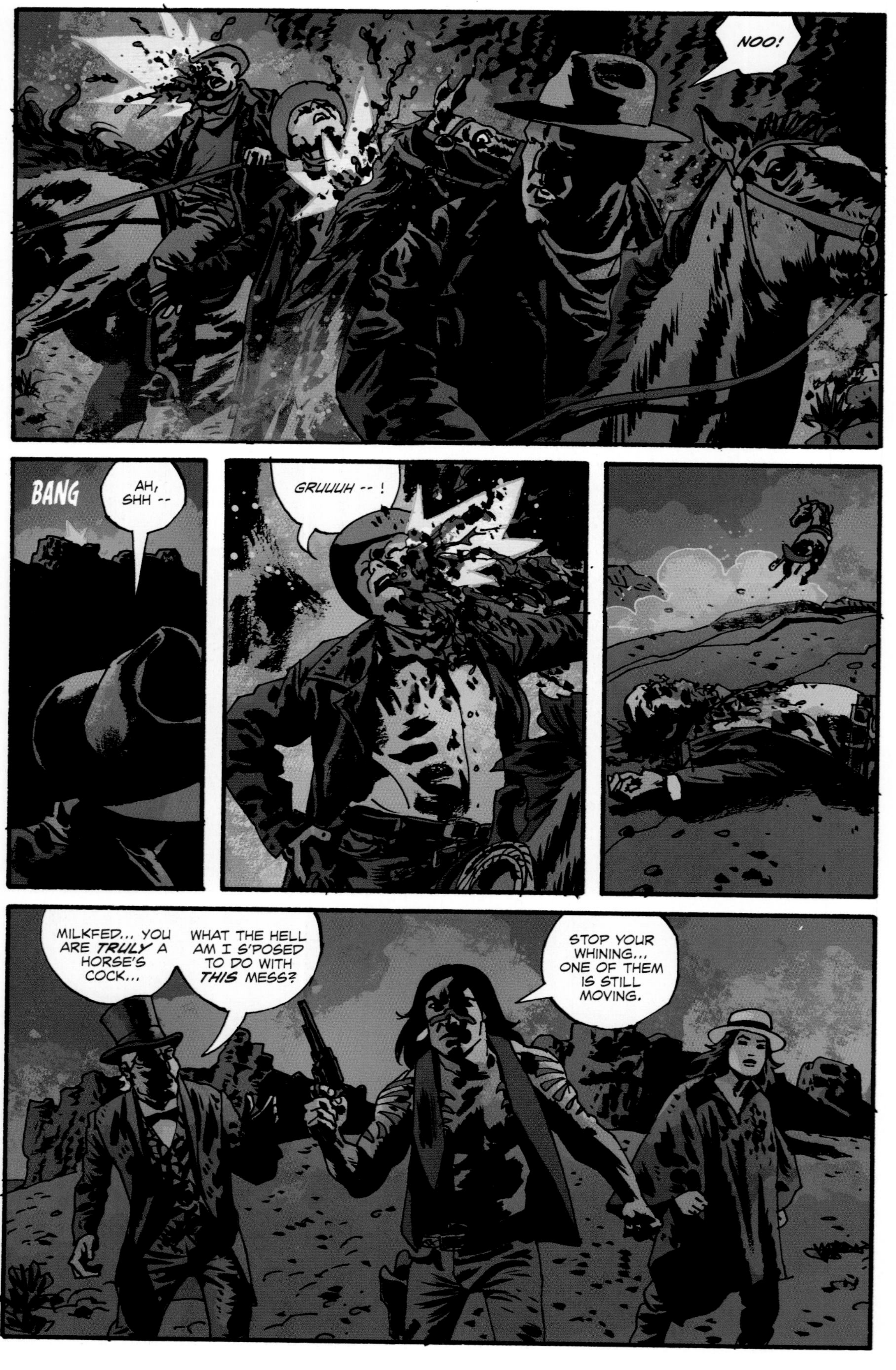
NOO!
BANG
AH, SHH --
GRUUUH -- !
MILKFED... YOU ARE TRULY A HORSE'S COCK...
WHAT THE HELL AM I S'POSED TO DO WITH THIS MESS?
STOP YOUR WHINING... ONE OF THEM IS STILL MOVING.

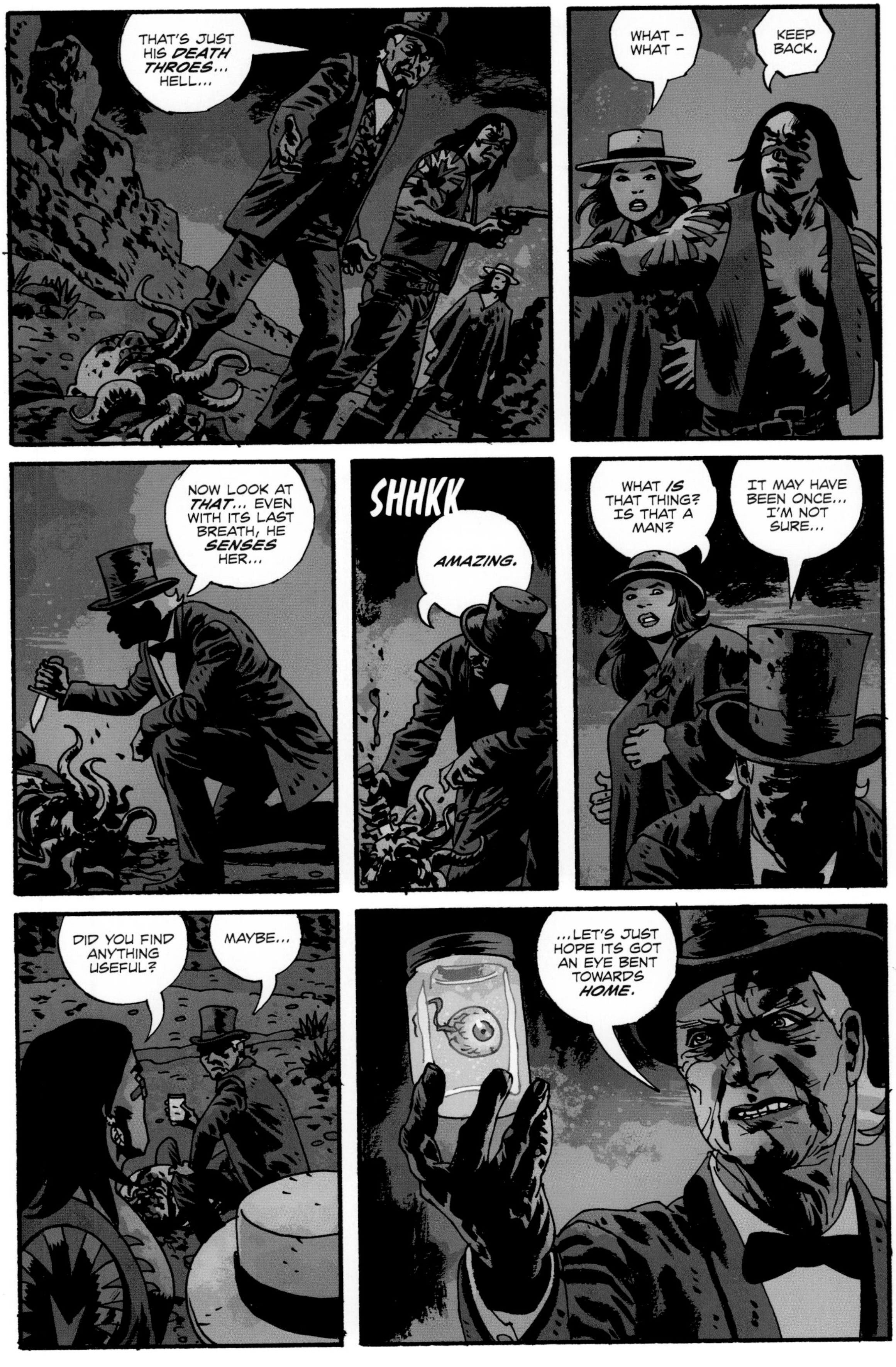
THAT'S JUST HIS *DEATH THROES*... HELL...
WHAT - WHAT -
KEEP BACK.
NOW LOOK AT *THAT*... EVEN WITH ITS LAST BREATH, HE *SENSES* HER...
SHHKK
AMAZING.
WHAT *IS* THAT THING? IS THAT A MAN?
IT MAY HAVE BEEN ONCE... I'M NOT SURE...
DID YOU FIND ANYTHING USEFUL?
MAYBE...
...LET'S JUST HOPE ITS GOT AN EYE BENT TOWARDS *HOME*.

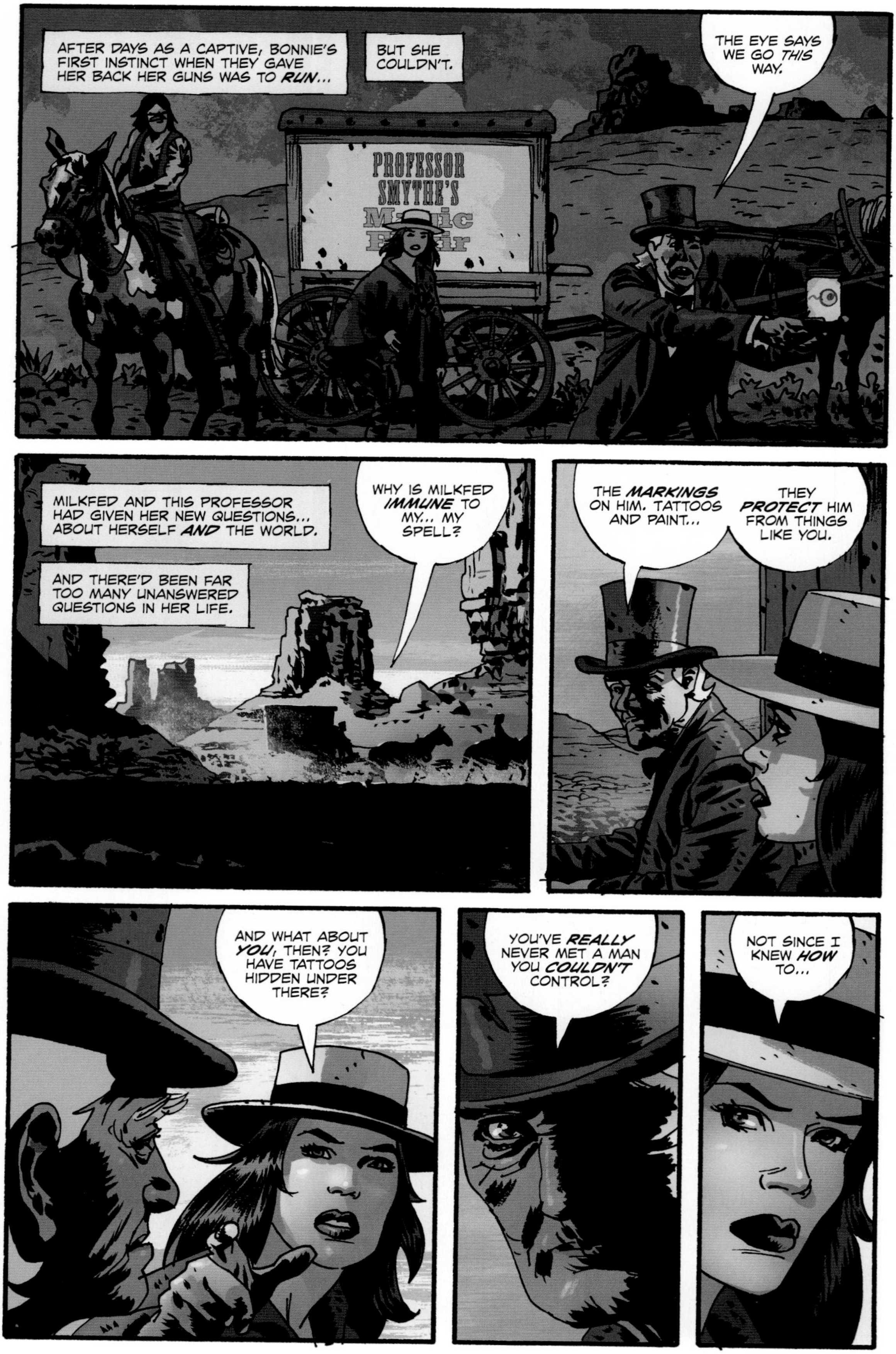

AFTER DAYS AS A CAPTIVE, BONNIE'S FIRST INSTINCT WHEN THEY GAVE HER BACK HER GUNS WAS TO *RUN*...
BUT SHE COULDN'T.
THE EYE SAYS WE GO *THIS* WAY.
PROFESSOR SMYTHE'S
MILKFED AND THIS PROFESSOR HAD GIVEN HER NEW QUESTIONS... ABOUT HERSELF *AND* THE WORLD.
AND THERE'D BEEN FAR TOO MANY UNANSWERED QUESTIONS IN HER LIFE.
WHY IS MILKFED *IMMUNE* TO MY... MY SPELL?
THE *MARKINGS* ON HIM. TATTOOS AND PAINT...
THEY *PROTECT* HIM FROM THINGS LIKE YOU.
AND WHAT ABOUT *YOU*, THEN? YOU HAVE TATTOOS HIDDEN UNDER THERE?
YOU'VE *REALLY* NEVER MET A MAN YOU *COULDN'T* CONTROL?
NOT SINCE I KNEW *HOW* TO...

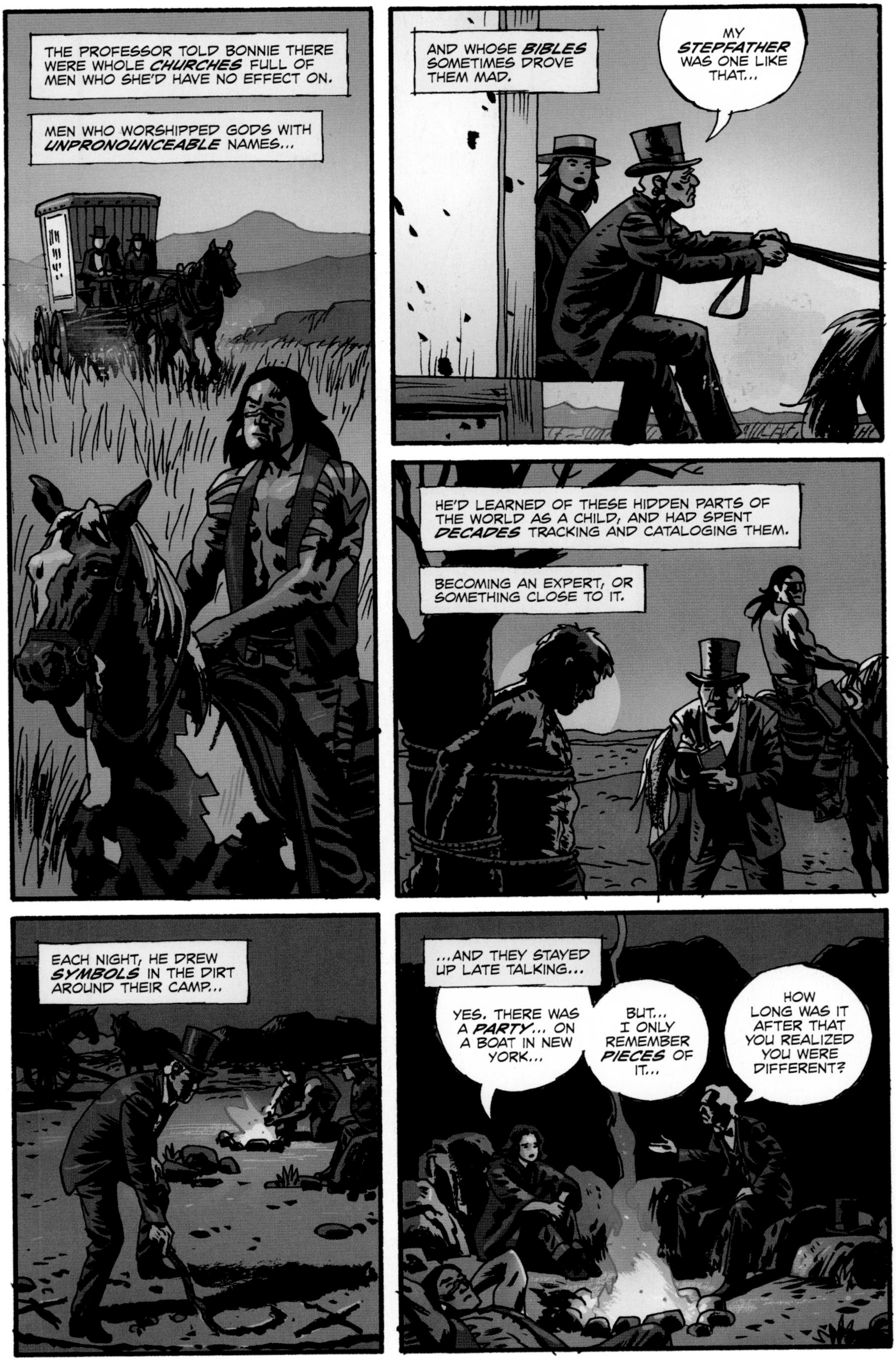
THE PROFESSOR TOLD BONNIE THERE WERE WHOLE CHURCHES FULL OF MEN WHO SHE'D HAVE NO EFFECT ON.
MEN WHO WORSHIPPED GODS WITH UNPRONOUNCEABLE NAMES...
AND WHOSE BIBLES SOMETIMES DROVE THEM MAD.
MY STEPFATHER WAS ONE LIKE THAT...
HE'D LEARNED OF THESE HIDDEN PARTS OF THE WORLD AS A CHILD, AND HAD SPENT DECADES TRACKING AND CATALOGING THEM.
BECOMING AN EXPERT, OR SOMETHING CLOSE TO IT.
EACH NIGHT, HE DREW SYMBOLS IN THE DIRT AROUND THEIR CAMP...
...AND THEY STAYED UP LATE TALKING...
YES. THERE WAS A PARTY... ON A BOAT IN NEW YORK...
BUT... I ONLY REMEMBER PIECES OF IT...
HOW LONG WAS IT AFTER THAT YOU REALIZED YOU WERE DIFFERENT?

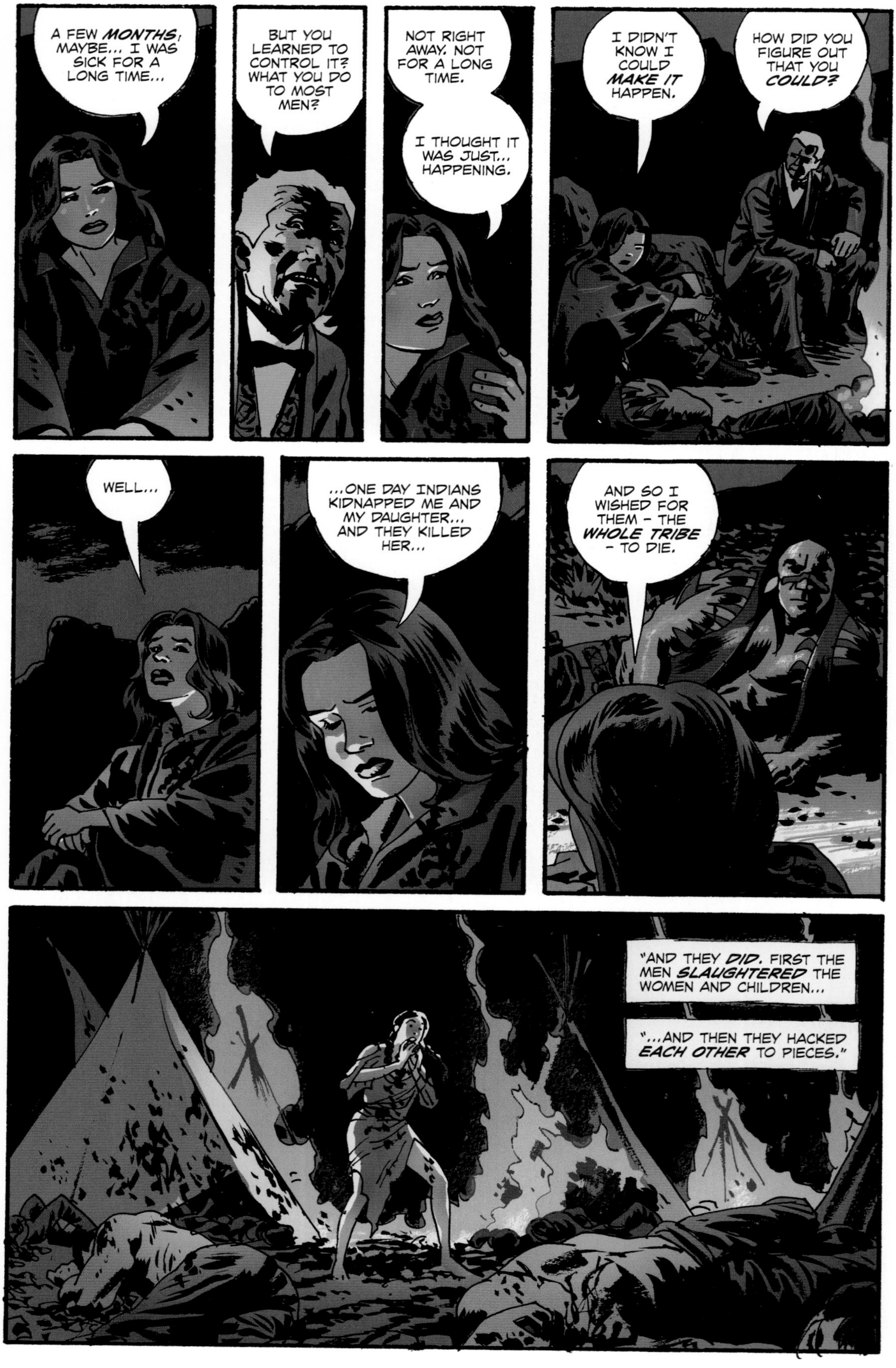
A FEW MONTHS, MAYBE... I WAS SICK FOR A LONG TIME...
BUT YOU LEARNED TO CONTROL IT? WHAT YOU DO TO MOST MEN?
NOT RIGHT AWAY. NOT FOR A LONG TIME.
I THOUGHT IT WAS JUST... HAPPENING.
I DIDN'T KNOW I COULD MAKE IT HAPPEN.
HOW DID YOU FIGURE OUT THAT YOU COULD?
WELL...
...ONE DAY INDIANS KIDNAPPED ME AND MY DAUGHTER... AND THEY KILLED HER...
AND SO I WISHED FOR THEM - THE WHOLE TRIBE - TO DIE.
"AND THEY DID. FIRST THE MEN SLAUGHTERED THE WOMEN AND CHILDREN...
"...AND THEN THEY HACKED EACH OTHER TO PIECES."

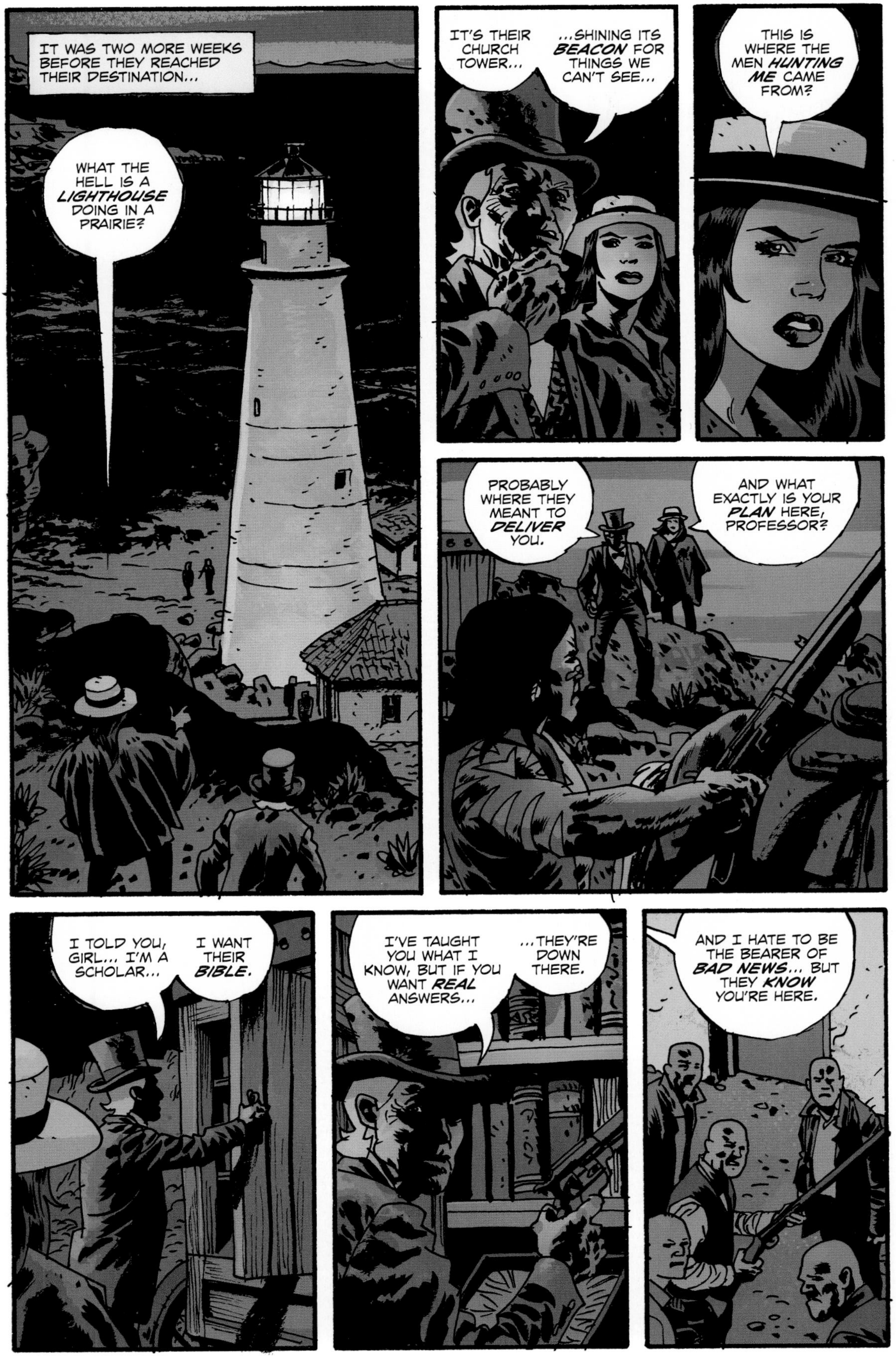
IT WAS TWO MORE WEEKS BEFORE THEY REACHED THEIR DESTINATION...
WHAT THE HELL IS A *LIGHTHOUSE* DOING IN A PRAIRIE?
IT'S THEIR CHURCH TOWER...
...SHINING ITS *BEACON* FOR THINGS WE CAN'T SEE...
THIS IS WHERE THE MEN *HUNTING ME* CAME FROM?
PROBABLY WHERE THEY MEANT TO *DELIVER* YOU.
AND WHAT EXACTLY IS YOUR *PLAN* HERE, PROFESSOR?
I TOLD YOU, GIRL... I'M A SCHOLAR...
I WANT THEIR *BIBLE.*
I'VE TAUGHT YOU WHAT I KNOW, BUT IF YOU WANT *REAL* ANSWERS...
...THEY'RE DOWN THERE.
AND I HATE TO BE THE BEARER OF *BAD NEWS*... BUT THEY *KNOW* YOU'RE HERE.

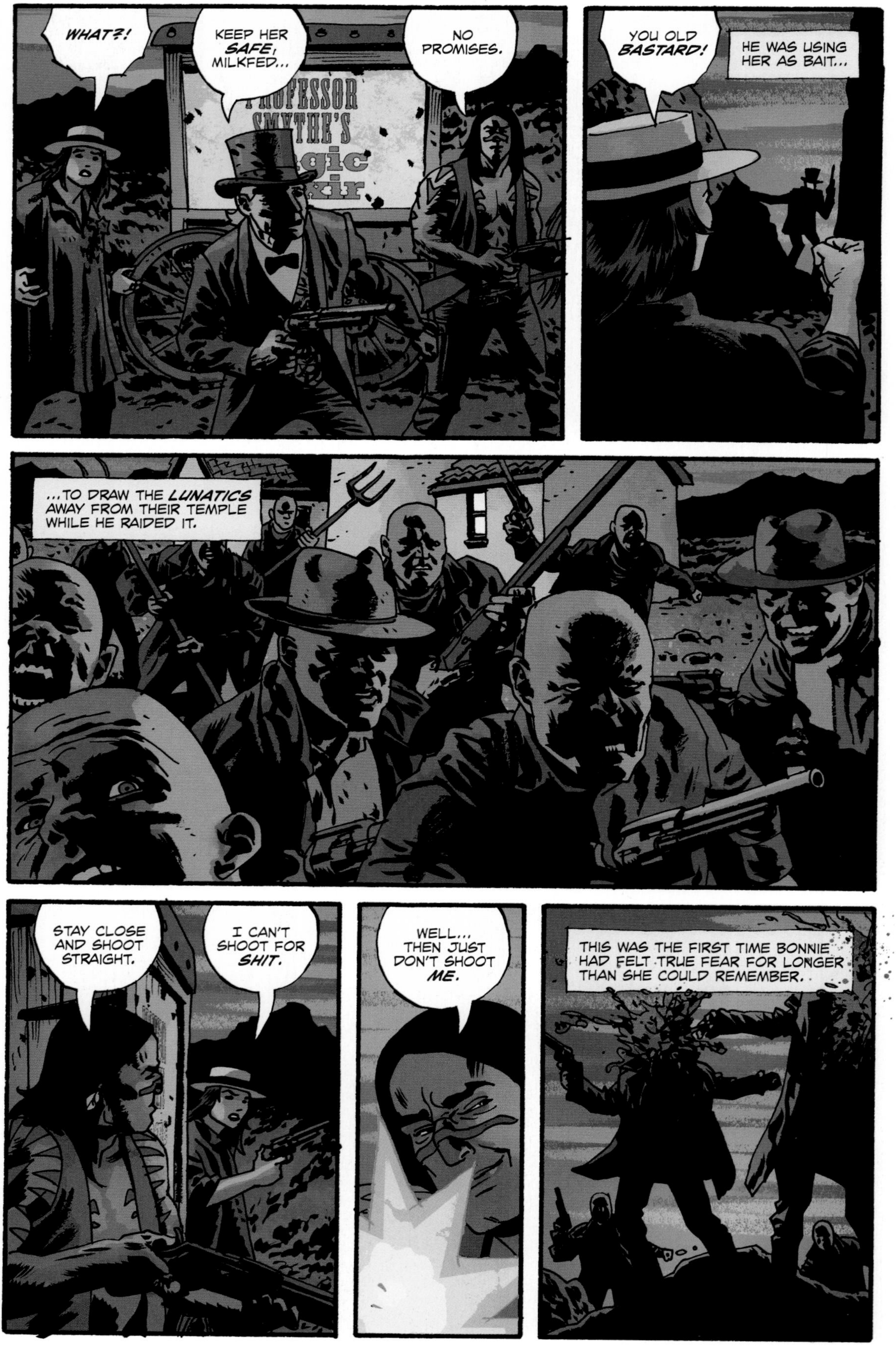
WHAT?!
KEEP HER SAFE, MILKFED...
NO PROMISES.
PROFESSOR SMYTHE'S
YOU OLD BASTARD!
HE WAS USING HER AS BAIT...
...TO DRAW THE LUNATICS AWAY FROM THEIR TEMPLE WHILE HE RAIDED IT.
STAY CLOSE AND SHOOT STRAIGHT.
I CAN'T SHOOT FOR SHIT.
WELL... THEN JUST DON'T SHOOT ME.
THIS WAS THE FIRST TIME BONNIE HAD FELT TRUE FEAR FOR LONGER THAN SHE COULD REMEMBER.

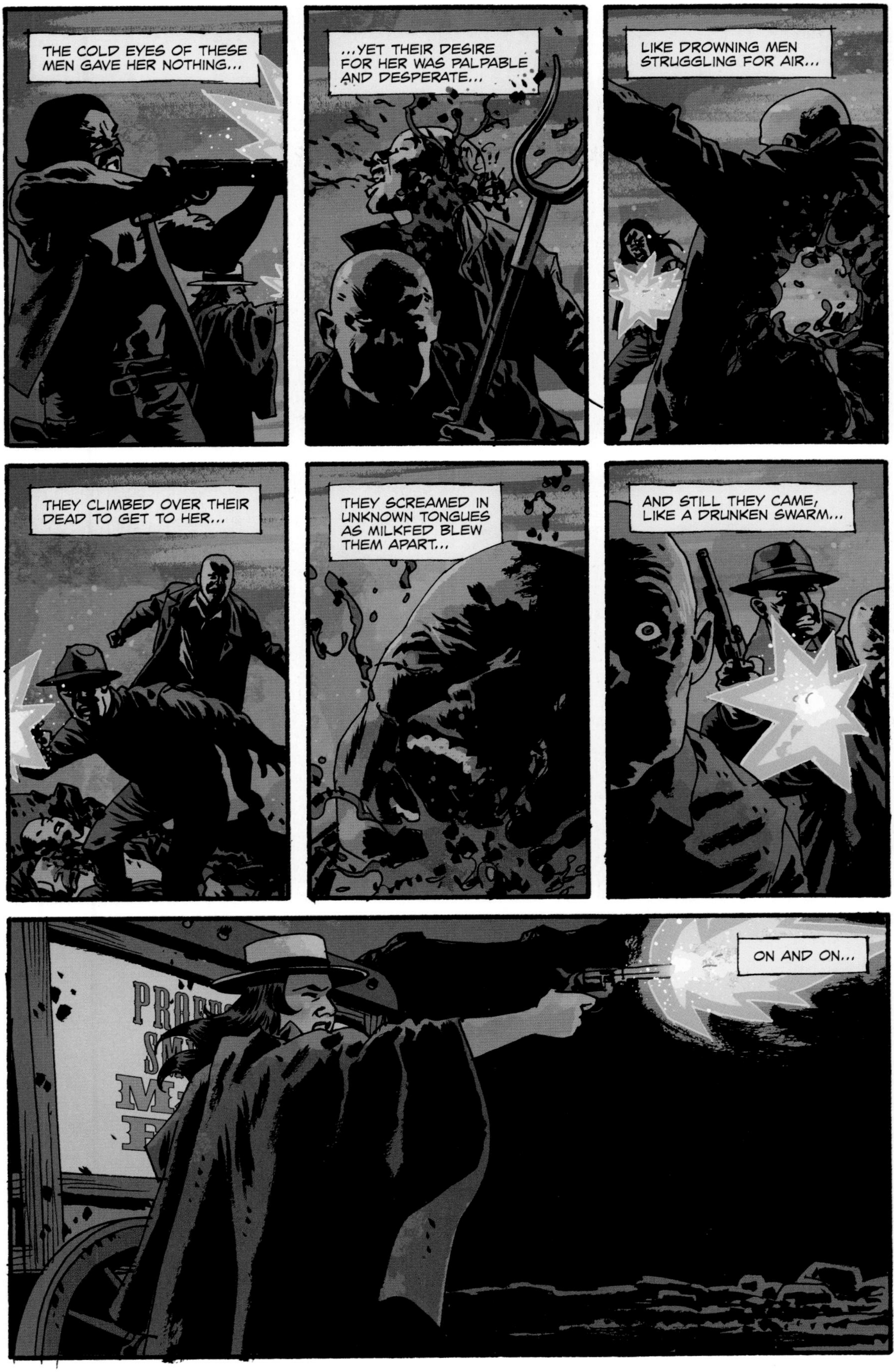
THE COLD EYES OF THESE MEN GAVE HER NOTHING...
...YET THEIR DESIRE FOR HER WAS PALPABLE AND DESPERATE...
LIKE DROWNING MEN STRUGGLING FOR AIR...
THEY CLIMBED OVER THEIR DEAD TO GET TO HER...
THEY SCREAMED IN UNKNOWN TONGUES AS MILKFED BLEW THEM APART...
AND STILL THEY CAME, LIKE A DRUNKEN SWARM...
ON AND ON...

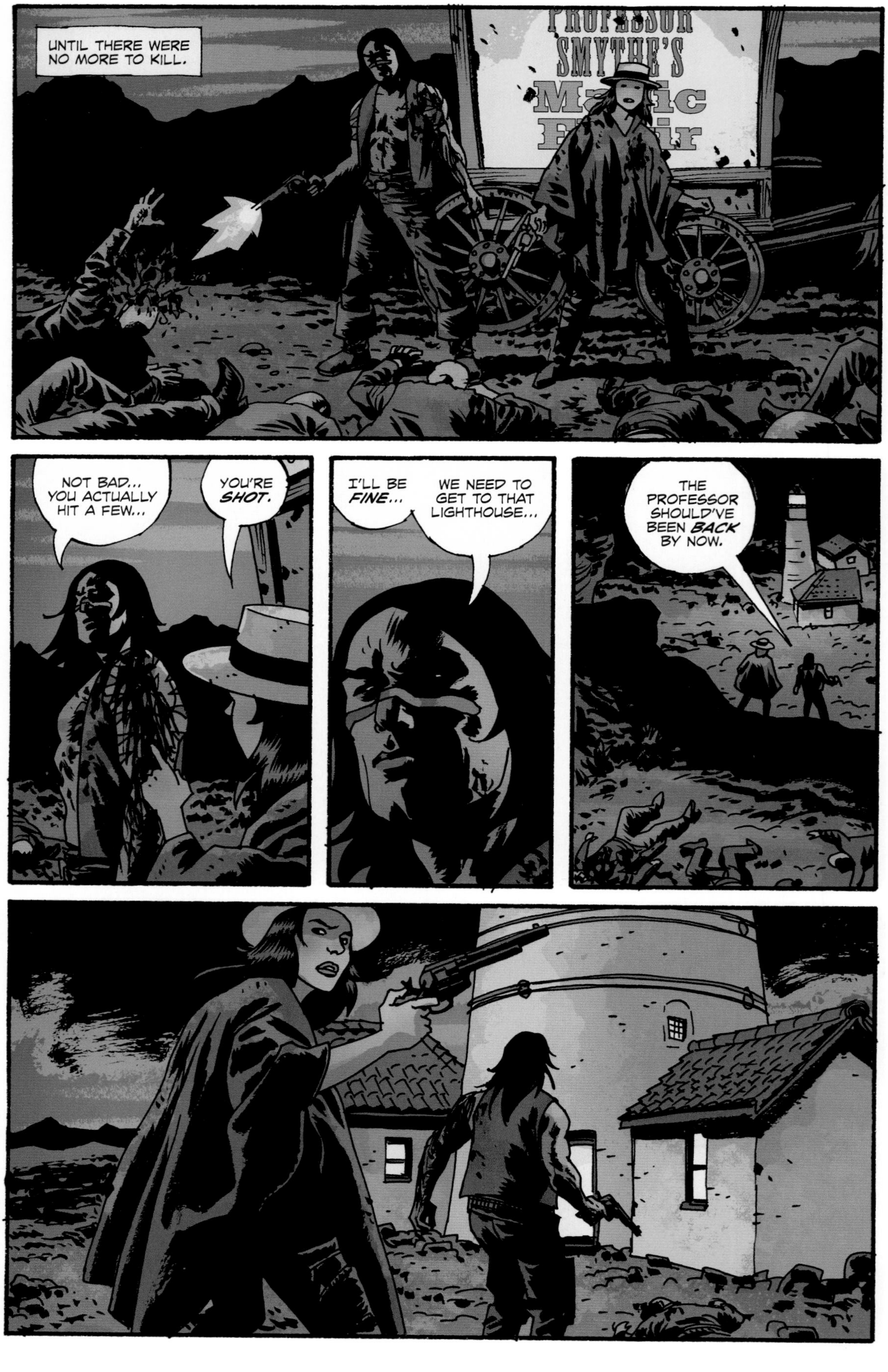
UNTIL THERE WERE NO MORE TO KILL.
PROFESSOR SMYTHE'S
NOT BAD... YOU ACTUALLY HIT A FEW...
YOU'RE *SHOT.*
I'LL BE *FINE*...
WE NEED TO GET TO THAT LIGHTHOUSE...
THE PROFESSOR SHOULD'VE BEEN *BACK* BY NOW.

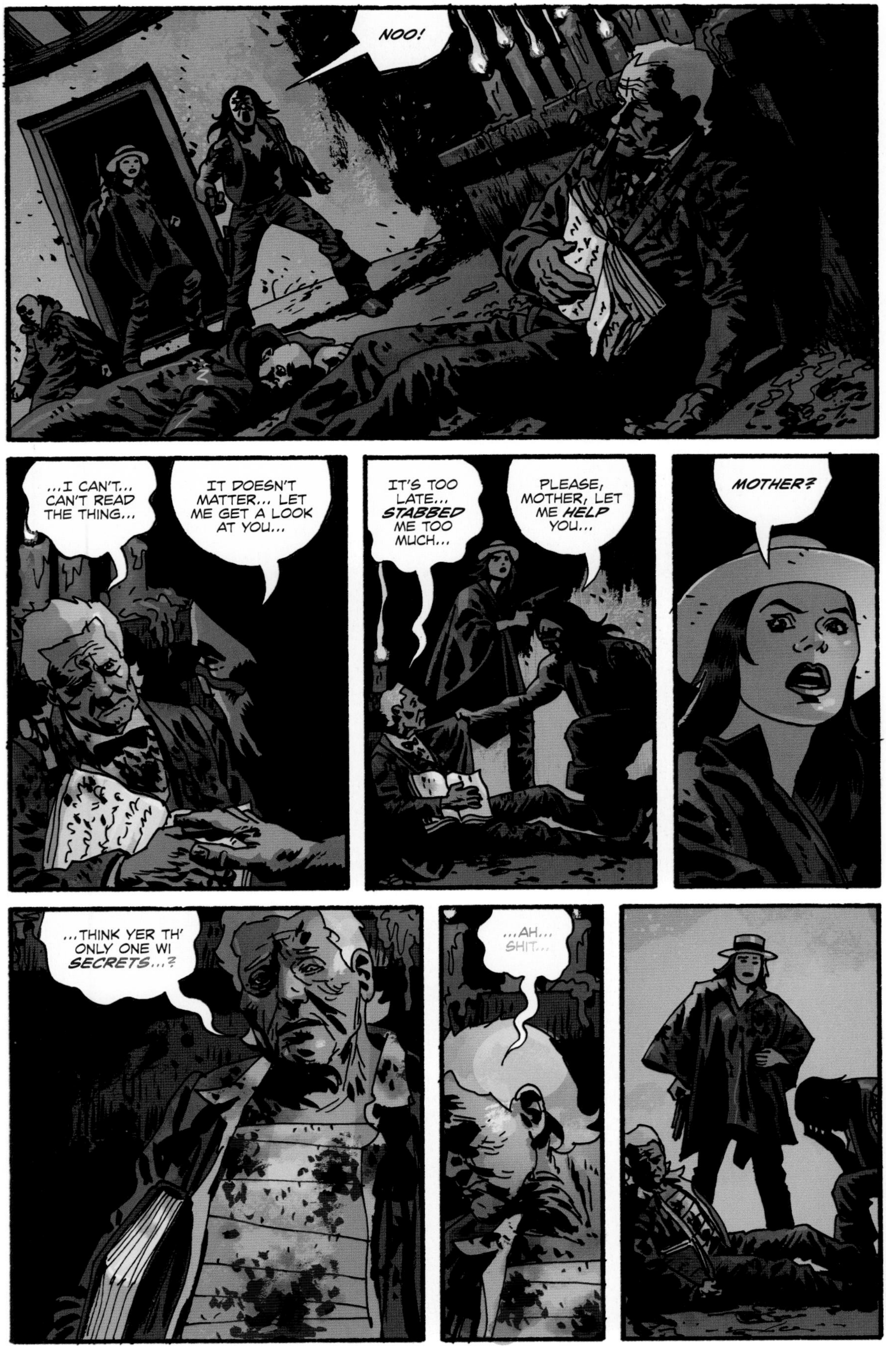
NOO!
...I CAN'T... CAN'T READ THE THING...
IT DOESN'T MATTER... LET ME GET A LOOK AT YOU...
IT'S TOO LATE... STABBED ME TOO MUCH...
PLEASE, MOTHER, LET ME HELP YOU...
MOTHER?
...THINK YER TH' ONLY ONE WI SECRETS...?
...AH... SHIT...

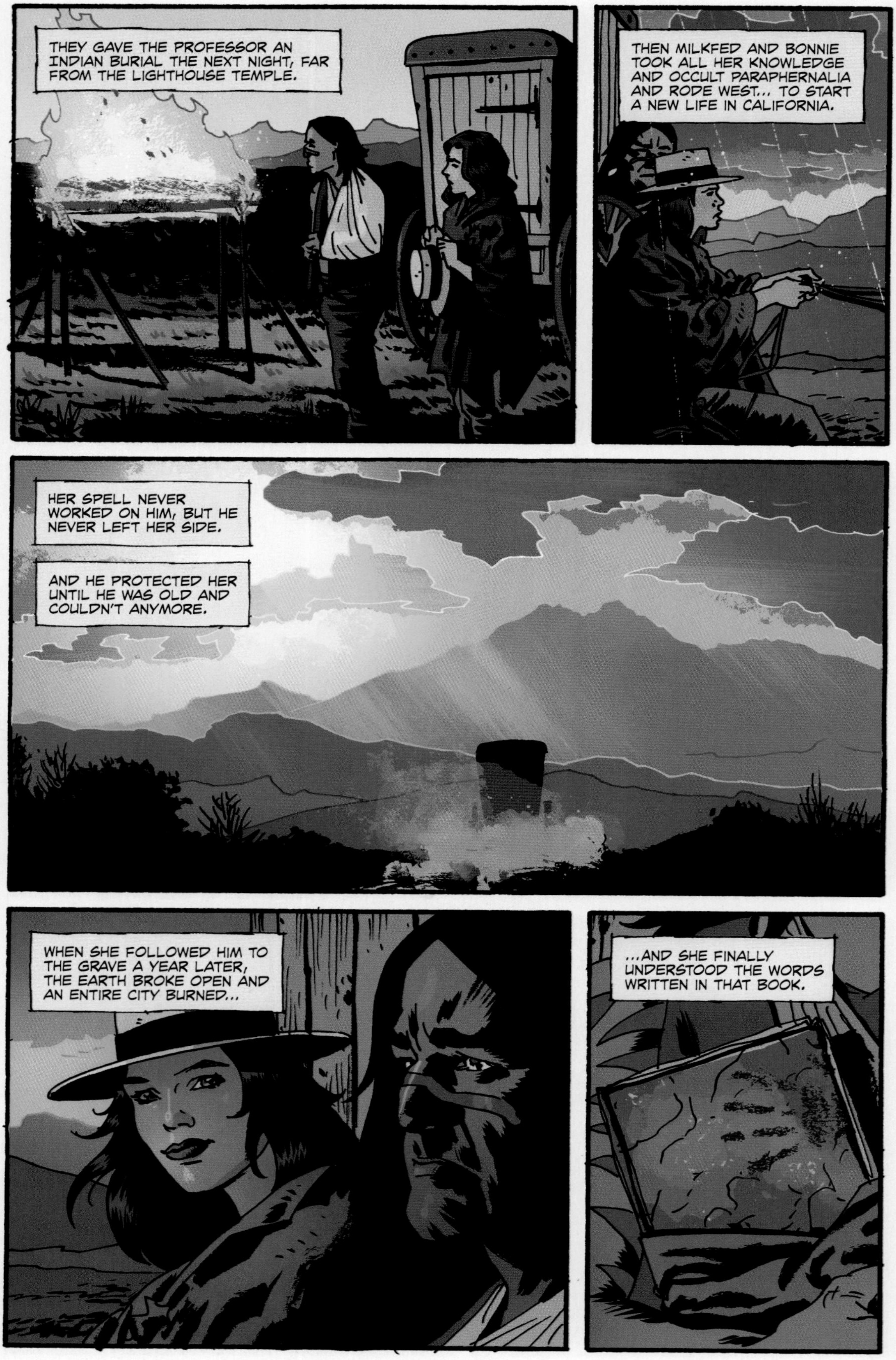
THEY GAVE THE PROFESSOR AN INDIAN BURIAL THE NEXT NIGHT, FAR FROM THE LIGHTHOUSE TEMPLE.
THEN MILKFED AND BONNIE TOOK ALL HER KNOWLEDGE AND OCCULT PARAPHERNALIA AND RODE WEST... TO START A NEW LIFE IN CALIFORNIA.
HER SPELL NEVER WORKED ON HIM, BUT HE NEVER LEFT HER SIDE.
AND HE PROTECTED HER UNTIL HE WAS OLD AND COULDN'T ANYMORE.
WHEN SHE FOLLOWED HIM TO THE GRAVE A YEAR LATER, THE EARTH BROKE OPEN AND AN ENTIRE CITY BURNED...
...AND SHE FINALLY UNDERSTOOD THE WORDS WRITTEN IN THAT BOOK.

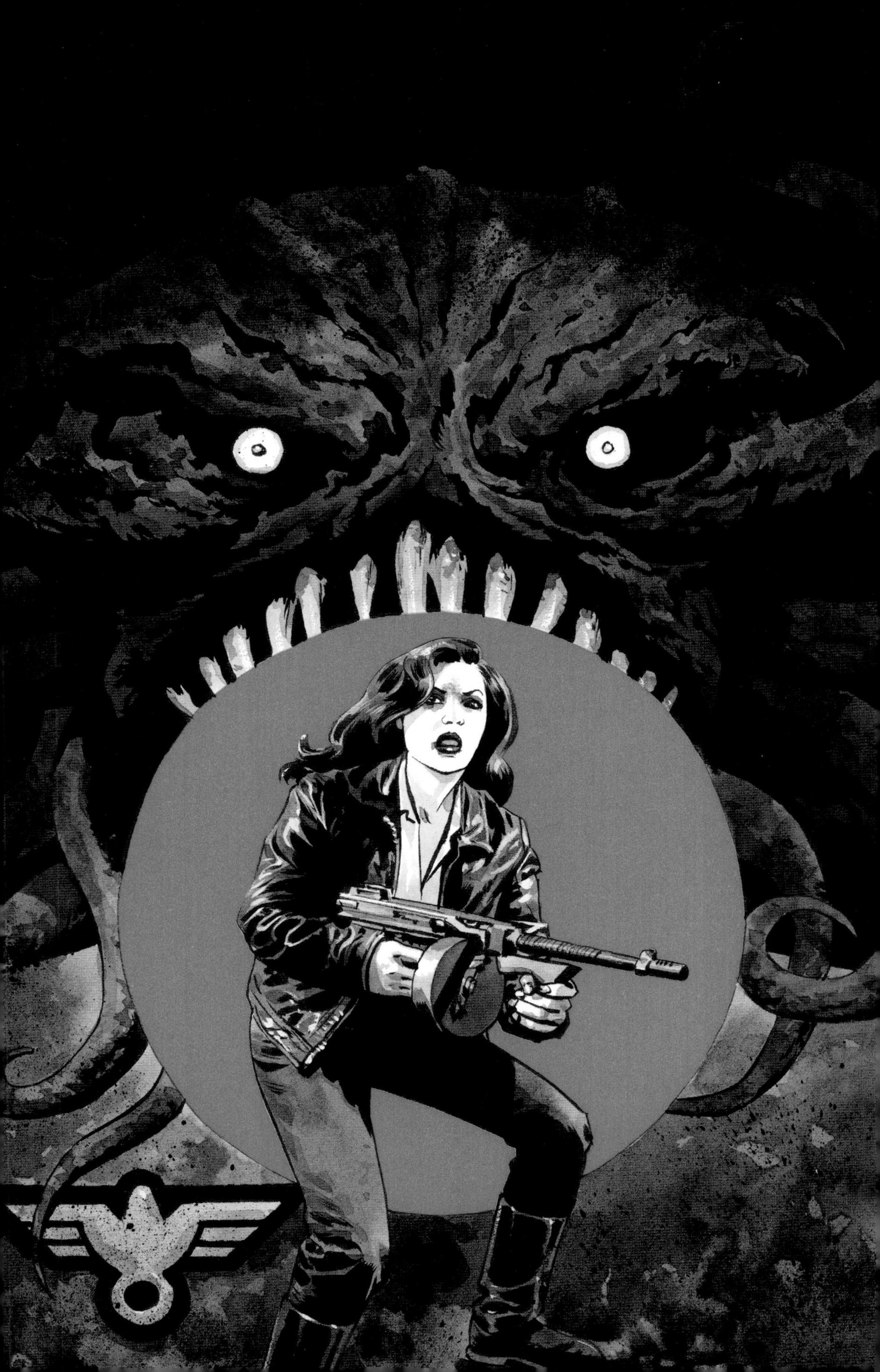

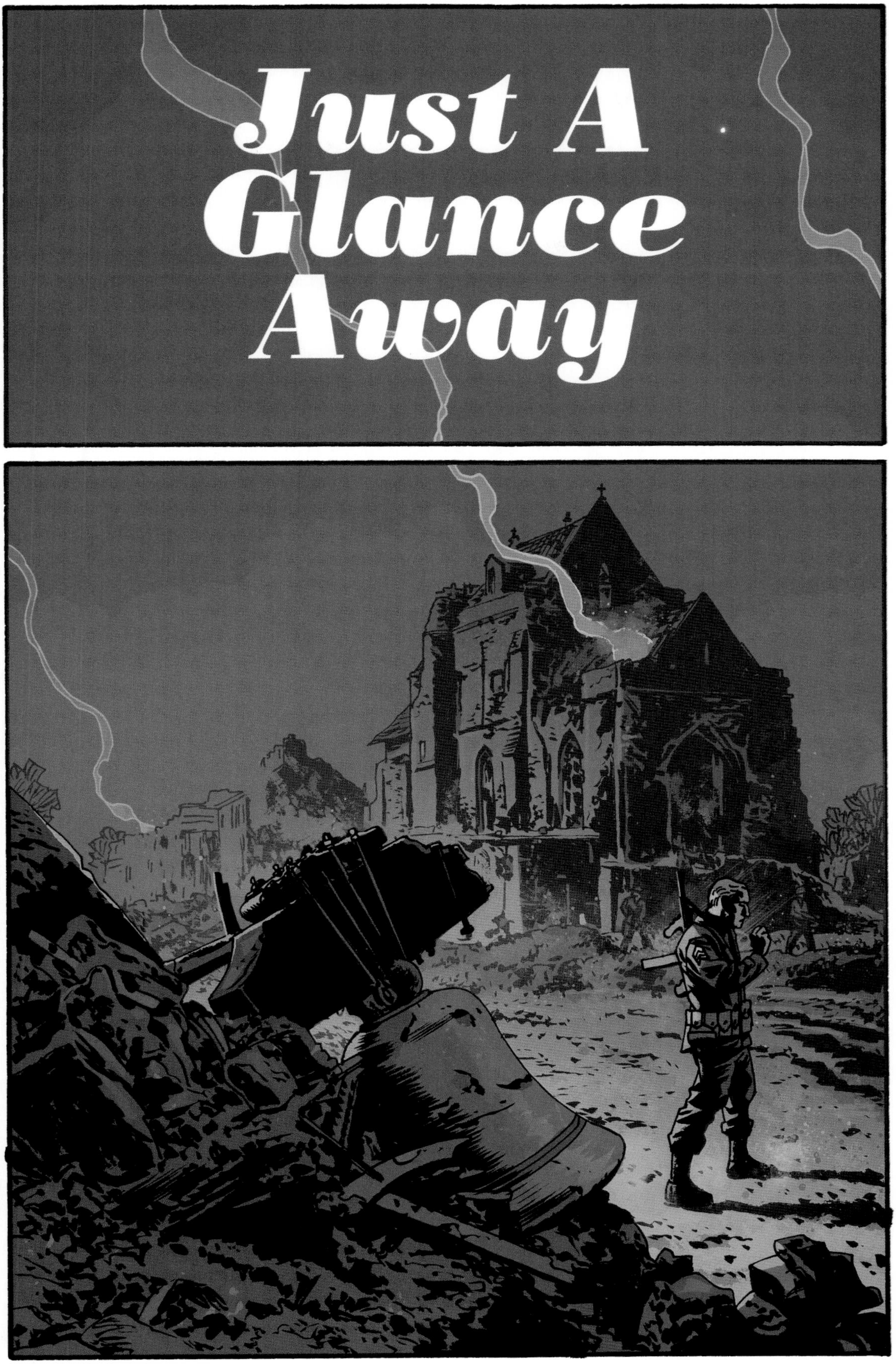
Just A Glance Away

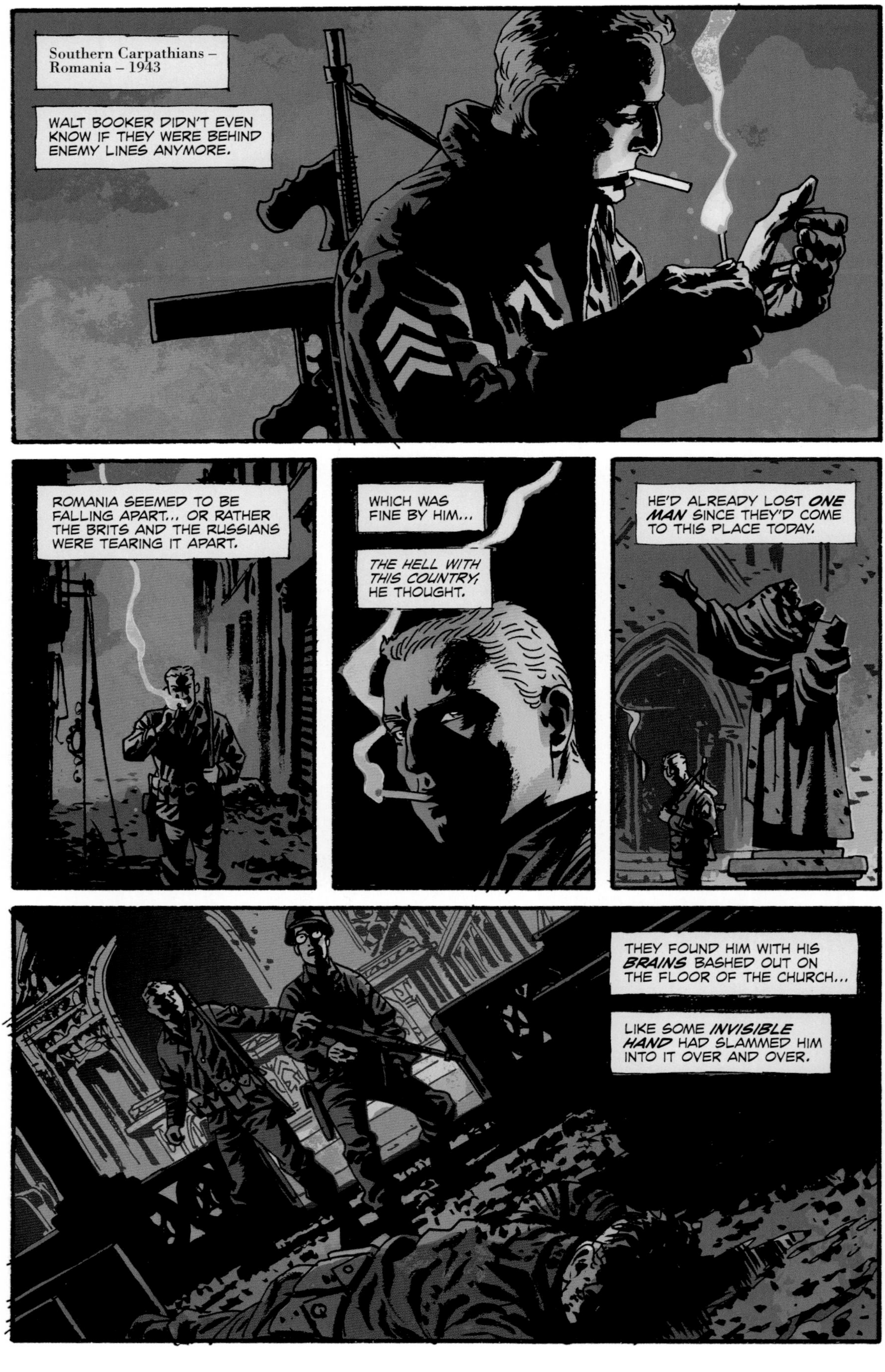
Southern Carpathians – Romania – 1943
WALT BOOKER DIDN'T EVEN KNOW IF THEY WERE BEHIND ENEMY LINES ANYMORE.
ROMANIA SEEMED TO BE FALLING APART... OR RATHER THE BRITS AND THE RUSSIANS WERE TEARING IT APART.
WHICH WAS FINE BY HIM...
THE HELL WITH THIS COUNTRY, HE THOUGHT.
HE'D ALREADY LOST ***ONE MAN*** SINCE THEY'D COME TO THIS PLACE TODAY.
THEY FOUND HIM WITH HIS ***BRAINS*** BASHED OUT ON THE FLOOR OF THE CHURCH...
LIKE SOME ***INVISIBLE HAND*** HAD SLAMMED HIM INTO IT OVER AND OVER.

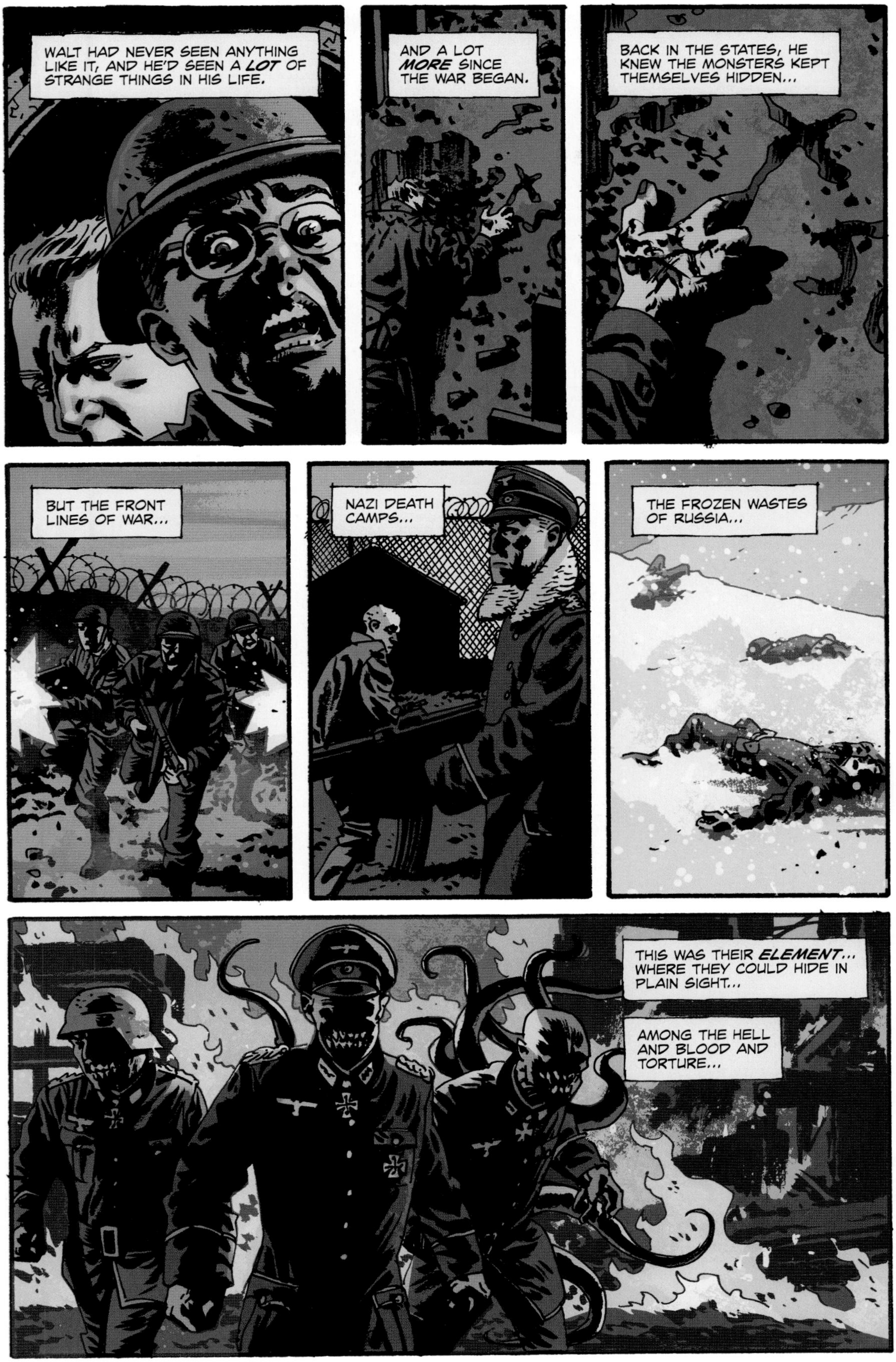
WALT HAD NEVER SEEN ANYTHING LIKE IT, AND HE'D SEEN A LOT OF STRANGE THINGS IN HIS LIFE.
AND A LOT MORE SINCE THE WAR BEGAN.
BACK IN THE STATES, HE KNEW THE MONSTERS KEPT THEMSELVES HIDDEN...
BUT THE FRONT LINES OF WAR...
NAZI DEATH CAMPS...
THE FROZEN WASTES OF RUSSIA...
THIS WAS THEIR ELEMENT... WHERE THEY COULD HIDE IN PLAIN SIGHT...
AMONG THE HELL AND BLOOD AND TORTURE...

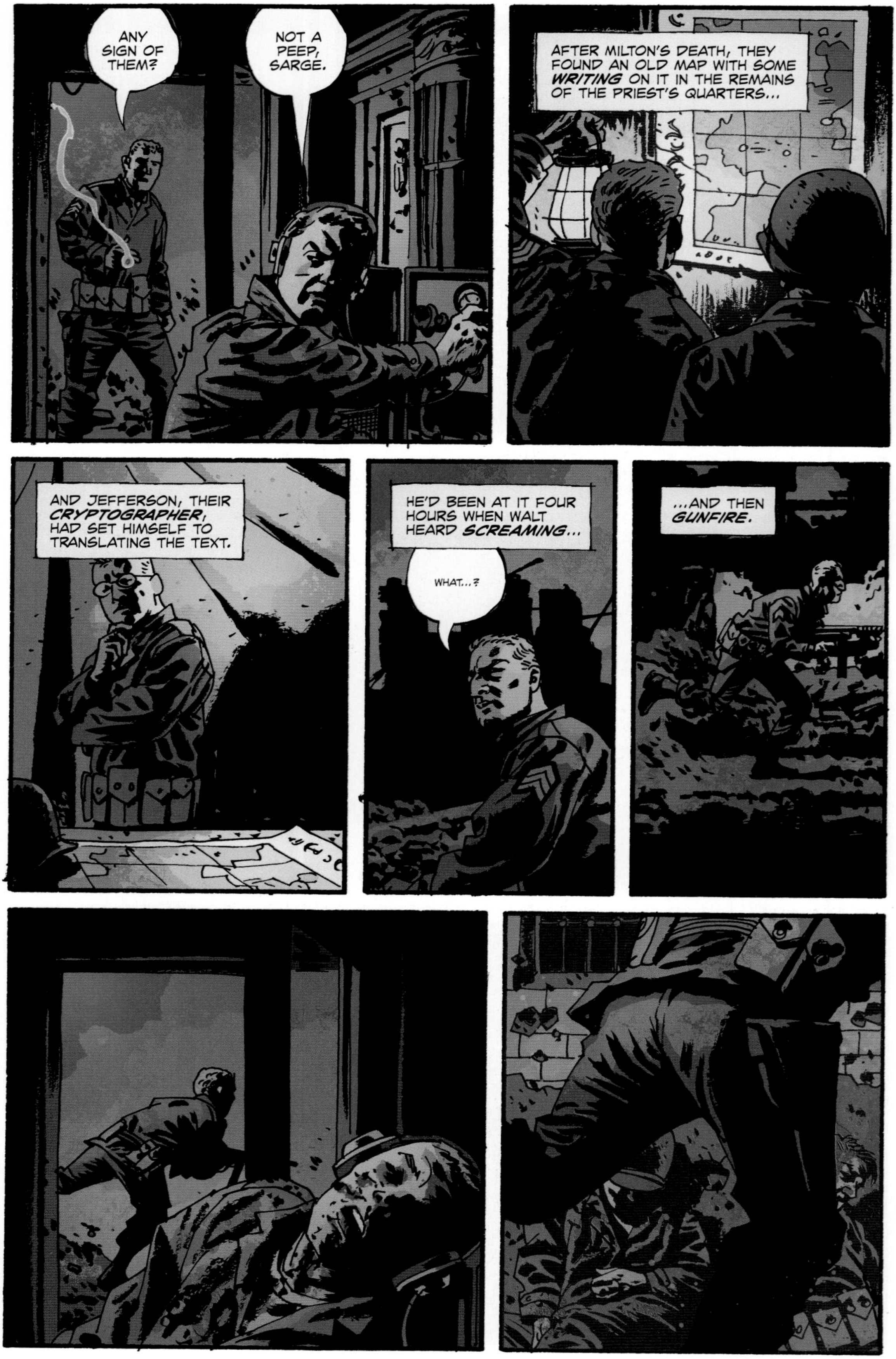
ANY SIGN OF THEM?
NOT A PEEP, SARGE.
AFTER MILTON'S DEATH, THEY FOUND AN OLD MAP WITH SOME *WRITING* ON IT IN THE REMAINS OF THE PRIEST'S QUARTERS...
AND JEFFERSON, THEIR *CRYPTOGRAPHER*, HAD SET HIMSELF TO TRANSLATING THE TEXT.
HE'D BEEN AT IT FOUR HOURS WHEN WALT HEARD *SCREAMING*...
WHAT...?
...AND THEN *GUNFIRE*.

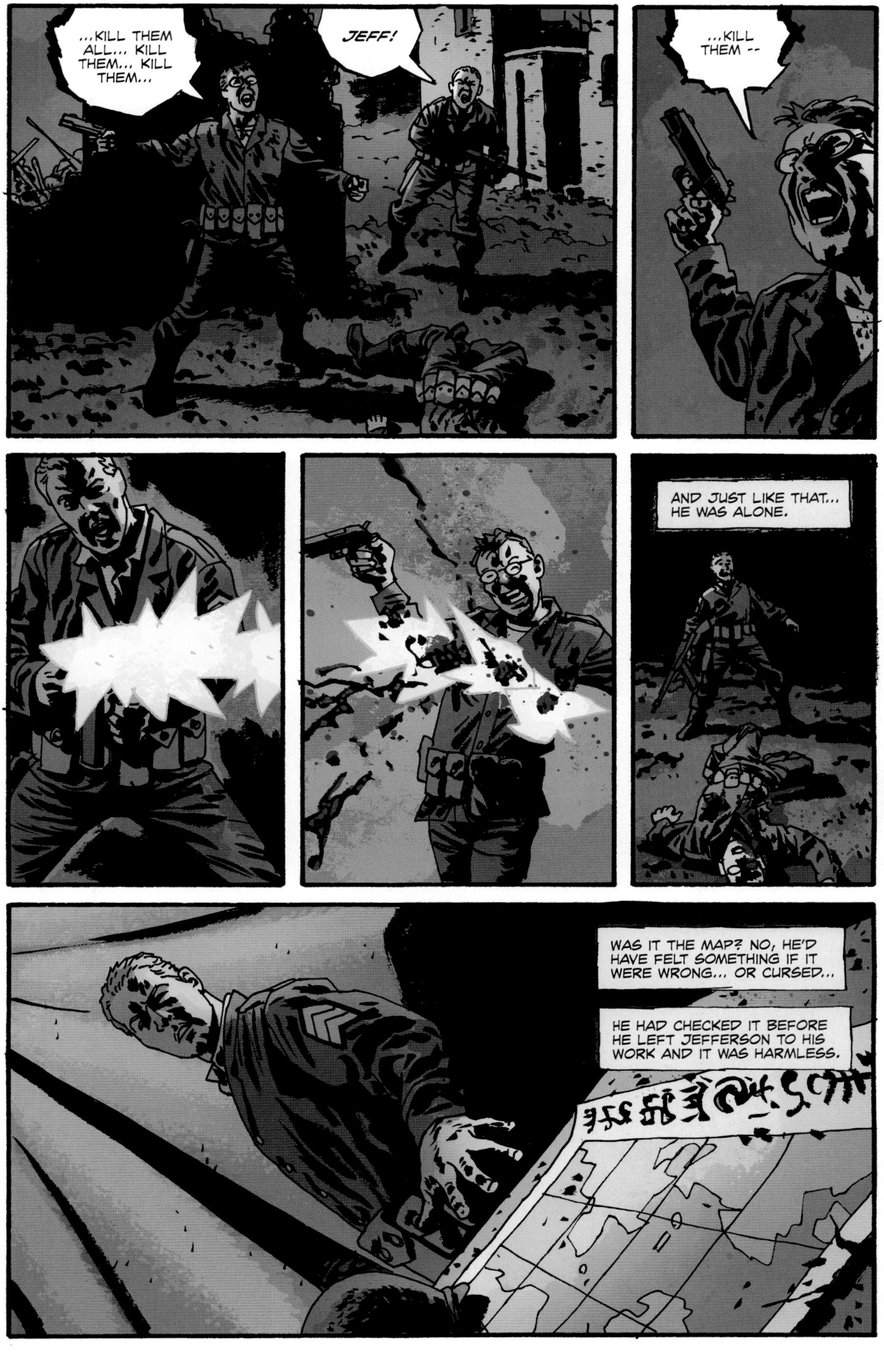

...KILL THEM ALL... KILL THEM... KILL THEM...
JEFF!
...KILL THEM --
AND JUST LIKE THAT... HE WAS ALONE.
WAS IT THE MAP? NO, HE'D HAVE FELT SOMETHING IF IT WERE WRONG... OR CURSED...
HE HAD CHECKED IT BEFORE HE LEFT JEFFERSON TO HIS WORK AND IT WAS HARMLESS.

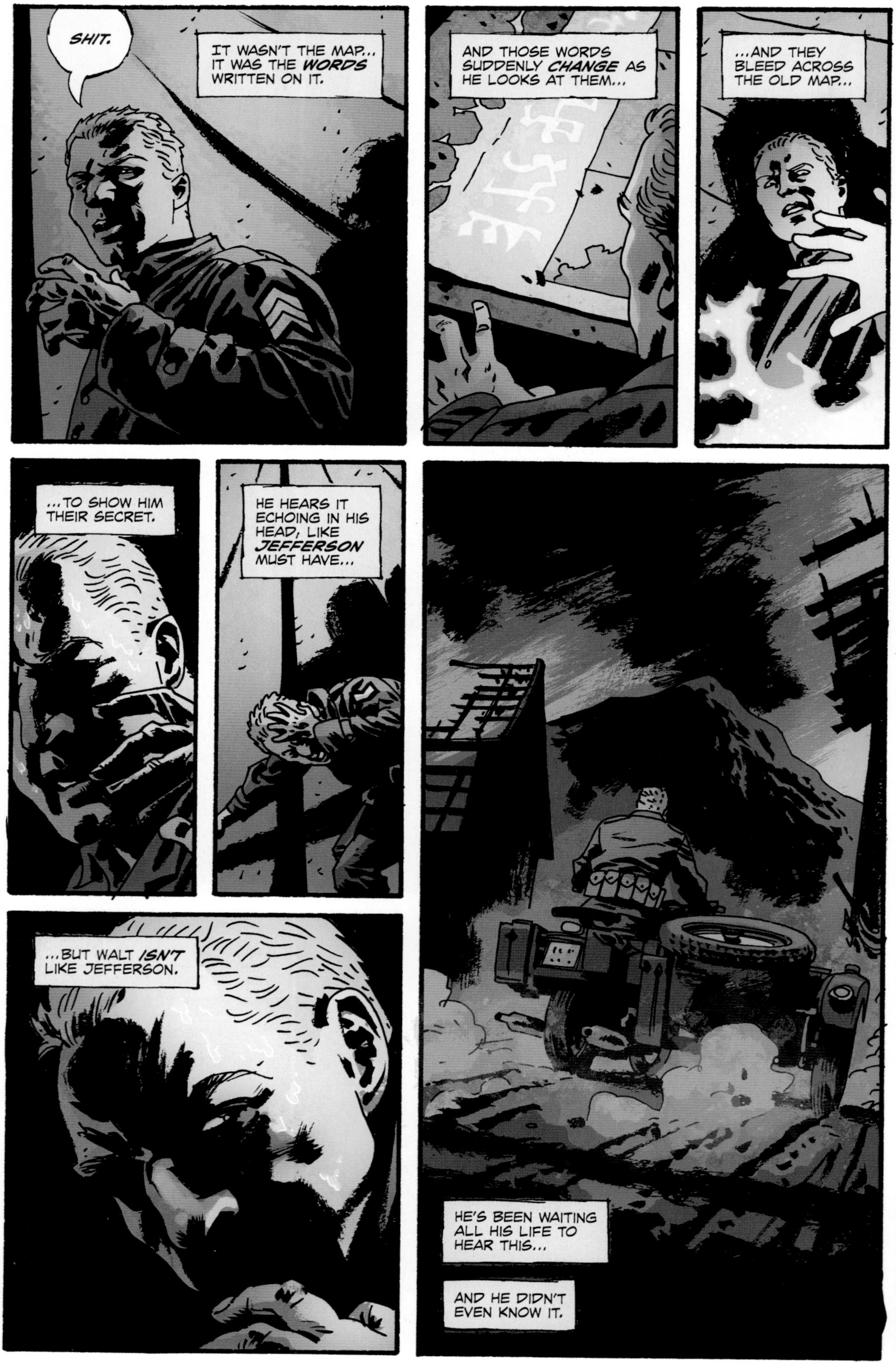
SHIT.
IT WASN'T THE MAP... IT WAS THE WORDS WRITTEN ON IT.
AND THOSE WORDS SUDDENLY CHANGE AS HE LOOKS AT THEM...
...AND THEY BLEED ACROSS THE OLD MAP...
...TO SHOW HIM THEIR SECRET.
HE HEARS IT ECHOING IN HIS HEAD, LIKE JEFFERSON MUST HAVE...
...BUT WALT ISN'T LIKE JEFFERSON.
HE'S BEEN WAITING ALL HIS LIFE TO HEAR THIS...
AND HE DIDN'T EVEN KNOW IT.

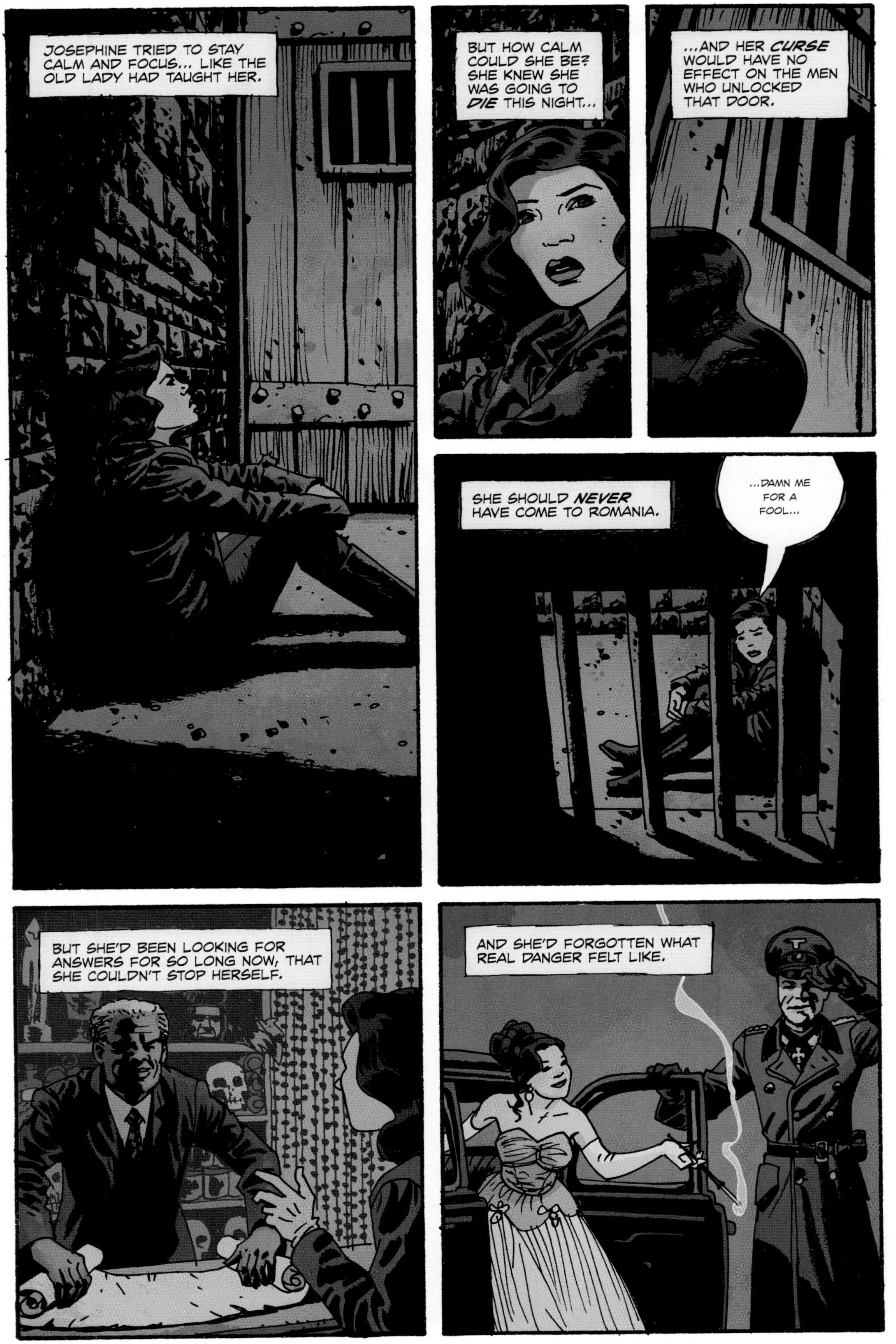
JOSEPHINE TRIED TO STAY CALM AND FOCUS... LIKE THE OLD LADY HAD TAUGHT HER.
BUT HOW CALM COULD SHE BE? SHE KNEW SHE WAS GOING TO DIE THIS NIGHT...
...AND HER CURSE WOULD HAVE NO EFFECT ON THE MEN WHO UNLOCKED THAT DOOR.
SHE SHOULD NEVER HAVE COME TO ROMANIA.
...DAMN ME FOR A FOOL...
BUT SHE'D BEEN LOOKING FOR ANSWERS FOR SO LONG NOW, THAT SHE COULDN'T STOP HERSELF.
AND SHE'D FORGOTTEN WHAT REAL DANGER FELT LIKE.

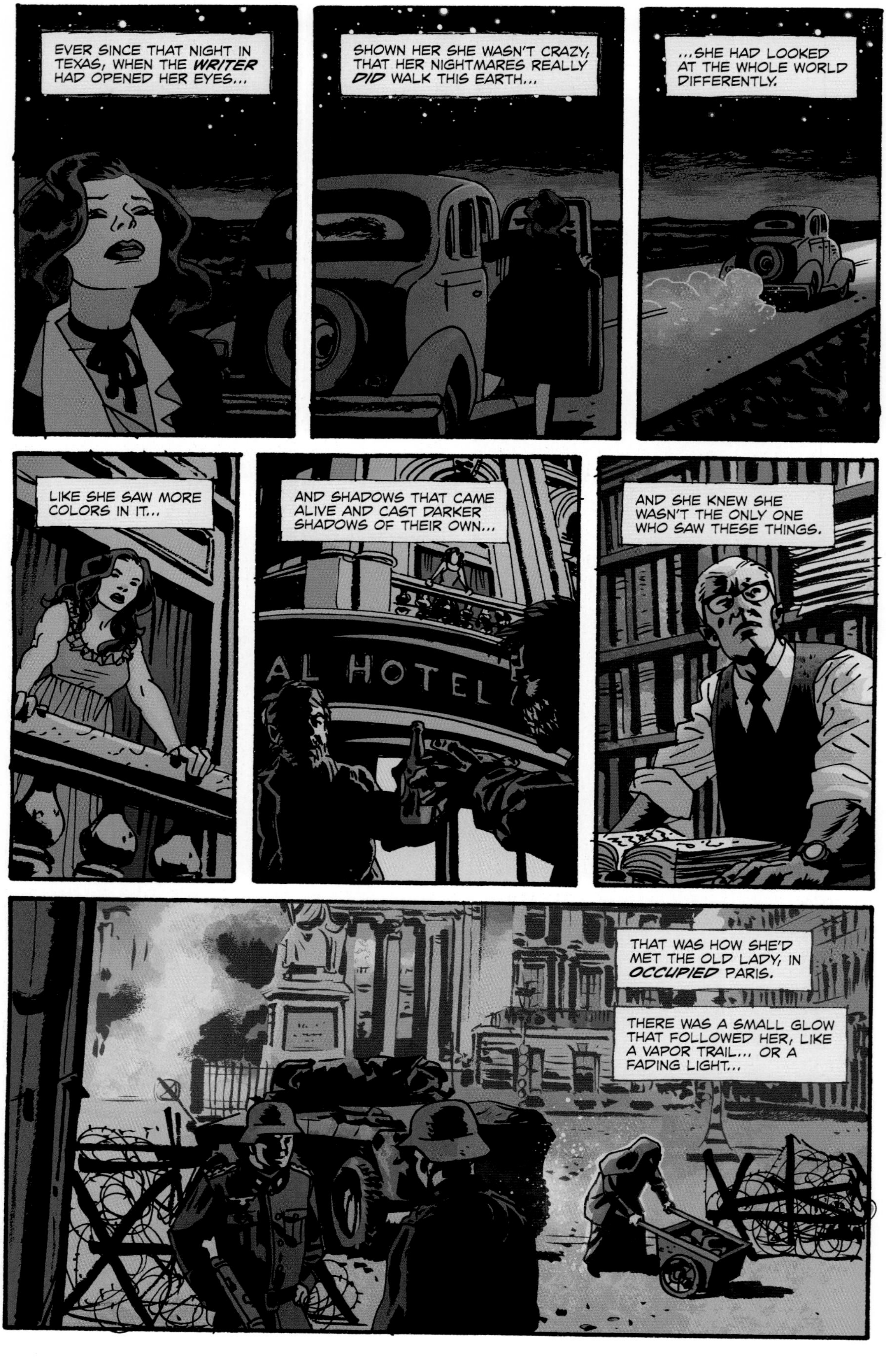
EVER SINCE THAT NIGHT IN TEXAS, WHEN THE WRITER HAD OPENED HER EYES...
SHOWN HER SHE WASN'T CRAZY, THAT HER NIGHTMARES REALLY DID WALK THIS EARTH...
...SHE HAD LOOKED AT THE WHOLE WORLD DIFFERENTLY.
LIKE SHE SAW MORE COLORS IN IT...
AND SHADOWS THAT CAME ALIVE AND CAST DARKER SHADOWS OF THEIR OWN...
AL HOTEL
AND SHE KNEW SHE WASN'T THE ONLY ONE WHO SAW THESE THINGS.
THAT WAS HOW SHE'D MET THE OLD LADY, IN OCCUPIED PARIS.
THERE WAS A SMALL GLOW THAT FOLLOWED HER, LIKE A VAPOR TRAIL... OR A FADING LIGHT...

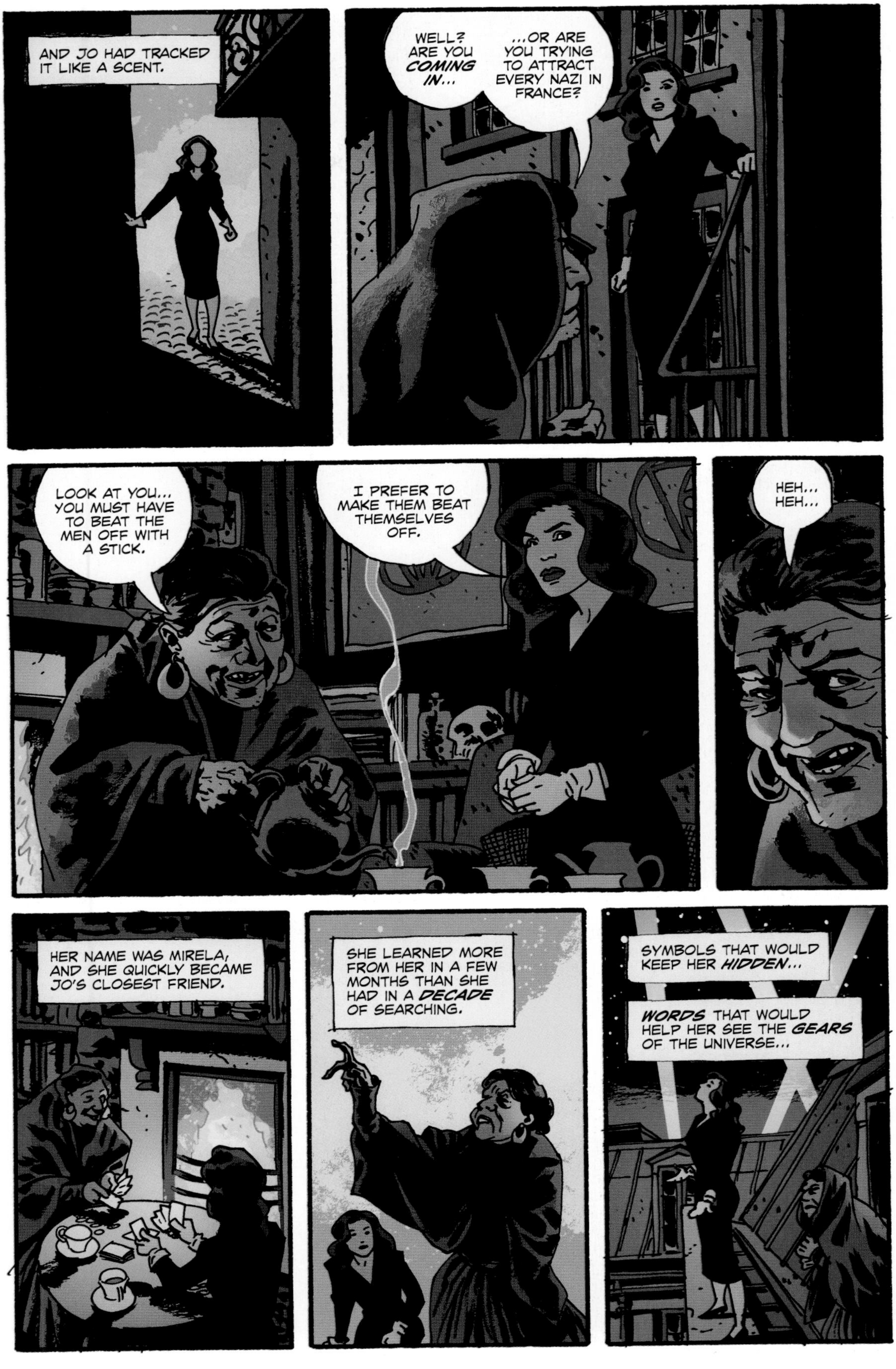
AND JO HAD TRACKED IT LIKE A SCENT.
WELL? ARE YOU COMING IN...
...OR ARE YOU TRYING TO ATTRACT EVERY NAZI IN FRANCE?
LOOK AT YOU... YOU MUST HAVE TO BEAT THE MEN OFF WITH A STICK.
I PREFER TO MAKE THEM BEAT THEMSELVES OFF.
HEH... HEH...
HER NAME WAS MIRELA, AND SHE QUICKLY BECAME JO'S CLOSEST FRIEND.
SHE LEARNED MORE FROM HER IN A FEW MONTHS THAN SHE HAD IN A DECADE OF SEARCHING.
SYMBOLS THAT WOULD KEEP HER HIDDEN...
WORDS THAT WOULD HELP HER SEE THE GEARS OF THE UNIVERSE...

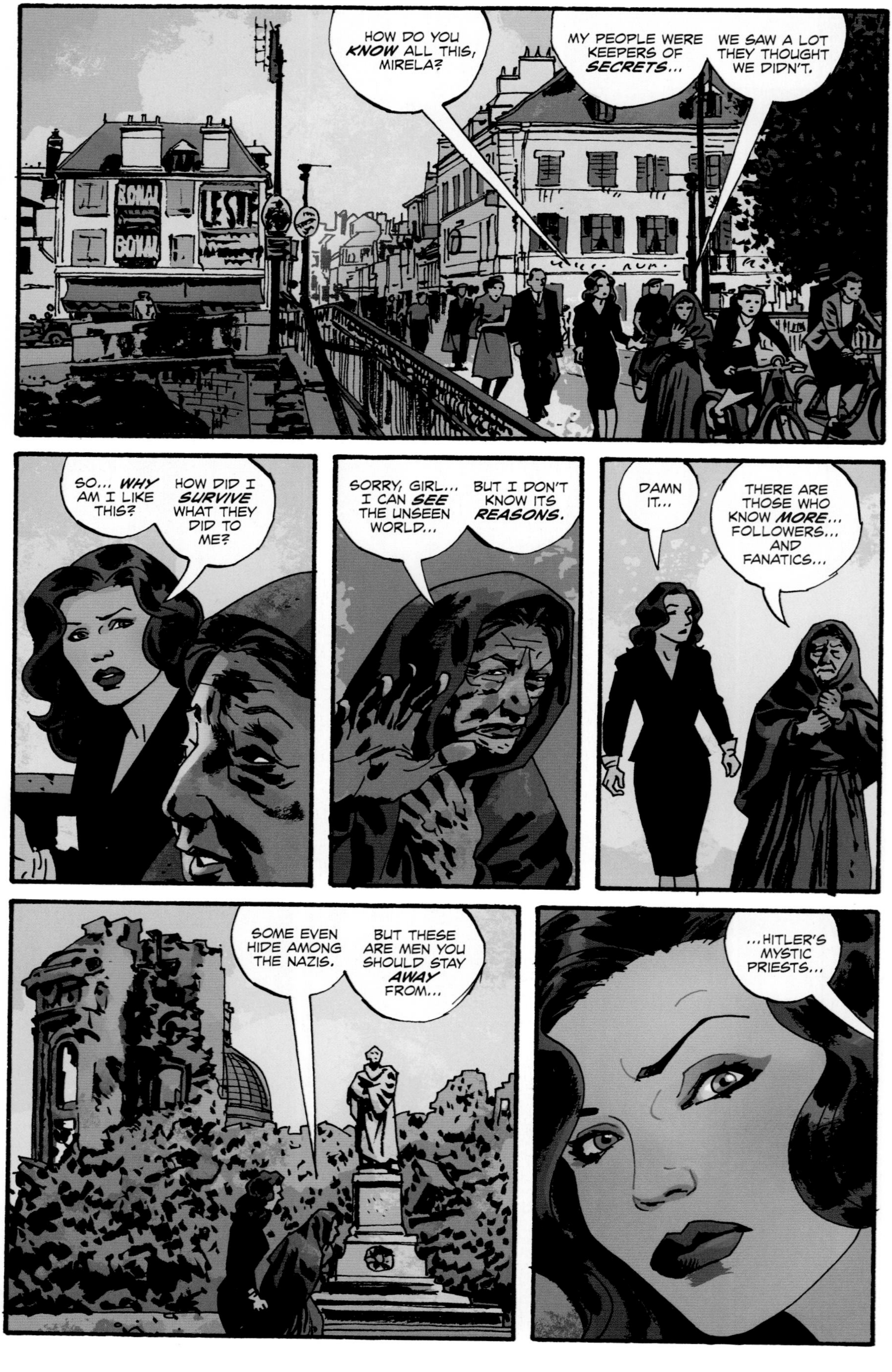
HOW DO YOU KNOW ALL THIS, MIRELA?
MY PEOPLE WERE KEEPERS OF SECRETS...
WE SAW A LOT THEY THOUGHT WE DIDN'T.
SO... WHY AM I LIKE THIS?
HOW DID I SURVIVE WHAT THEY DID TO ME?
SORRY, GIRL... I CAN SEE THE UNSEEN WORLD...
BUT I DON'T KNOW ITS REASONS.
DAMN IT...
THERE ARE THOSE WHO KNOW MORE... FOLLOWERS... AND FANATICS...
SOME EVEN HIDE AMONG THE NAZIS.
BUT THESE ARE MEN YOU SHOULD STAY AWAY FROM...
...HITLER'S MYSTIC PRIESTS...

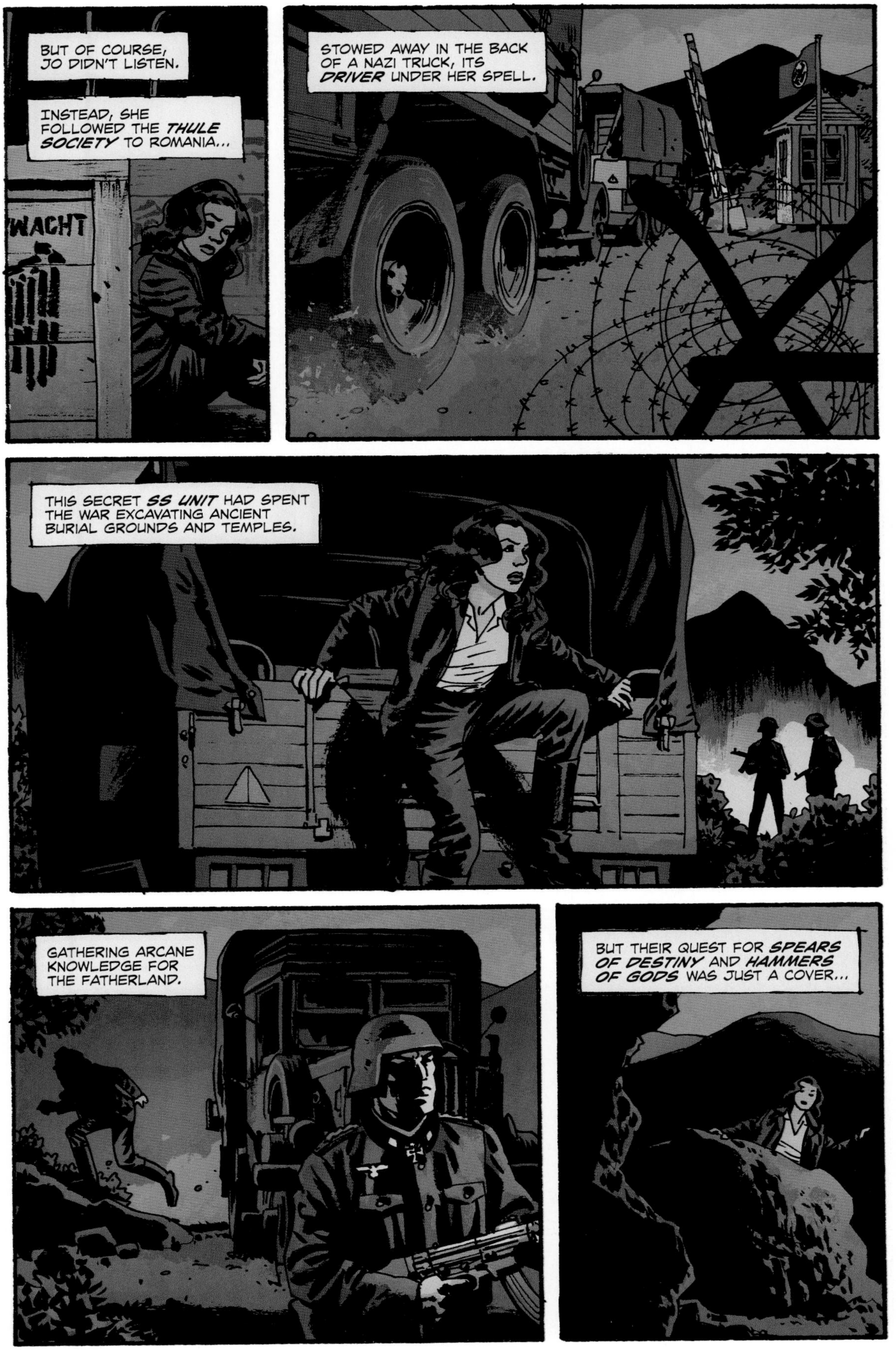

BUT OF COURSE, JO DIDN'T LISTEN.
INSTEAD, SHE FOLLOWED THE *THULE SOCIETY* TO ROMANIA...
WACHT
STOWED AWAY IN THE BACK OF A NAZI TRUCK, ITS *DRIVER* UNDER HER SPELL.
THIS SECRET *SS UNIT* HAD SPENT THE WAR EXCAVATING ANCIENT BURIAL GROUNDS AND TEMPLES.
GATHERING ARCANE KNOWLEDGE FOR THE FATHERLAND.
BUT THEIR QUEST FOR *SPEARS OF DESTINY* AND *HAMMERS OF GODS* WAS JUST A COVER...

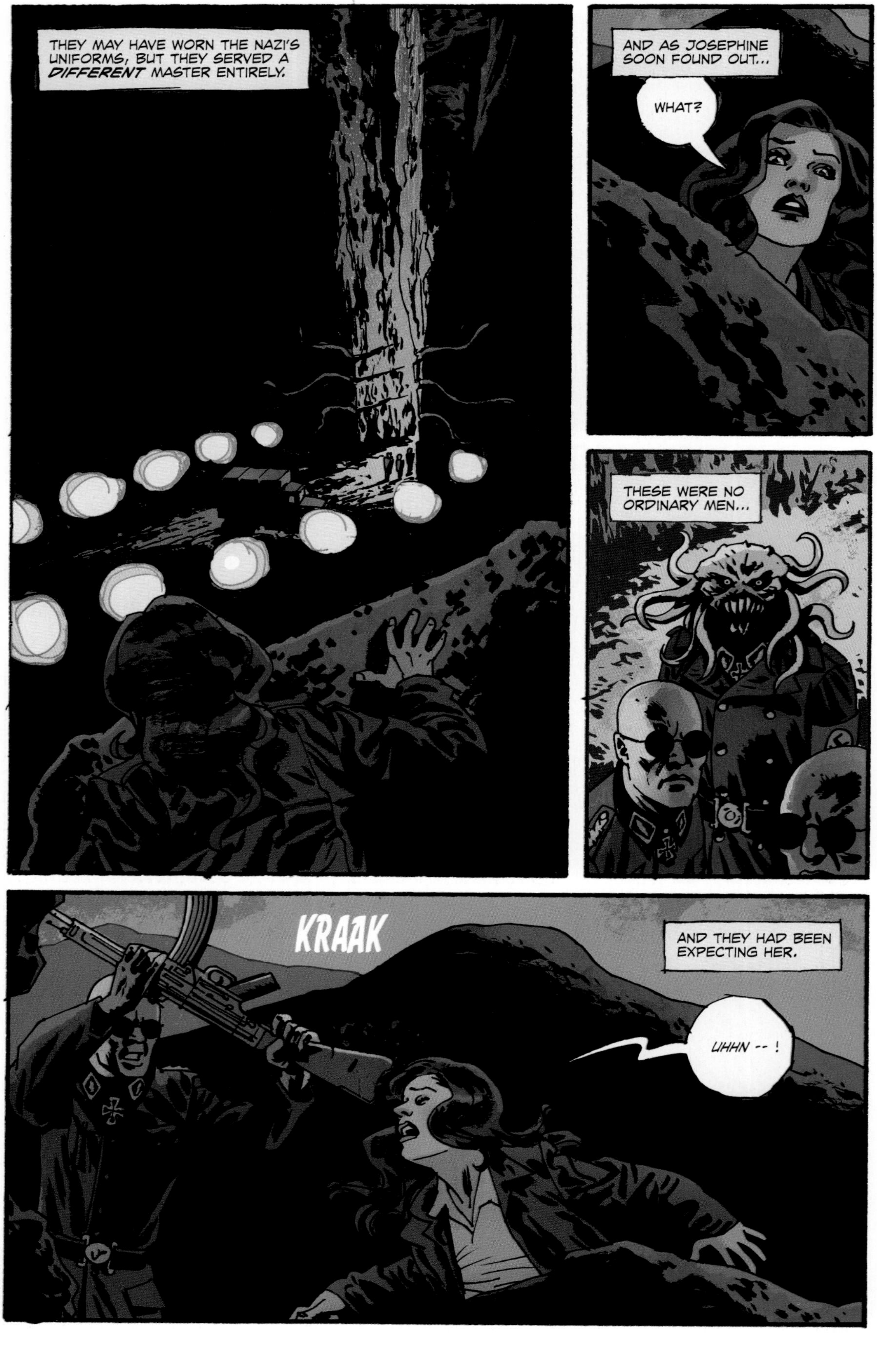
THEY MAY HAVE WORN THE NAZI'S UNIFORMS, BUT THEY SERVED A *DIFFERENT* MASTER ENTIRELY.
AND AS JOSEPHINE SOON FOUND OUT...
WHAT?
THESE WERE NO ORDINARY MEN...
KRAAK
AND THEY HAD BEEN EXPECTING HER.
UHHN -- !

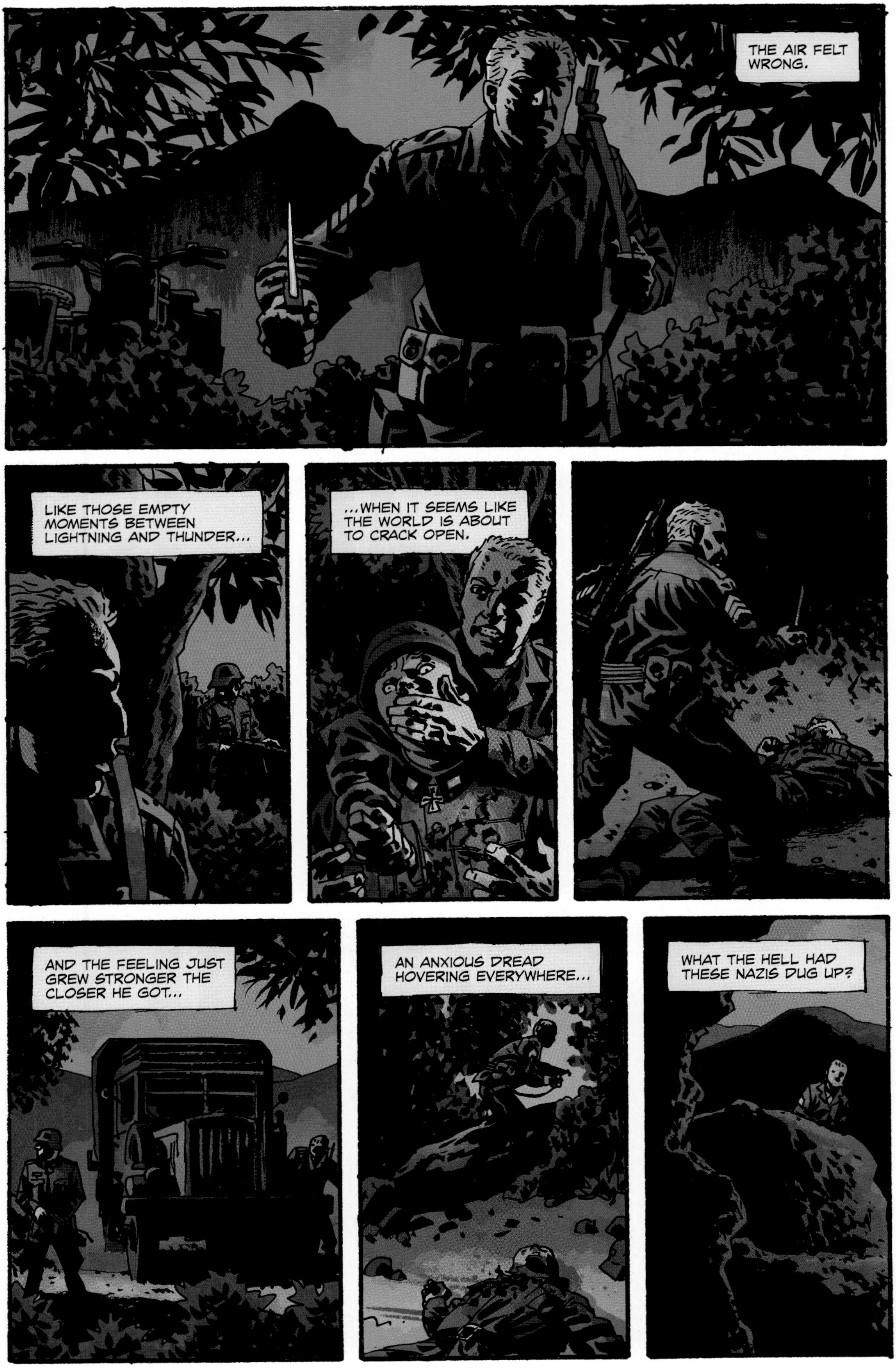
THE AIR FELT WRONG.
LIKE THOSE EMPTY MOMENTS BETWEEN LIGHTNING AND THUNDER...
...WHEN IT SEEMS LIKE THE WORLD IS ABOUT TO CRACK OPEN.
AND THE FEELING JUST GREW STRONGER THE CLOSER HE GOT...
AN ANXIOUS DREAD HOVERING EVERYWHERE...
WHAT THE HELL HAD THESE NAZIS DUG UP?

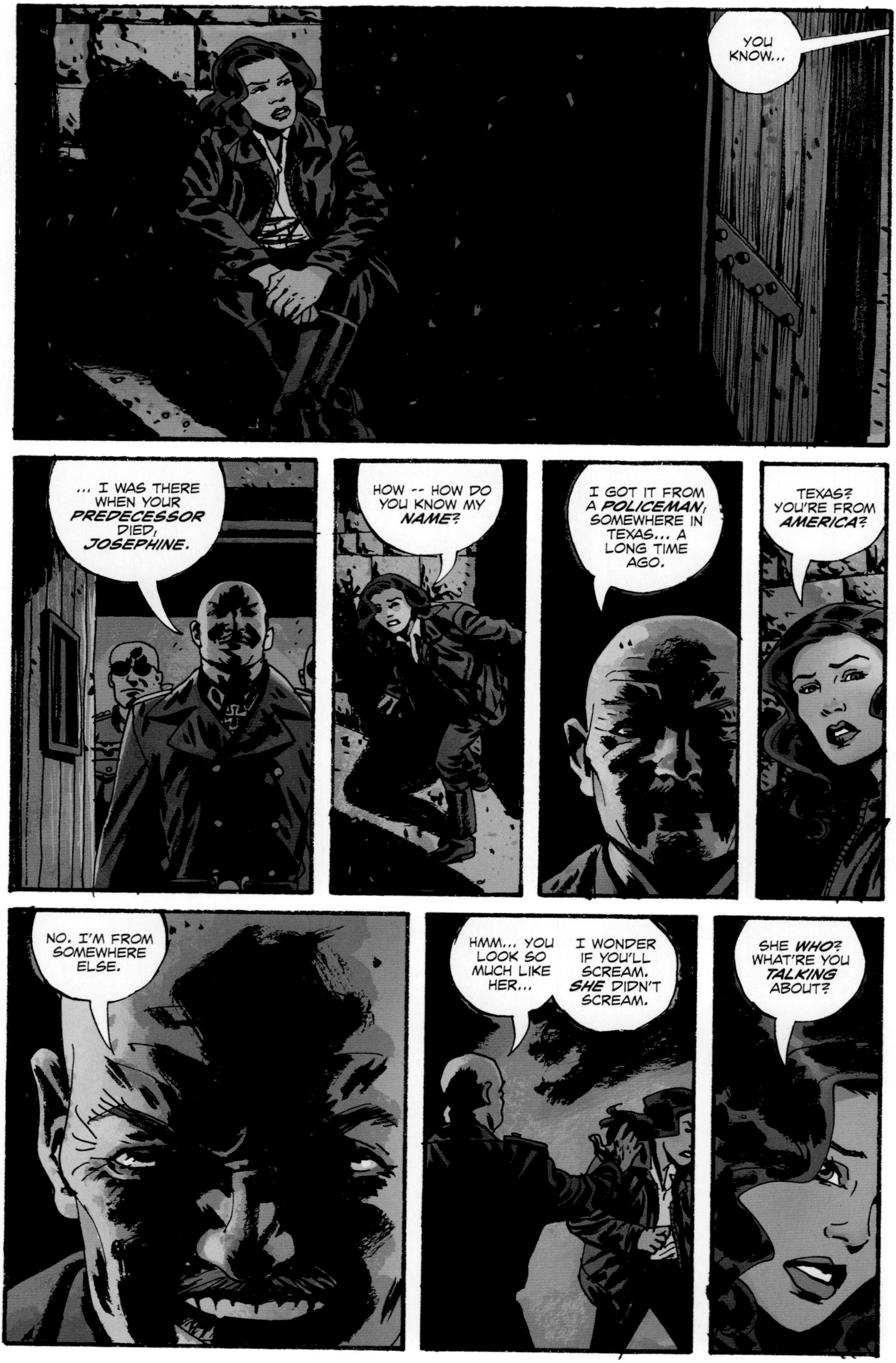
YOU KNOW...
... I WAS THERE WHEN YOUR PREDECESSOR DIED, JOSEPHINE.
HOW -- HOW DO YOU KNOW MY NAME?
I GOT IT FROM A POLICEMAN, SOMEWHERE IN TEXAS... A LONG TIME AGO.
TEXAS? YOU'RE FROM AMERICA?
NO. I'M FROM SOMEWHERE ELSE.
HMM... YOU LOOK SO MUCH LIKE HER...
I WONDER IF YOU'LL SCREAM. SHE DIDN'T SCREAM.
SHE WHO? WHAT'RE YOU TALKING ABOUT?

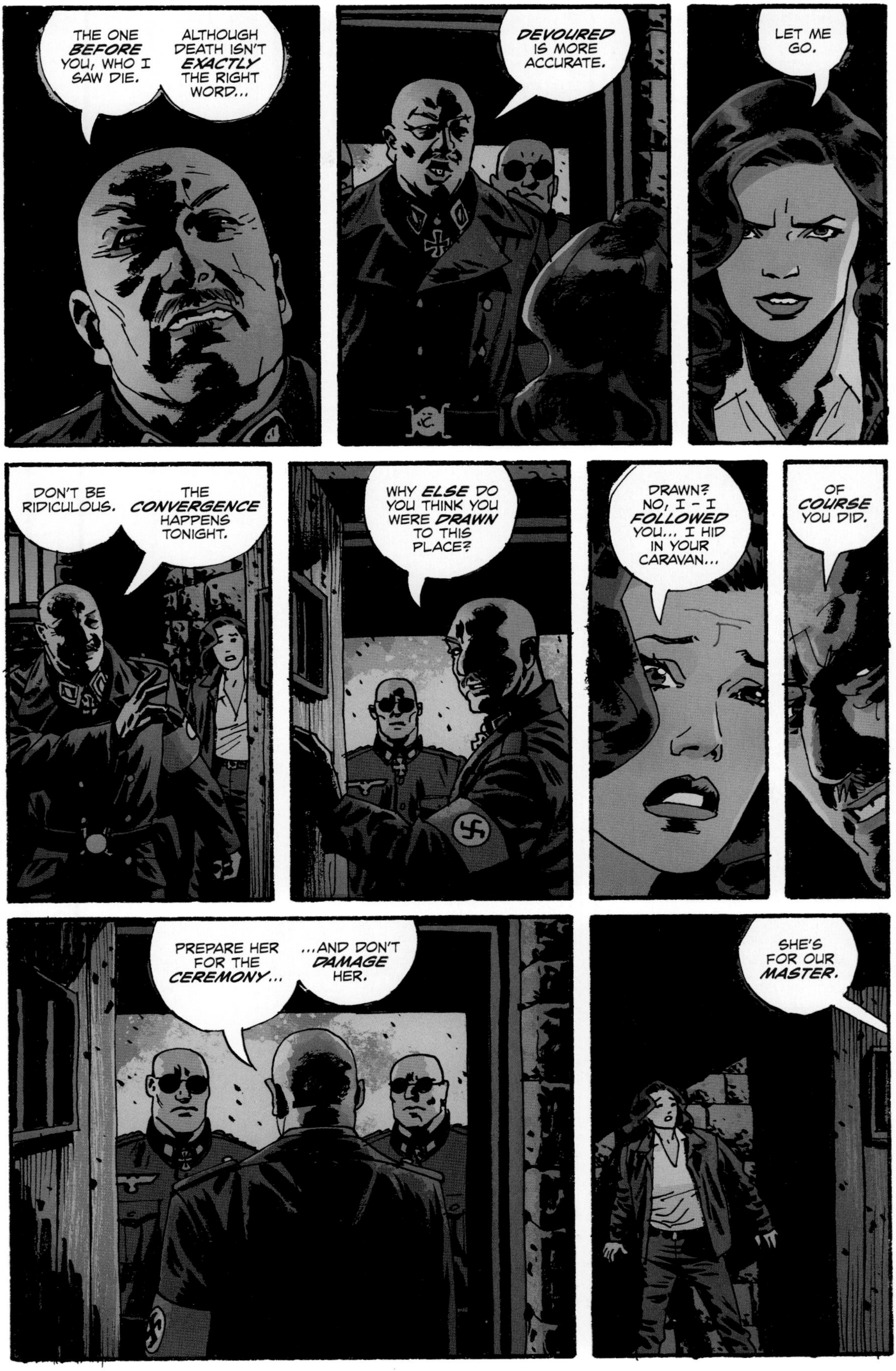
THE ONE BEFORE YOU, WHO I SAW DIE.
ALTHOUGH DEATH ISN'T EXACTLY THE RIGHT WORD...
DEVOURED IS MORE ACCURATE.
LET ME GO.
DON'T BE RIDICULOUS.
THE CONVERGENCE HAPPENS TONIGHT.
WHY ELSE DO YOU THINK YOU WERE DRAWN TO THIS PLACE?
DRAWN? NO, I - I FOLLOWED YOU... I HID IN YOUR CARAVAN...
OF COURSE YOU DID.
PREPARE HER FOR THE CEREMONY...
...AND DON'T DAMAGE HER.
SHE'S FOR OUR MASTER.

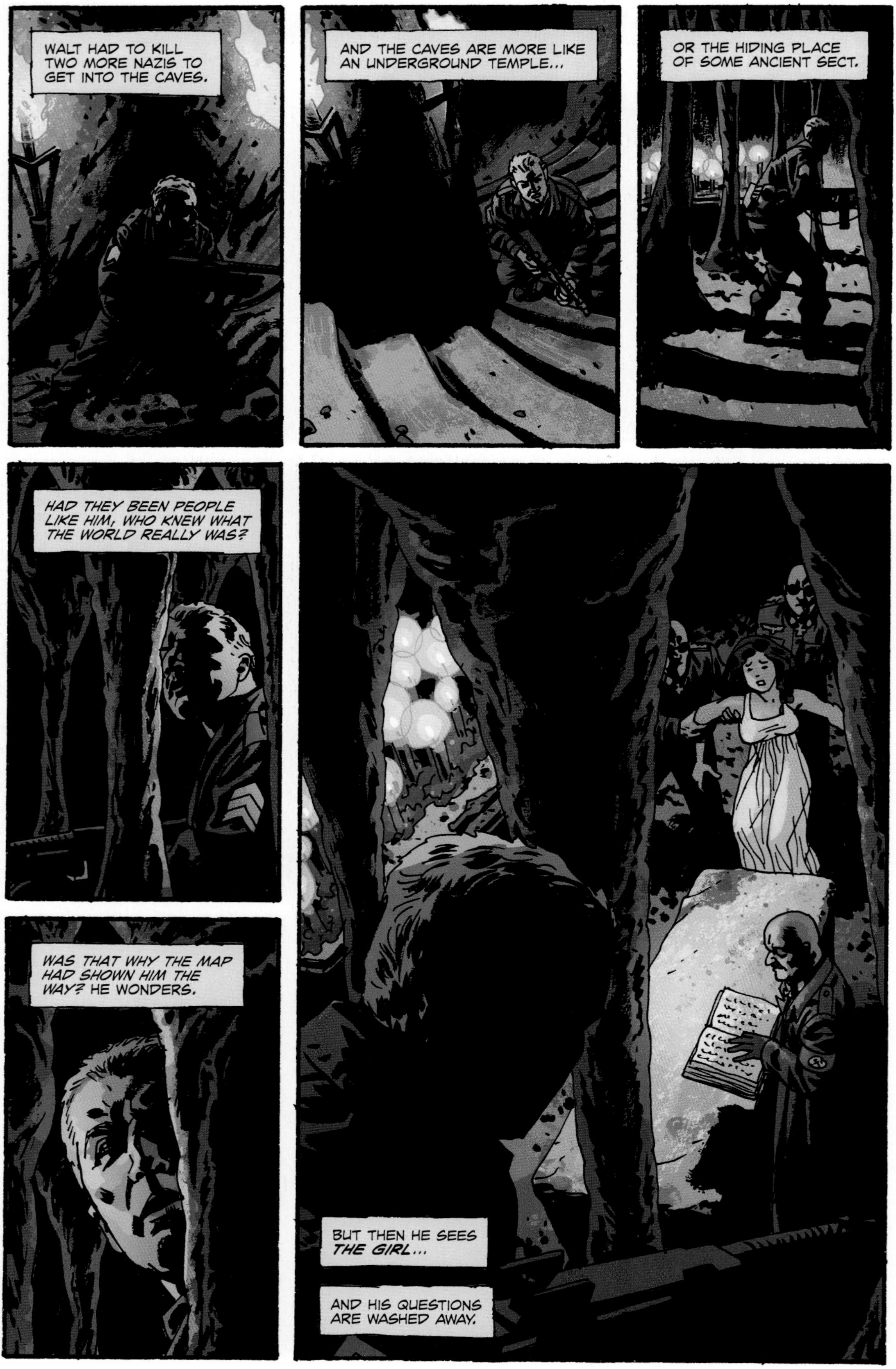
WALT HAD TO KILL TWO MORE NAZIS TO GET INTO THE CAVES.
AND THE CAVES ARE MORE LIKE AN UNDERGROUND TEMPLE...
OR THE HIDING PLACE OF SOME ANCIENT SECT.
HAD THEY BEEN PEOPLE LIKE HIM, WHO KNEW WHAT THE WORLD REALLY WAS?
WAS THAT WHY THE MAP HAD SHOWN HIM THE WAY? HE WONDERS.
BUT THEN HE SEES *THE GIRL*...
AND HIS QUESTIONS ARE WASHED AWAY.

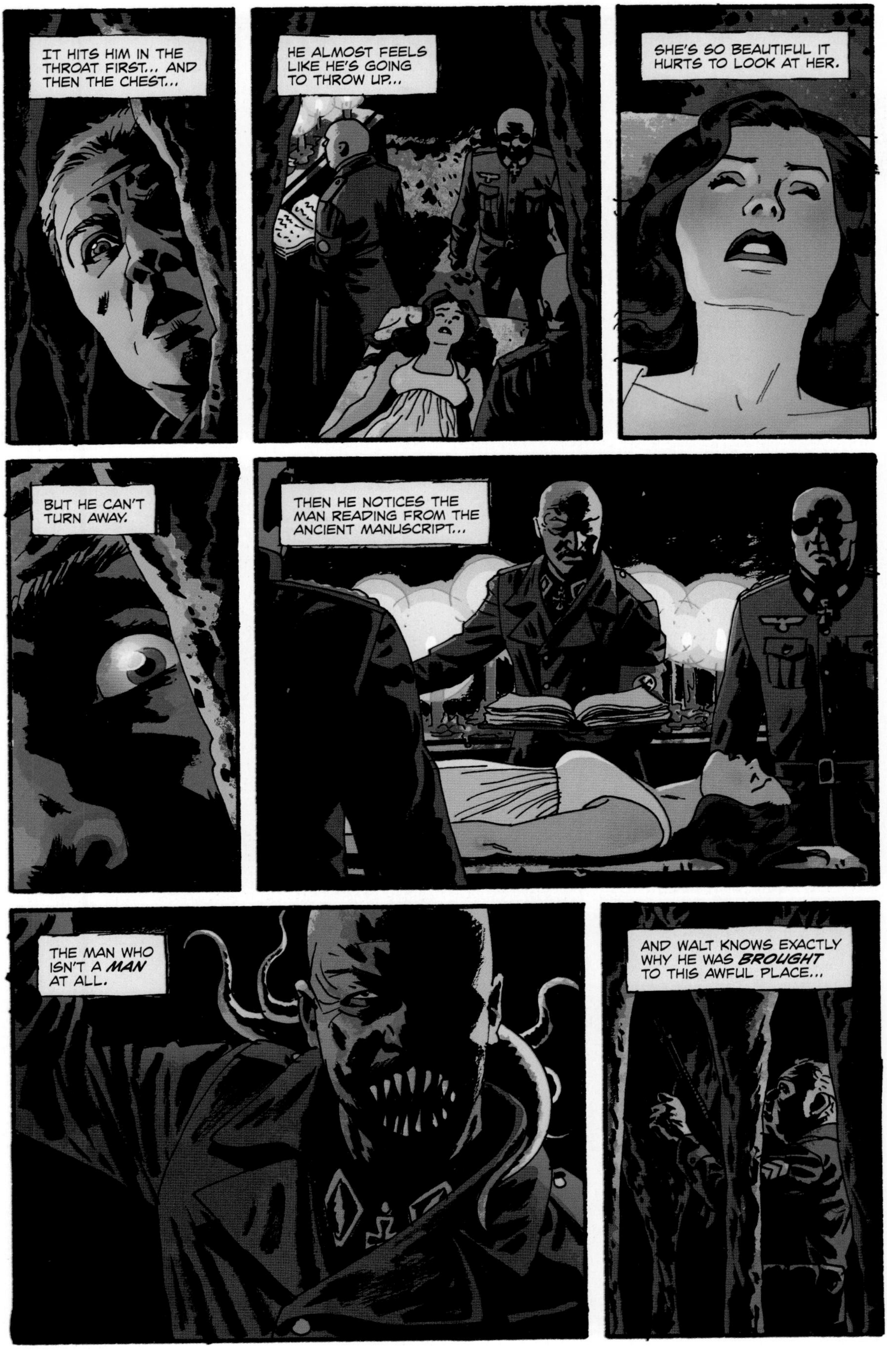
IT HITS HIM IN THE THROAT FIRST... AND THEN THE CHEST...
HE ALMOST FEELS LIKE HE'S GOING TO THROW UP...
SHE'S SO BEAUTIFUL IT HURTS TO LOOK AT HER.
BUT HE CAN'T TURN AWAY.
THEN HE NOTICES THE MAN READING FROM THE ANCIENT MANUSCRIPT...
THE MAN WHO ISN'T A *MAN* AT ALL.
AND WALT KNOWS EXACTLY WHY HE WAS *BROUGHT* TO THIS AWFUL PLACE...

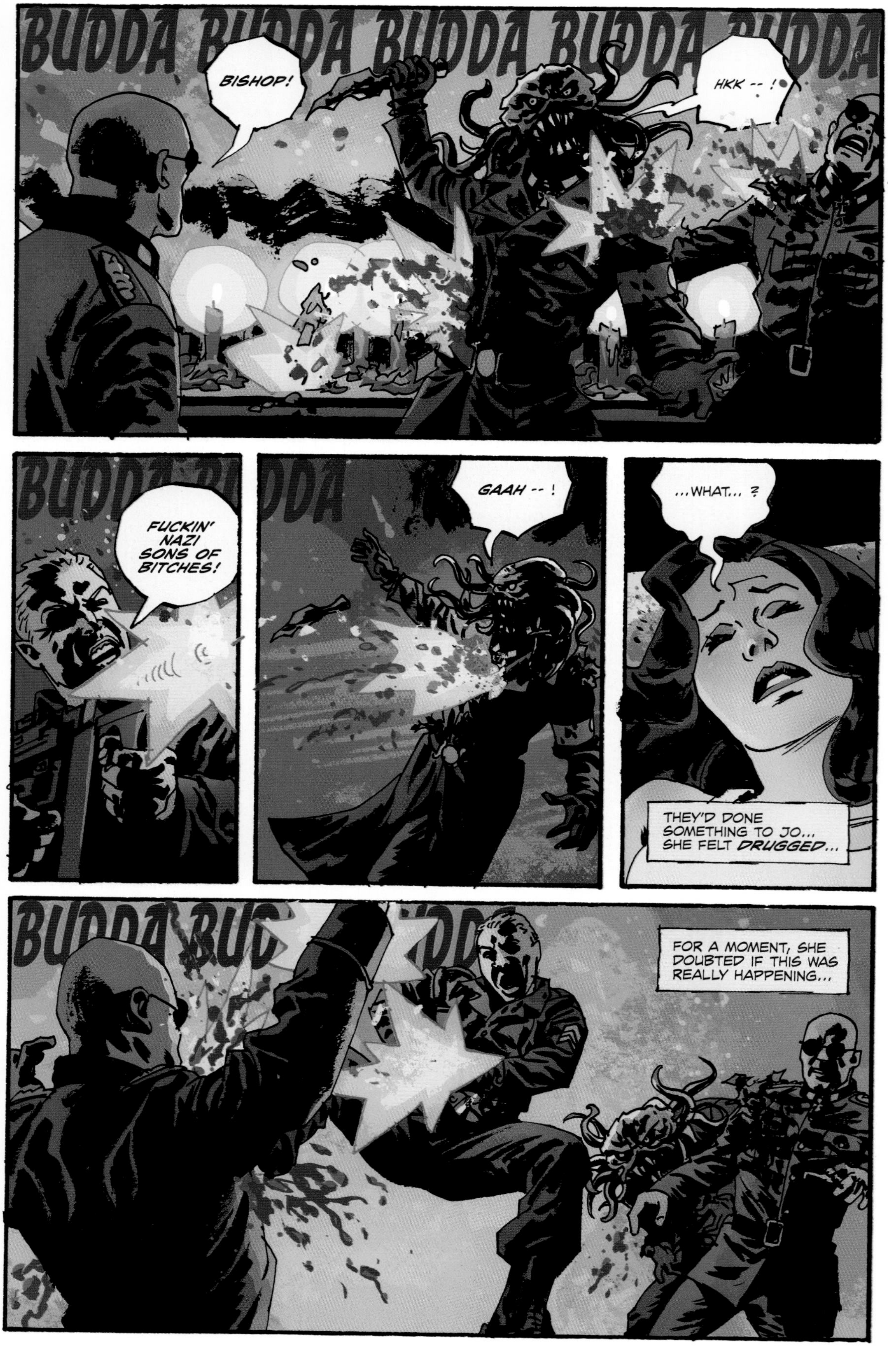
BUDDA BUDDA BUDDA BUDDA
BISHOP!
HKK -- !
BUDDA BUDDA
FUCKIN' NAZI SONS OF BITCHES!
GAAH -- !
...WHAT... ?
THEY'D DONE SOMETHING TO JO... SHE FELT DRUGGED...
BUDDA BUD
FOR A MOMENT, SHE DOUBTED IF THIS WAS REALLY HAPPENING...

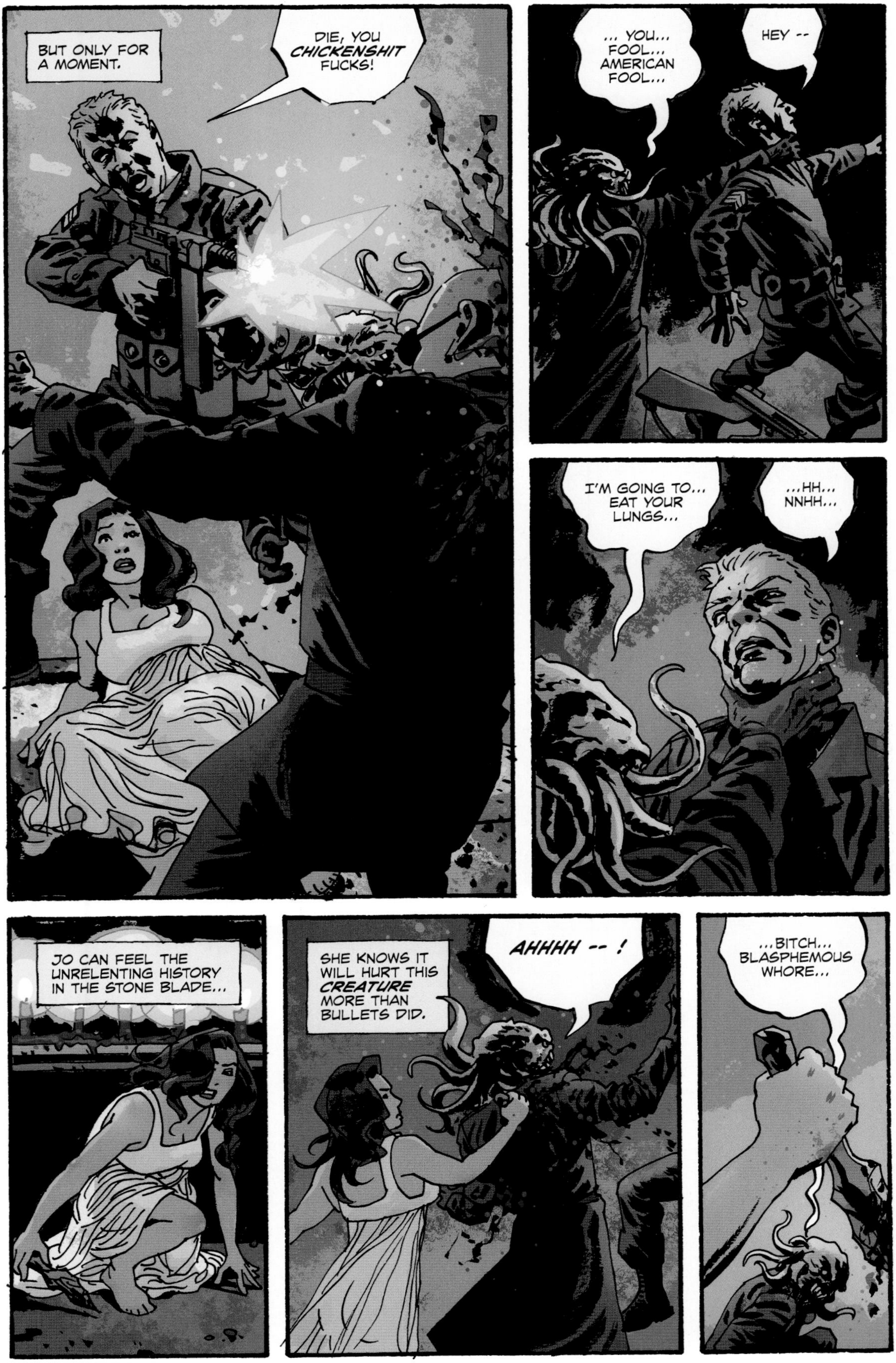
BUT ONLY FOR A MOMENT.
DIE, YOU *CHICKENSHIT* FUCKS!
... YOU... FOOL... AMERICAN FOOL...
HEY --
I'M GOING TO... EAT YOUR LUNGS...
...HH... NNHH...
JO CAN FEEL THE UNRELENTING HISTORY IN THE STONE BLADE...
SHE KNOWS IT WILL HURT THIS *CREATURE* MORE THAN BULLETS DID.
AHHHH -- !
...BITCH... BLASPHEMOUS WHORE...

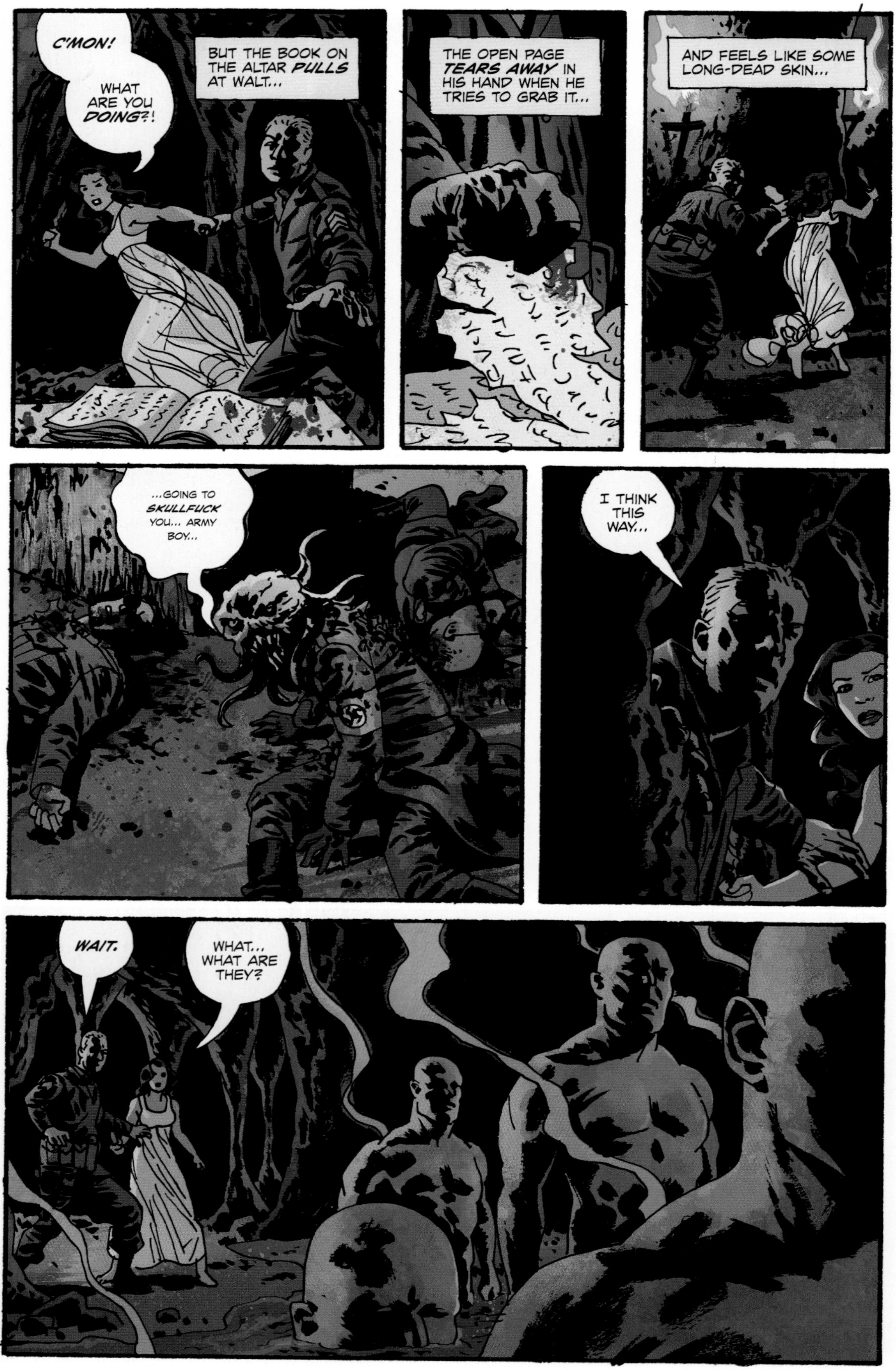
C'MON!
WHAT ARE YOU DOING?!
BUT THE BOOK ON THE ALTAR PULLS AT WALT...
THE OPEN PAGE TEARS AWAY IN HIS HAND WHEN HE TRIES TO GRAB IT...
AND FEELS LIKE SOME LONG-DEAD SKIN...
...GOING TO SKULLFUCK YOU... ARMY BOY...
I THINK THIS WAY...
WAIT.
WHAT... WHAT ARE THEY?

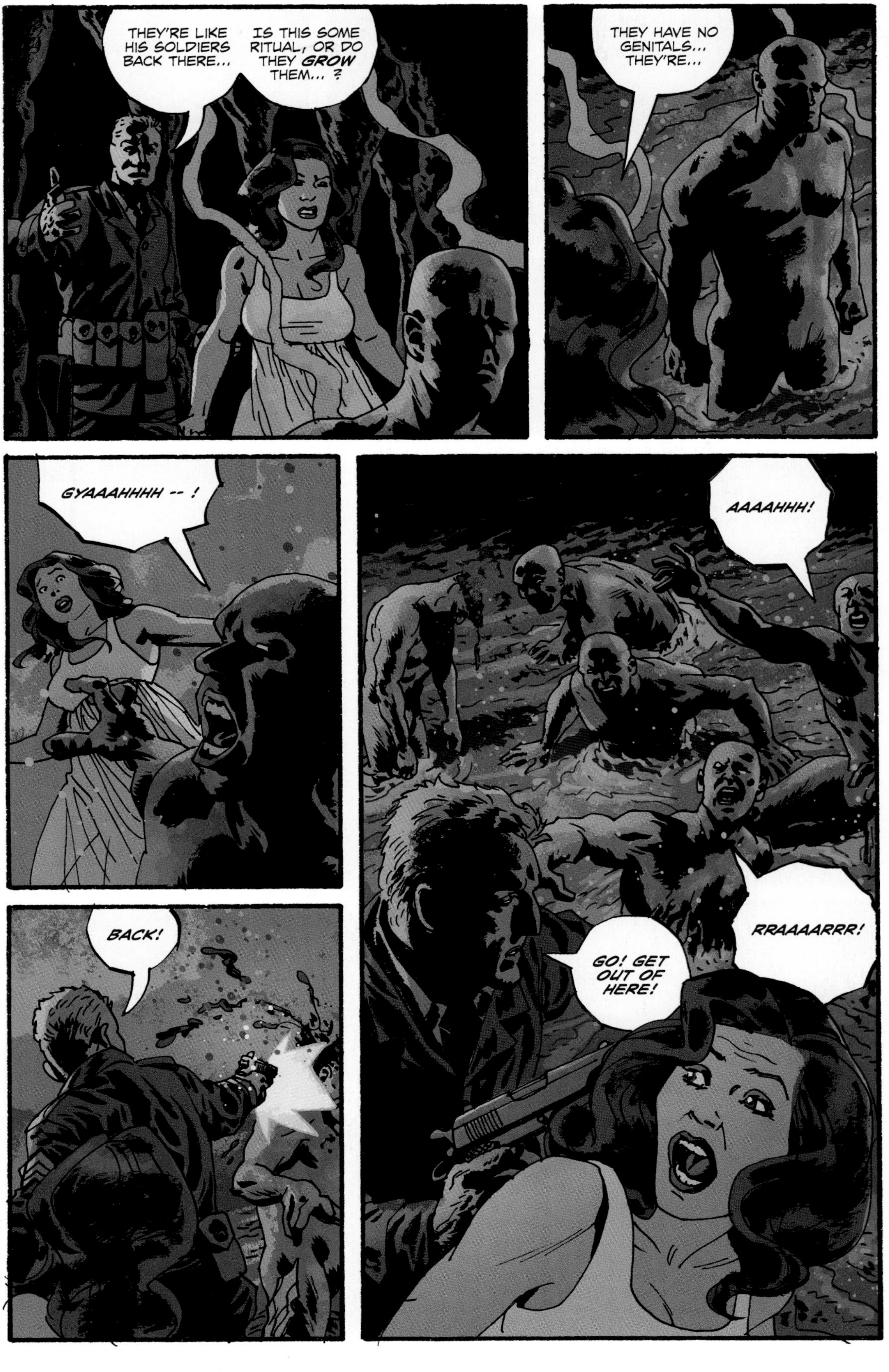

THEY'RE LIKE HIS SOLDIERS BACK THERE...
IS THIS SOME RITUAL, OR DO THEY GROW THEM... ?
THEY HAVE NO GENITALS... THEY'RE...
GYAAAHHHH -- !
BACK!
AAAAHHH!
RRAAAARRR!
GO! GET OUT OF HERE!

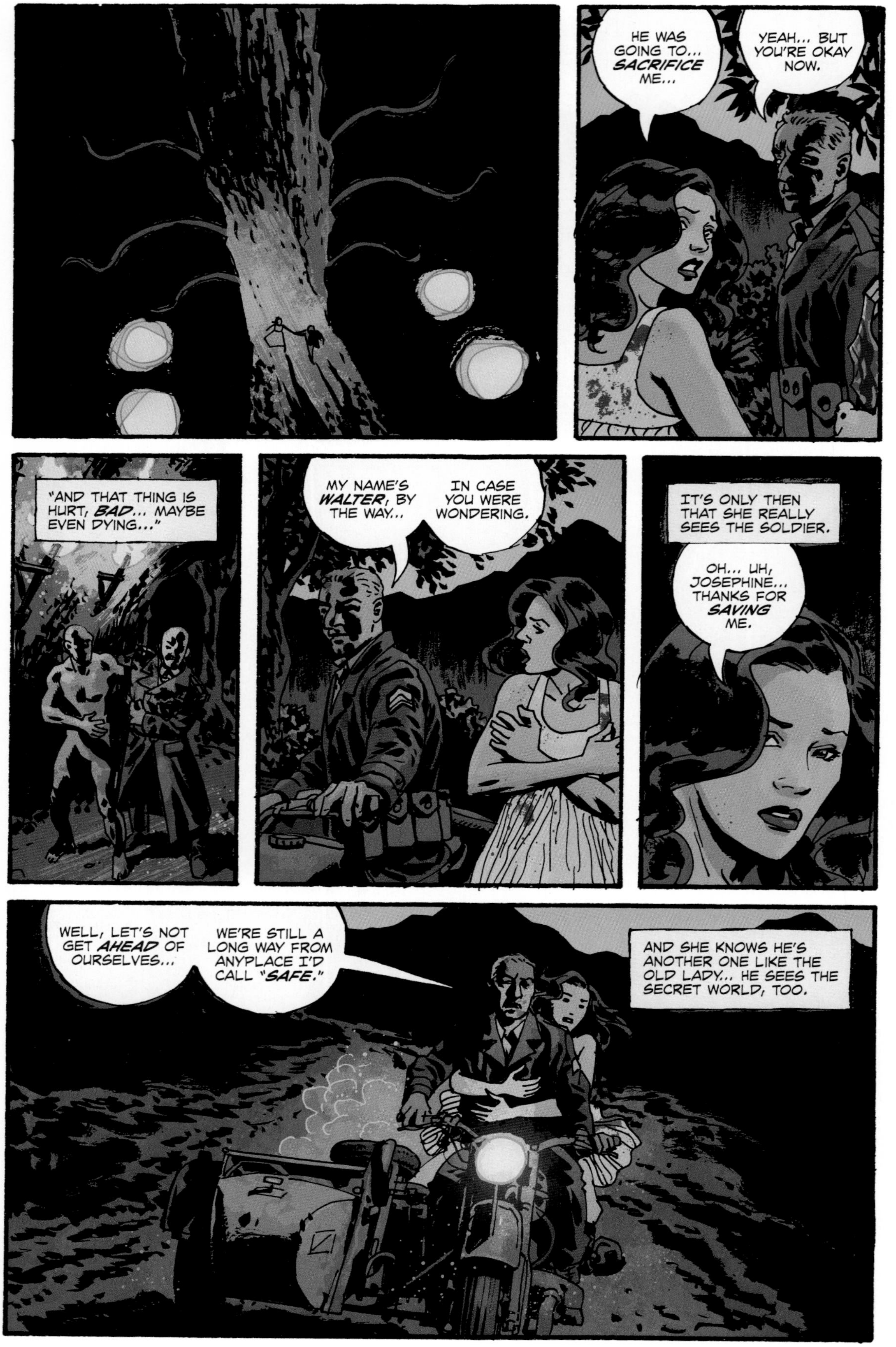
HE WAS GOING TO... SACRIFICE ME...
YEAH... BUT YOU'RE OKAY NOW.
"AND THAT THING IS HURT, BAD... MAYBE EVEN DYING..."
MY NAME'S WALTER, BY THE WAY...
IN CASE YOU WERE WONDERING.
IT'S ONLY THEN THAT SHE REALLY SEES THE SOLDIER.
OH... UH, JOSEPHINE... THANKS FOR SAVING ME.
WELL, LET'S NOT GET AHEAD OF OURSELVES...
WE'RE STILL A LONG WAY FROM ANYPLACE I'D CALL "SAFE."
AND SHE KNOWS HE'S ANOTHER ONE LIKE THE OLD LADY... HE SEES THE SECRET WORLD, TOO.

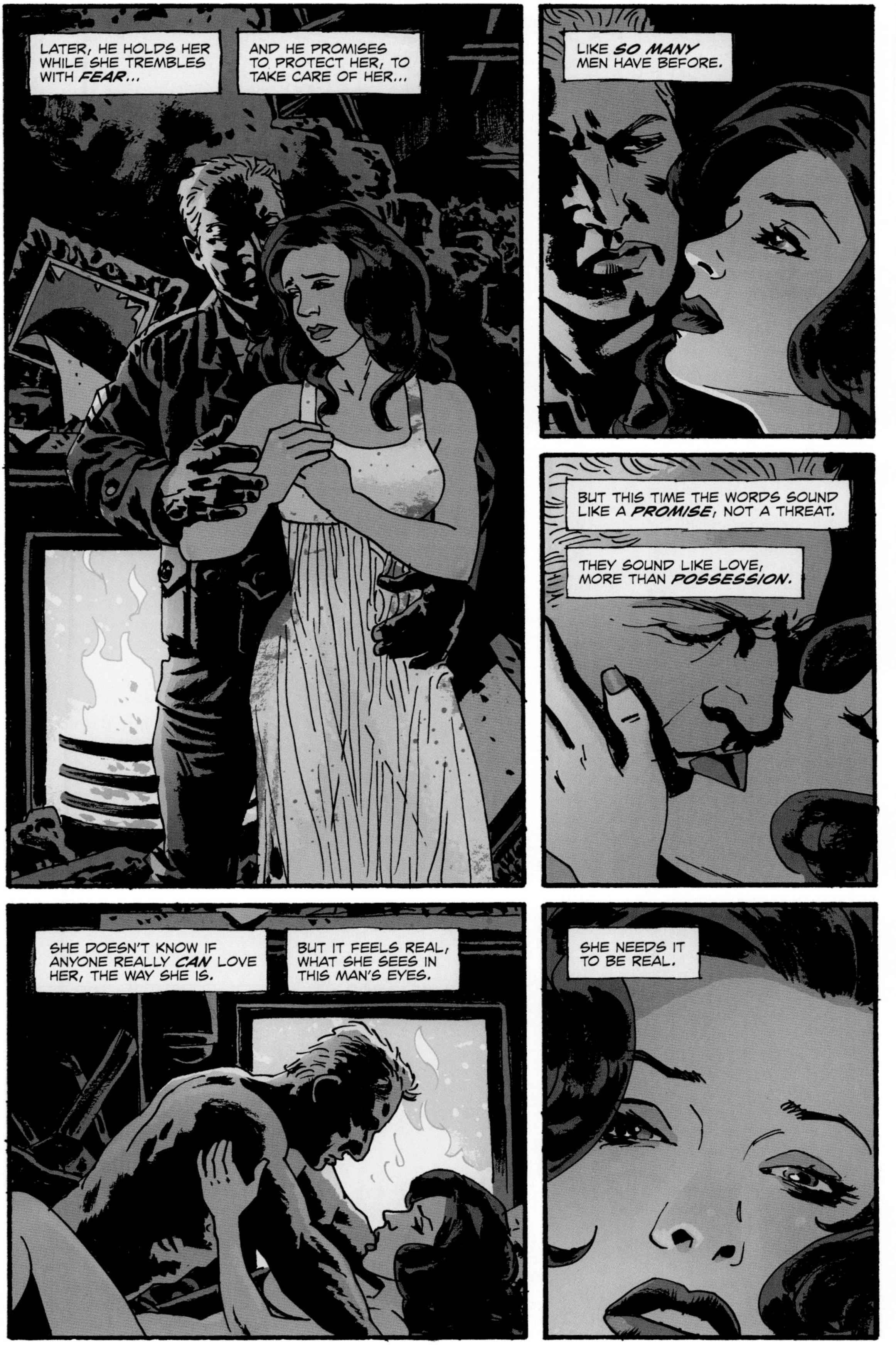
LATER, HE HOLDS HER WHILE SHE TREMBLES WITH FEAR...
AND HE PROMISES TO PROTECT HER, TO TAKE CARE OF HER...
LIKE SO MANY MEN HAVE BEFORE.
BUT THIS TIME THE WORDS SOUND LIKE A PROMISE, NOT A THREAT.
THEY SOUND LIKE LOVE, MORE THAN POSSESSION.
SHE DOESN'T KNOW IF ANYONE REALLY CAN LOVE HER, THE WAY SHE IS.
BUT IT FEELS REAL, WHAT SHE SEES IN THIS MAN'S EYES.
SHE NEEDS IT TO BE REAL.

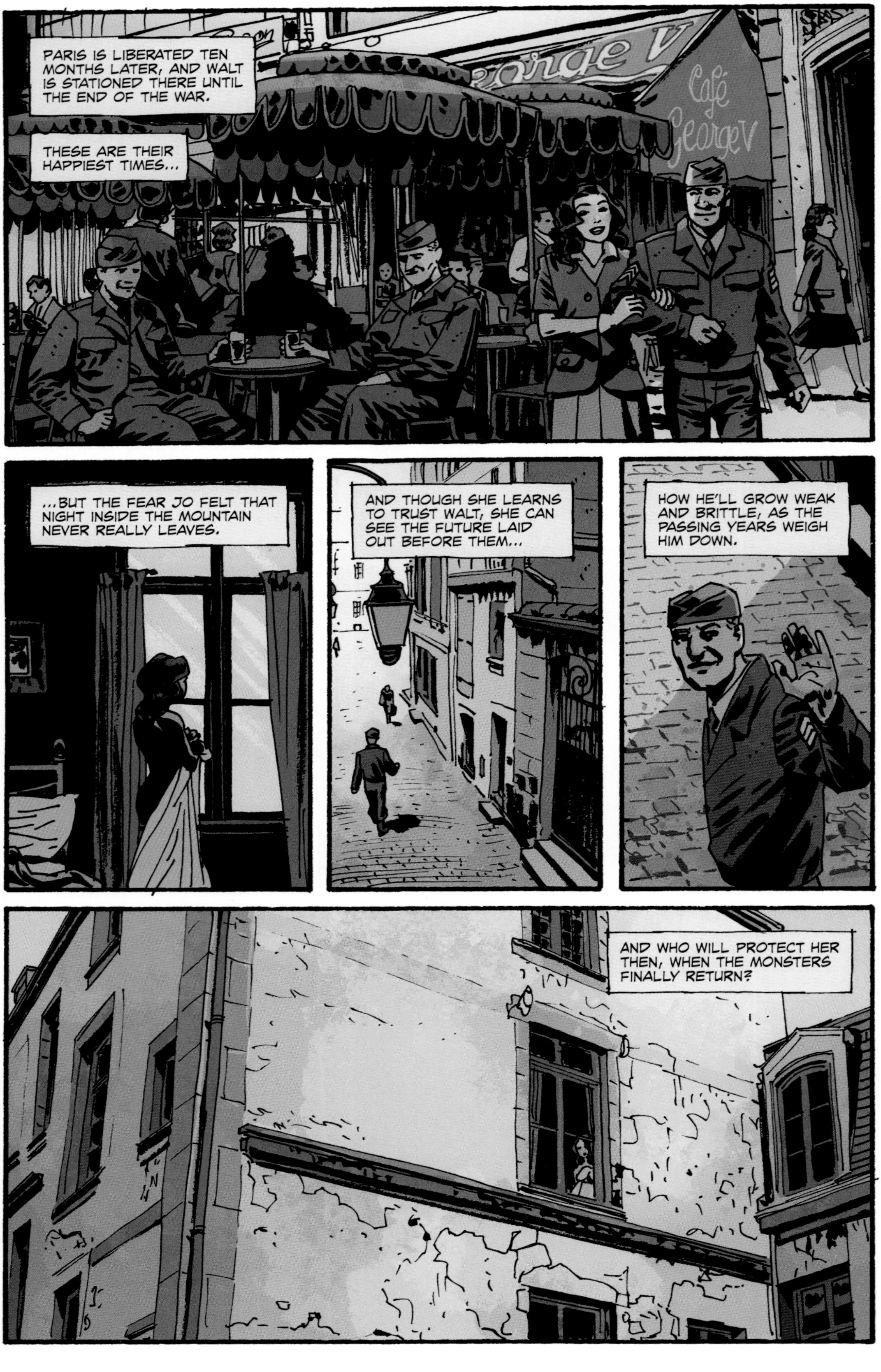
PARIS IS LIBERATED TEN MONTHS LATER, AND WALT IS STATIONED THERE UNTIL THE END OF THE WAR.
THESE ARE THEIR HAPPIEST TIMES...
Café George V
...BUT THE FEAR JO FELT THAT NIGHT INSIDE THE MOUNTAIN NEVER REALLY LEAVES.
AND THOUGH SHE LEARNS TO TRUST WALT, SHE CAN SEE THE FUTURE LAID OUT BEFORE THEM...
HOW HE'LL GROW WEAK AND BRITTLE, AS THE PASSING YEARS WEIGH HIM DOWN.
AND WHO WILL PROTECT HER THEN, WHEN THE MONSTERS FINALLY RETURN?

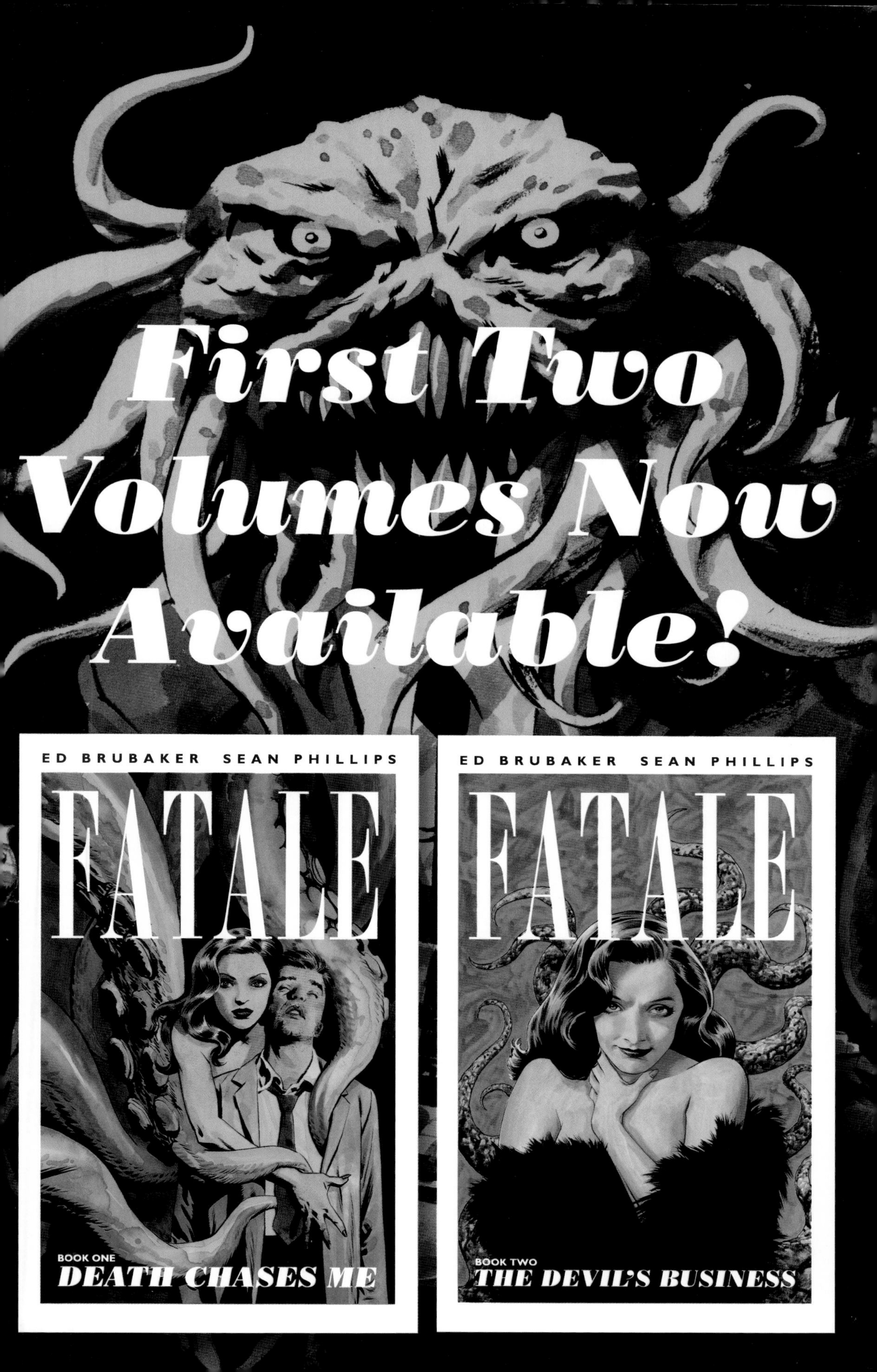
First Two Volumes Now Available!
ED BRUBAKER SEAN PHILLIPS
FATALE
BOOK ONE
DEATH CHASES ME
ED BRUBAKER SEAN PHILLIPS
FATALE
BOOK TWO
THE DEVIL'S BUSINESS